RAVES FOR ARCHER MAYOR, JOE GUNTHER, AND *TUCKER PEAK*

"The writing is strong, with sharp social observations throughout. . . . Gunther grows on you from novel to novel."
—*Washington Post Book World*

"The book's beauty lies in how smoothly Mayor incorporates disparate elements into a coherent and suspenseful plot, with some of the strands winding back around each other."
—*Publishers Weekly* (starred review)

"Clever. . . . Mayor again vividly portrays the hardscrabble life of southern Vermont.
—*Library Journal*

"This series is superior."
—**Charles Champlin**, *Los Angeles Times Book Review*

"Among the best cop stories being written today. The sense of place Mayor creates is vivid and real."
—*Booklist*

"One of the sharpest writers of police procedurals."
—*Midwest Book Reviews*

"Mayor keeps getting better with age. . . . Few writers deliver such well-rounded novels of such consistently high quality."
—*Arizona Daily Star*

more . . .

"The strength of this durable series has always been its insularity: local settings, sharp small-town characterizations, homegrown police procedures."
—*Kirkus Reviews*

"A believable, appealing hero."
—*Cleveland Plain Dealer*

"Gunther is a bloodhound of unusual depth and insight."
—*Los Angeles Times*

"Mayor's strength lies in his dedication to the old-fashioned puzzle, brought to a reasonable conclusion."
—*San Jose Mercury News*

"Mayor knows how to keep you turning pages."
—*Trenton Times*

"A great storyteller."
—*Maine Sunday Telegram*

"Lead a cheer for Archer Mayor and his ability not only to understand human relationships, but to convey them to his readers."
—*Washington Sunday Times*

TUCKER PEAK

Other Books by Archer Mayor

The Marble Mask

Occam's Razor

The Disposable Man

Bellows Falls

The Ragman's Memory

The Dark Root

Fruits of the Poisonous Tree

The Skeleton's Knee

Scent of Evil

Borderlines

Open Season

TUCKER
PEAK

ARCHER MAYOR

WARNER BOOKS

An AOL Time Warner Company

WARNER BOOKS EDITION

Copyright © 2001 by Archer Mayor
All rights reserved. No part of this book may be reproduced in any form or by any electronic or mechanical means, including information storage and retrieval systems, without permission in writing from the publisher, except by a reviewer who may quote brief passages in a review.

Cover design and art by Robert Santora

Warner Books, Inc.
1271 Avenue of the Americas
New York, NY 10020

Visit our Web site at
www.twbookmark.com.

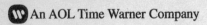 An AOL Time Warner Company

Printed in the United States of America

Originally published in hardcover by The Mysterious Press
First Paperback Printing: September 2002

10 9 8 7 6 5 4 3 2 1

ACKNOWLEDGMENTS

As will be immediately clear to readers of past books of mine, the following acknowledgments are shorter than they have been. This is in large part due to the fact that several sources who helped me to detail the behind-the-scenes view of the Vermont ski resort industry preferred to remain anonymous. This discretion in no way diminishes their contribution, however. Their help was invaluable and greatly appreciated.

Others who were equally helpful were:

Peter Barton   Anita Bobee
John Sinclair   Lloyd Ucko
Phil Sarcione   Von Labare
Green Mountain Power   John Martin
Paco Aumand   The Brattleboro Police Dept.
The Vermont State Police   The Windham Co. Sheriff's Dept.
The U.S. Marshals Service   Bill and Karen Sampson

To all, my deepest thanks; and to all, my apologies for any mistakes I may have committed in transposing your knowledge to the following pages. Any such errors, should they exist, are mine alone.

TUCKER
PEAK

CHAPTER ONE

I GLANCED OVER SNUFFY DAWSON'S WELL-PADDED SHOULDER at the snow drifting by out the window. It was falling in thick, light flakes, like goose down meandering earthward after a well-conducted pillow fight.

An avuncular man, Snuffy was the sheriff from the county next door—called Daniel only by his oldest female relatives—and as canny a politician as he was old-fashioned a police officer. He liked things simple and straightforward, or so he said, which put him increasingly at odds with a complex and confusing world. It also prompted him to affect a slow and deliberate manner, which helped explain why my attention was beginning to wander. He'd been standing awkwardly in the woodworking shop attached to my small Brattleboro, Vermont, house for fifteen minutes already, and I still hadn't figured out why.

"You sure you don't want some coffee?" I asked for the second time. "I have a fresh pot in the kitchen."

He looked around at all the tools I'd lovingly, even compulsively, hung on several Peg-Board sheets along the walls. They were almost like a museum display, they were so tidy. A keen observer might have ventured that such neatness implied more show than action. And it was true that the shop was more a personal escape valve than it was some master craftsman's studio. I was happy enough to be what my brother called a "wood butcher."

"How're you liking your outfit so far, Joe?" Snuffy suddenly asked.

The "outfit" was the Vermont Bureau of Investigation, or VBI, a new statewide detective squad drawn from the best officers of every law enforcement agency in Vermont—previously a plainclothes function belonging exclusively to the state police's Bureau of Criminal Investigation, or BCI. This new, more democratic, seemingly reasonable configuration, created by the legislature just one year ago, had caused some serious ripples across the law enforcement community. It had provoked deep resentment from the state police, whose BCI officers were now restricted to more localized coverage areas, and had to hand over their major crimes to VBI.

"I like it a lot," I told him, absentmindedly running a piece of sandpaper along some wood I'd just cut out on the table saw. "People are still getting used to us, but we've gotten high marks from the ones we've helped. Is that why you're here?"

But he wasn't being rushed. "I heard the state cops weren't too happy."

I repressed a sigh, irritated both by the familiarity of the topic, and that it was being voiced in this one place of retreat. I hadn't done much woodworking since I was a kid on the family farm upstate, but once my brother Leo made me a gift of our late father's refurbished tools—

right after I'd moved in here—it had become a reborn passion.

"Some are, others aren't. If any of their detectives want to go back to doing statewide major crimes, they can sign up and join us, *and* keep their bennies intact. Not that that's any secret—most of our agents are ex-troopers, anyhow. My bet is the majority of bent noses either belong to people who don't know what we do, or who were turned down when they applied. We are tough to get into, as we should be."

I didn't state the obvious, that the additional rub was the perceived affront of it all—that the VBI was proof that the BCI wasn't capable of doing its job. In fact, the opposite was true. BCI had been so successful, the politicians had merely opened up the opportunities it offered to a wider pool of qualified people.

Snuffy didn't look overly impressed. Police officers are a conservative bunch. The test of time is what they use to tell a good idea from a bad one—and we hadn't been around nearly long enough.

"I suppose," he said vaguely, idly running his finger through a thin film of sawdust on the table saw's otherwise gleaming black surface.

I figured I'd now fulfilled my social obligations. It was Saturday, and despite Snuffy's having driven so far for whatever reason, I was eager to get back to what I'd been doing. "So, you got something on your mind, or are you just running away from your paperwork?"

He smiled and shook his large, close-cropped head. "Nah. I either don't do it or I give it to somebody else. I just wanted to run something by you—sort of to be polite, you know?"

I wasn't sure I did, but I nodded to keep him going now that he'd finally gotten started.

"We had a burglary at Tucker Peak last night—one of the condos. The owner had a watch stolen, and a bunch of other stuff. We spread the word as usual, but it's probably a little early yet."

He paused as if expecting a response. For lack of options, I played straight man. "Nice watch, huh?"

He raised his eyebrows. I had apparently done well. "Oh, yeah. Twenty thousand dollars worth."

I whistled. "Jesus. What else did he lose?"

"Some jewelry, plus the standard portable stuff: a small TV, a cordless phone, a couple of radios, some silverware. About thirty grand total, but it was the watch that turned his crank."

Another lull, another nod from me. "Too bad."

"Yeah, well. He said he wanted you guys in on the investigation."

That caught me by surprise. I put the piece of wood down on the bench before me. "No kidding. He asked for VBI by name?"

Snuffy frowned slightly. "Yup. Said he was a friend of the governor—wanted the best of the best, not a bunch of Deputy Dawgs."

He stopped again, but this time I knew he was fishing for more than an encouraging head nod. "You tell him to eat shit?" I asked.

He laughed, obviously pleased with my response. "Not in those words, but yeah, sort of. What pissed him off is that one of my men moonlights as security for the mountain, which made the rent-a-cops and us look like one and the same. That was after he implied the security people might be in cahoots with the crooks. Real jerk."

He hesitated briefly, and then ruefully admitted to his credit, "Not that it's not possible—in theory, anyway."

I dusted my hands on my jeans. "Well, he's out of luck. That's not how we work."

His eyes narrowed. "This below you?"

"No," I answered pleasantly. "It's felony theft—we handle that. But we only come in when the home turf agency invites us."

That wasn't a hundred percent true, of course. The VBI's charter allowed it more room than that. But I wasn't about to ruin a good mood for no reason—Snuffy's presence here spoke for itself.

"What if he does call the governor?"

I shrugged. "Same answer. We're a support service, not a lead unit. You don't want us, we don't come. If we do, though, I should add that we come equipped with our own prosecutor, especially assigned to us from the AG's office. You know her—Kathy Bartlett—tough as nails, been there for years, and makes the lawyering end of any problems we run into fast and efficient, always a plus if you need legal advice in the middle of the night."

He mulled that over as I added, "And we always report to whoever calls us in—no separate press conferences, no leaks to the media. Just like we did in Stowe last month."

His expression showed he understood the reference. Our last big case had been under Stowe Police aegis, and our profile had been so low, most of the public hadn't even heard about us. Law enforcement had, though, we'd made sure of it.

"Okay," Snuffy said, but he didn't sound elated.

"This theft the only thing you got going?"

"Hardly," he answered. "Just the latest in a string of burglaries, and the worst. And then there's a bunch of tree-huggers bitching about new developments planned for over there, too. Tucker Peak's become a pain in the ass."

"You don't have any leads?"

"Nah, and I'm stretched for coverage."

I chose my phrasing carefully. "Tough spot—tight on manpower and a potential conflict of interest if the victim's right about your deputy."

"The victim's full of crap. I already looked into that. I can't swear the security outfit's clean, but my guy is."

I ducked that debate. "What's the victim's name, by the way?"

"William Manning. Flatlander, of course—New York."

This time, I was the one to let silence fill the room. Snuffy knew the political realities. Not to use us would be foolish, given the circumstances. But he had his pride, and I didn't want him claiming later that I'd twisted his arm.

Finally, he rubbed his chin with one large hand, stared at his shoes for a moment, and then slowly looked up at me. "So, how's this work exactly?"

Willy Kunkle stared incredulously at me from across the office, his coat still on and his standard dour expression darker by several degrees. "A stolen watch? It's Saturday, for Christ's sake. I thought we were like the Un-frigging-touchables—murder and mayhem only. We'll be ticketing cars next."

We were on the top floor of Brattleboro's Municipal

Building, two flights above the police department we both used to call home. Only now, instead of sprawling across half the ground level and most of the basement in a cluster of mismatched rooms and windowless caverns, we and two other so-called special agents shared a single large office, our desks backed like wary opponents into all four corners. Willy and I were alone for the moment, making the room look emptier than usual. This sensation was only enhanced by a general barrenness. Nothing had been hung on the walls yet, and while we'd been given a few file cabinets and computers, the use of things like a copier and a fax machine could only be had through the good graces of our downstairs neighbors. VBI's budgeting and equipment needs were still works in progress.

"It's the latest in a string," I said, not really expecting to win him over. "This last victim suspects the rent-a-cops are in on it."

Kunkle waved his hand dismissively in the air. "Hell, they all say shit like that. Rich guy in a fancy condo, leveraged up the whazoo—probably pawned his junk for the insurance. Why can't Dawson handle it, beside the fact that he's too dumb?"

"We got it, Willy," I told him, my tone indicating the conversation had run its course. "Saturday or not."

He studied me for a moment, perhaps reflecting on how many times we'd jousted in the past. Proud, judgmental, cynical, dismissive of others, and incredibly rude to almost everyone he met, Willy was also a workaholic who'd used law enforcement as a lifeline to pull himself free of a coterie of devils, from the Vietnam War, to alcohol abuse and a self-destructive, violent divorce, to a crippling bullet wound he'd received when we'd both worked downstairs which had left him with a withered, useless left arm. Through it all, and despite many who'd urged me to cut Willy loose, I'd made it a point to ensure he was measured by his abilities instead of his attitude. Which is how he'd paradoxically ended up among the VBI's first recruits. The commissioner of public safety had tapped me as the Bureau's field force commander and the Southeast Division's agent-in-charge. I'd accepted both jobs, but only in exchange for Willy's being considered on his merits, and not his personality.

Which had resulted in my being, once more, his immediate boss.

Willy finally raised his eyebrows. "Guess that means we're supposed to risk our lives, drive out to Tucker Peak in the middle of a snowstorm, and see if we can't help the good sheriff tell the difference between his butt and a hole in the ground?"

I rose to my feet and crossed over to where my own parka hung on the wall, noticing that the snow had pretty much stopped falling. "Right."

CHAPTER TWO

TUCKER PEAK LIES IN SOUTHERN VERMONT, WHICH FOR A ski resort is both good and bad news. Like its sisters—Stratton, Mount Snow, and Bromley—it's closer to the money states of Massachusetts and Connecticut, and to New York City, but unlike more northern mountains, such as Stowe, Killington, and Jay Peak, Tucker suffers from the south's chronic climatic stinginess. As with almost every other resort, it's piped for snowmaking, if only partially, but even artificial snow requires freezing weather, and there are winters in Vermont, especially recently, when that kind of cold, not to mention plain old-fashioned, natural snow, has been a precious and rare commodity.

Of course, that's one reason the pipes appeared in the first place, and with them other, less winter-dependent options for financial survival. Golf courses, tennis courts, horseback riding, summer alpine slides, swimming pools, old-car shows, antique fairs—along with the requisite hotels and condos—have slowly crowded around base lodges all across the state to help make Vermont's occasionally threadbare skiing a smaller piece of the economic pie.

Which is not to say that this type of mixing and matching isn't still a tricky recipe, conditional as it is on such imponderables as customer loyalty, community and governmental support, and the ability of a resort to turn its customers into its own best ambassadors. In fact, while I'd heard of Tucker Peak's ambitions to diversify, this last ingredient was something rumored to be in short supply.

"You're close to the grapevine," I told Willy as we left Brattleboro for the Green Mountains that ran up the state's middle like a spine. "Give me the lowdown on Tucker Peak."

Willy was staring glumly out at the barely falling snow that was both dry and sparse enough to make windshield wipers unnecessary. "Bunch of bored people sliding down a mountain so they can drink too much and jump each other's bones after a night at the disco. Never made much sense to me."

I ignored the preamble, knowing there was no information about his fellow human beings Willy didn't find interesting, and waited patiently for him to address the actual topic.

"According to the barflies I know who work there," he admitted after a pause, "up to last year, no one could count on being paid for the full season—attendance was down, equipment was falling apart, and maintenance was sucking hind tit. Now, it looks like they're betting the farm."

I knew they'd added condos, boutiques, and a nightclub, to negligible effect, but this was obviously something bigger. "How's that?"

"They've lined up some big investors to spruce up everything at once. Summer and winter stuff, both: a hotel, twice the condo units, tennis courts, and a golf course. They're talking over fifteen million dollars, which is huge on our pissant scale."

"Why haven't I read about it in the paper?"

"They haven't hit stride yet. They got a fancy model in the base lodge, a few contracts out for hardware and engineering studies, and surveyors and guys cutting trees for new trails and a lift line, but basically they're limping through this winter so they can make a big splash in the spring."

I absorbed all this without comment. Willy took my silence as encouragement.

"My sources are hardly Wall Street types, but they see no reason this should work."

"Why not? A total mountain makeover might be a home run."

He was shaking his head. "My people feed these wannabes, clean their toilets, change their sheets, pick up after 'em. They hear the bitching about ticket prices, lousy service, how boring the slopes are. It's the proverbial pig's ear, according to them. You can gussy it up all you want, you can't change the basics."

I drove through the tiny village of Lifton in three seconds flat and then turned onto Tucker Peak's access road a couple of miles farther on. It was identified by a slightly weather-beaten sign next to a small cluster of retail buildings, including a bar. "So you're not buying stock?"

"How're they going to pay for it, even with investors? Prices'll have to go up, and the mountain'll still be what it's always been, a mole hill with attitude, just like the rest of this woodchuck state."

Sad to say, even if untrue, that had a ring of familiarity to it. Vermont's economy wasn't far different from the rest of the country's, but it was miniaturized to where it looked quaintly third world. No matter what we did commercially up here, or how well, our best was always a blip when compared to places budgeted in the billions. The one exception was maple syrup, where we topped the nation by a fat margin, but even there, who really cared? A half-million gallons a year still only supplied a demand less than that for caviar. So, I understood what Willy was saying about little Tucker Peak. Spend what it might, it could never hold a candle to resorts in Utah and Colorado. Worse still, it couldn't even compete in sheer size and height to the best in Vermont. In a market rewarding bigger, steeper, faster slopes, Tucker didn't look slated for survival, much less rebirth.

But then, I'd thought the Internet was a pipe dream, too.

And I had to give it to Tucker Peak on aesthetics. Like Stratton, although smaller, it lay encased in a bowl of mountains. A single road led into it, up and over a humpbacked cleft, and the initial view of the resort, as the car turned the last curve at a low-flying, bird's-eye level, was straight from a fairy tale. The base lodge, surrounded by buildings, stores, sheds, and the nightclub, looked like an alpine village, the slopes and lifts fanning out like anchor lines from the heart of a spider's web. The sprinkling of slopeside condos resembled outlying rural homes.

The most striking feature, however, towered far overhead, above the buildings, the access road, and even the broad, carved mountain bowl cradling the ski trails. Lining the horizon, with the blank white sky as a backdrop, looking spectrally indistinct in the barely falling snow, was a row of modern windmills—stark, pale, streamlined, and huge—eight of them with rotors so wide, it seemed unlikely they could move. And yet move they did, with the same ghostly, silent, otherworldly grace that elephants have drifting through the night in a herd.

In another effort to pay the bills, Tucker Peak had leased its ridgeline to a local power company for this experiment in alternative energy, granting itself in the process the single most unusual feature of any ski resort in the country.

All of it—the village, the fan of trails, the beautiful mountains, the surreal windmill farm, and the colorful sprinkling of brightly clad skiers across the white snow—made me think that in a world so given to appearance over substance, I might have been too harsh in giving Tucker Peak an early requiem. Faced with such an ethereal picture, this isolated, small, vertically challenged ski bowl just might find a way to compete with its brawnier rivals.

"Where do we go?" Willy asked, as impressed as if we'd just come to a crossroads in Kansas.

"Western slope. Something called Laurel Lane. Number three-one-eight."

I drove down into the pseudovillage, noticing how its alpine image fell apart under closer scrutiny. The buildings, of ersatz Swiss design, began losing their picturesque appeal. Dark, supposedly shingle roofs emerged as painted metal, the crisscross of wooden beams on fake stucco walls turned out to be only brown paint. The whole vision became threadbare, cheap, and perilously impermanent. I was abruptly forced to wonder if fifteen million would make much of a dent, a thought driven home by the addition of a quiet group of placard-wielding protesters camped out by the base lodge's front entrance.

I passed between the lodge and the nightclub opposite, paused where the road split into a Y, and headed uphill to the left, skirting one side of the crazy quilt of interlocking ski trails. I noticed that the skiers I'd seen earlier, traversing the slopes like ants crisscrossing a sugar spill, weren't present in the kind of numbers to give a resort owner much joy, especially during a weekend. I also saw there were as many empty building lots as condo sites.

Willy was checking off road signs. "Summit Road, Powder Lane, Snowflake Circle . . . Christ almighty, Joe, why don't they give it a rest? Here we go, the tree section: Maple, Fir, Hemlock . . . Laurel's on the right."

The scattered houses we'd passed had varied in opulence from the functional, tucked away with no view apart from a few trees, to the marginally upscale, with a glimpse of a meadow or a nearby ski trail. Laurel Lane brought us up a significant notch.

"What d'ya think?" Willy asked. "A half million each? Three-quarters?"

I watched the procession slide by as the road emerged from the trees and stretched taut behind one perched palace after another, like a ribbon with gaudy baubles glued to one edge. Most of the houses were cantilevered out over a steep incline, allowing them the panorama their less affluent neighbors merely aspired to. For the first time since our arrival, here were signs of real wealth—and of potential salvation for the whole.

"I have no idea," I said quietly, suspecting the economies of such places had little to do with true value.

Number 318 looked vaguely western to me, low and spread out with an expansive, oversize roof that was more flat than peaked, unlike most New England buildings. It was built of logs, had huge windows, and a wraparound deck that looked deep enough to hold a tennis court.

We parked next to a sports utility vehicle deserving of a rope ladder and stepped out into the cold air. The snowfall had completely petered out.

As we set foot on the porch, the front door facing us opened abruptly, revealing a short, round, balding man wearing a bulky, expensive white knit sweater and a permanently angry crease between his eyes.

"Who are you?" he asked abruptly, his tone of voice matching his expression.

I couldn't stop Willy in time.

"Be nice, asshole," he said without hesitation, "we're cops."

The owner's mouth dropped open. Feeling like the straight man in a comedy act, I pulled out my shield and announced as nonchalantly as possible, "Vermont Bureau of Investigation—Special Agents Gunther and Kunkle. I gather you asked to see us?"

To my surprise, our presumably Type-A host merely gave Willy a grudging look of admiration and stepped back into the open doorway. "'Bout time. Come in."

We walked past him as he continued, "I'm glad that

idiot sheriff got the message. I thought I might have to call the governor."

"We're only here because the sheriff invited us," I explained. "It's still his case."

The short man waved his hand dismissively. "Whatever. I just wanted someone who could read and write. Guess you'll have to do."

"Wild guess," Willy interjected, "you must be William Manning, from New York."

The crease deepened between Manning's eyebrows. "You got by the first time, sonny. Don't push it."

"Could we cut this out?" I asked them both.

They looked at me as if I'd just spoiled a good windup. Manning was the first to recover. "Right. This has really pissed me off. I didn't come to the boonies to get robbed like it was the city."

He preceded us toward a glass-walled living room beyond the entryway. I held up a hand to stop Willy from responding.

"Why don't you take it from the top, Mr. Manning?" I suggested.

He motioned us toward one of three large sofas, all positioned to enjoy the scenery outside. Everything was there, from the sweep of ski slopes, to the base lodge far below, to the windmills looming high in the distance like gigantic praying mantises. I noticed there was a long, graceful ramp connecting the deck to the nearest trail, allowing Manning and his guests to ski directly from home.

Despite the overcast day, the living room was saturated with light.

"You're not going to ask for coffee, are you?" Manning suddenly asked.

We both shook our heads.

He sat back and crossed his legs. "There's not much to tell. My wife and I come up weekends this time of year. Last weekend, everything was fine. This one, they ripped us off."

I pulled a sheet of paper from my pocket, rose, and crossed the thick wool rug to hand it to him. "That's the list of missing items Sheriff Dawson prepared from your statement. Any changes you'd like to make?"

Manning pulled a pair of half-glasses out of his breast pocket and scrutinized the list, eventually saying, "That's it. The watch was the only thing I couldn't replace."

"What was so special about it?" Willy asked. "Besides the cost?"

Manning responded to the implication. "Yeah, that would stick out for you guys. The cost is irrelevant. It was a custom job, from my son on my sixtieth birthday. It's a sentimental thing, one of a kind."

"You have a picture of it?"

He gave us a sour smile. "Yeah, I do. The insurance company made a big deal out of it, bastards." He reached over to a long table behind the sofa, opened a wooden box, and pulled out a wad of photographs. "I had these delivered to me this morning. It's everything that's missing, including the watch."

He extended the pictures to me but didn't bother getting up, forcing me to cross the rug again to take them. I was half tempted to tear a page from Willy's manual of style by fake kissing the man's ring.

Instead, I returned to my roost and handed the photos to Willy to study. He pointedly tucked them into his pocket without a glance.

The sooner I was out of this gladiator pit, the better, I thought.

"Did you sense anything unusual when you drove up this last time?" I asked.

Manning shook his head, but then answered in contradiction, "Yeah. Some snow had drifted onto the deck, in front of the front door, but it had been swept clean. I thought it was the caretaker, at first, why, I don't know. Dumb yokel wouldn't know a broom if he fell over it. It was obviously to get rid of footprints, but I didn't figure that out till later, when I found the broken window they used to get in, around the far side of the porch."

"You asked him anyway?" I asked.

"'Course I did—he was clueless."

"Mr. Manning," I asked, "when did you notice you'd been robbed?"

"As soon as we got inside. For one thing, it was cold, from the broken window. But the small TV was missing from the kitchen. Peggy noticed that right off, no surprise."

We both noticed the sardonic tone of voice again.

"Where's your wife now?" Willy asked.

"She went back to the city. Anyhow, after that, I started looking around. Whoever did it was obviously low rent— missed the paintings and ceramics and grabbed whatever he could sell fast."

"And the watch was on your bedroom dresser?" I asked, recalling Snuffy's report.

"Yeah, out in plain view. You want to see where everything was?"

I shook my head. "The sheriff's people took photographs and made diagrams. Just out of curiosity, though, pretending this isn't the smash-and-grab we're all assuming it is, can you think of anyone who might've done this to get back at you for some reason?"

The other man was genuinely nonplussed. "Get *back* at me? For what?"

Willy rose abruptly and studied Manning, cradled by his overpriced sofa like a silver spoon on velvet. "Can't think of a thing," he said in an angry, flat voice and headed toward the front door. "I'll be in the car."

Manning and I watched him leave.

"Touchy guy," he commented.

I stood up also. "Yeah . . . Well, I don't think so. You told the sheriff you thought one of his deputies might've been involved in this and that you also suspected the mountain's security force."

Manning shook his head disdainfully. "I said that to get his attention—like hitting a mule with a two-by-four."

"So, there's no truth to it?"

"I don't know," he said with disgust. "That's your job."

I found Willy sitting quietly in the car, staring out the window at the view.

I didn't start the engine immediately. "Am I going to have problems with you on this?"

He remained looking straight ahead. "I was just asking myself the same thing."

"And?"

"Not if I don't have to spend any more time with him."

I turned the ignition key. "Deal."

CHAPTER THREE

IT HAD BEEN WHOLLY APPROPRIATE TO DRIVE OUT TO
Tucker Peak on a Saturday on Snuffy Dawson's request,
but given the low profile of the crime and our own bud-
getary constraints, I was now happy to drop Willy off outside the office and just quickly double-check by phone
that the sheriff's deputies had filed the initial paperwork,
processed the evidence, and set all the appropriate electronic inquiries into motion. After that, I headed back
home to my woodworking shop.

Not that my project there was anything monumental.
In fact, I was replacing an elaborately shaped but cracked
wooden seat from a chair belonging to Gail Zigman, the
woman with whom I'd eccentrically shared my life for
just under twenty years.

We weren't married, and we didn't live together, although we had briefly not long before. But through thick
and thin, some of it quite traumatic, we'd proven to ourselves and to each other that we were as closely intertwined as any couple we knew.

Gail was younger than I, born to privilege in New

York City. Well traveled and highly educated, she had come to Brattleboro at the height of the commune movement to try living a life far different from that of her parents. Living the countercultural life in Vermont hadn't been a waste of time. It had opened her eyes to values she still held dear. But it had also been relatively short-lived. Within a few years, she'd yielded to an ingrained and natural ambition and had joined the town's business and political world, growing and evolving over a couple of decades from successful Realtor to selectman to deputy state's attorney, to where she'd recently become legal counsel to VermontGreen, the state's preeminent environmental group, based in the capital city of Montpelier.

Now, Gail was one of that growing class of professionals who'd taken advantage of computers, faxes, and cell phones to stretch the lines connecting her to the office. When the state's citizen legislature was in session, roughly from January to April or May, she lived in a condo in Montpelier so she could watch the political pot. The rest of the time, she worked out of the house we'd once shared in West Brattleboro, from which the chair I was repairing had come.

As foolish as it sounded for a man of my years, I was intent on returning to my repair job less for the daunting task of making a new piece match an old chair, and more because handling it brought me at least tangentially closer to Gail.

We didn't live apart because of any friction. We didn't argue, or dislike each other's politics or eating habits or taste in late-night movies. It was more that since we'd met later in life—I a widower and a settled, lifelong cop; she a professional woman increasingly eager for a new challenge—we'd already come to terms with the bachelor lives we'd adopted. We instinctively needed more breathing space than a younger couple and were less willing to compromise for the sake of steady companionship.

In the end, it had been neither easier nor harder than an old-fashioned marriage. It had merely evolved into something rich and rewarding enough to keep us coming back for more.

So, I kept at my project for the rest of the weekend, until by Sunday night I fitted a reasonably antiqued seat between the old and slightly battered legs, arms, and back of a hundred-year-old wooden chair, knowing that the effort I'd put into it would count for more with Gail than just good craftsmanship.

It was with similar anticipation that I returned to the office on Monday morning to see what the computers had coughed up concerning William Manning's missing items. For me, an investigation, no matter how apparently trivial, shared many of the elements of a woodworking project. They both demanded thoughtfulness, patience, and attention to detail, and both promised to disappoint if handled carelessly. But neither one was entirely successful if only followed by the numbers. Strong elements of intuition and creativity always featured in the end result.

It was also true, however, that encouraging momentum was sometimes slow to build. When I checked for reports from our queries of two days ago, I found nothing.

Or, as Willy put it more succinctly, "We got shit. No

hits on the fingerprints, the MO, the sheriff's neighborhood canvass, nothing from the caretaker, who I interviewed yesterday, and no news on any of our rich boy's toys. I still think he did it himself for the insurance."

Sammie Martens was standing by a small counter that held a coffeemaker and a few cups. Small, slight, and as tough as sinew, Sammie was ex-military like Willy and me, but—perhaps because she was barely in her thirties—she still maintained the spit and polish both of us had long since dropped. She was also intense, ambitious, and extremely loyal, a combination that occasionally got uncomfortably tangled up in itself and dropped her into dark moods of self-doubt and frustration. She and Willy were the only erstwhile Brattleboro police officers to accompany me in the shift to VBI, a move that had effectively robbed the town's detective bureau of three-fifths of its manpower. We'd been working as a team for over ten years, as a result, and had become more like family members than mere colleagues.

"You know most of that stuff won't be coming in for days," she told him. "You're just pissed off because you don't like the guy and you think the case is beneath you, but you still can't resist being interested in it."

Willy looked at her balefully. "Oh, right. Like I'm staying up late at night sweating this out."

"You drove me all the way back to Tucker Peak to talk to the caretaker on a Sunday," she said, smiling and taking her first sip of coffee. "The sheriff'd already done that."

Willy scowled.

"Did you learn anything new?" I asked, surprised and curious.

But feeling cornered by now, he didn't take it well. "Right—you, too. Don't be bashful. Pile it on. You saying we shouldn't double-check the other guy's work?"

Sammie was walking slowly across to her desk so she wouldn't spill her drink. "Willy, give us a break. It's too early for opera."

He didn't respond, but I noticed him hiding a smile as he pretended to dig around in a lower drawer. Willy and Sammie, after years of bickering while working for me downstairs, had recently and suddenly become a romantic item, just prior to joining VBI. It was very low-key. I was one of the few who even knew of it, and it had seemed at the time as likely as a bird courting a bullfrog. But it appeared to be working. Sammie's nearly obsessive, jagged, driven style had been softened, and the angry fire that raged perpetually inside Willy was running just a few degrees cooler.

The office door opened with a bang and a tall, skinny man with a tousled shock of blond hair entered, saying something pleasantly suggestive over his shoulder to Judy, our secretary, who sat alone in the small waiting area between our office and the hallway.

Lester Spinney was the final member of the "Southeast" team, VBI being divided into four cardinal divisions around the state, with the fifth residing at the Department of Public Safety headquarters in centralized Waterbury. Lester and I had known each other since we'd worked together on a homicide in the state's isolated Northeast Kingdom region a decade earlier. He'd been a detective with the state police's Bureau of Criminal Investigation then, and (as far as I was concerned) had now become the perfect poster boy of how and why VBI benefited all capable, ambitious Vermont cops, regardless of where they'd started out.

One paradoxical aspect of the Vermont State Police—or VSP in acronym-happy law enforcement parlance—was that while it was Vermont's premier law enforcement agency, in terms of size, budget, and quality, it was also a traditionally structured organizational pyramid. The more capable and upwardly mobile an officer became, the less likely it was he or she would be given an open slot in a timely manner. Highly deserving, experienced people were finding themselves either standing in line, praying for providence, or looking for jobs elsewhere.

Spinney had opted for an alternate route, in fact declining a VSP promotion that would have anchored him to a desk in order to join the attorney general's office and keep working investigations. The only downside was that he'd exchanged being a part of a large, companionable organization of fellow cops for working with a bunch of lawyers. Educational perhaps, but also socially isolating—and he was a famously sociable person.

Enter VBI.

"Hello, boys and girls," he said, trying to simultaneously shuck his coat and not drop an oversize box of Dunkin' Donuts. "I thought I'd take the edge off a Monday by putting your minds on your stomachs."

"It'll take more'n that," Willy grumbled.

Spinney smiled broadly and reached into the box. "Just what I thought, Grumpy, which is why I got *you* an extrabig cinnamon roll." He laid it with a flourish on Kunkle's desk, complete with a napkin. Willy rolled his eyes but was eating Lester's offering within five minutes. The rest of us didn't bother being coy.

"How's your caseload, Lester?" I asked with my mouth full, having already quizzed the other two on their work.

He'd replaced Sammie at the coffee machine and was pouring himself a cup. "The homicide in Springfield looks pretty straightforward, just lining everything up for the prosecution. The arson at that farm in Rockingham might take a bit more. It's still a toss-up between the son and the neighbor. I'm leaning toward the neighbor. Why? Got something going?"

"Yeah," Willy said sarcastically. "Better put all that on hold. We're in the big leagues now."

"Burglary at Tucker Peak," I answered. "About fifty grand worth of stuff. We got it from Snuffy Dawson because of a twenty-thousand dollar watch and the fact that he's already got his hands full with a bunch of protesters."

Lester whistled, and unlike Willy, didn't question our involvement. Instead, he came up with an immediate suggestion. "You try the Internet auction houses yet?"

Sammie looked up from her paperwork. "You're kidding."

"Nope. Next best thing to a pawn shop, and with a much wider clientele. If I ended up with something like that, that's how I'd move it."

He crossed over to one of the several computers we had around the room. "Want me to try?"

To pay Willy his due, he was the first one by Lester's side as he sat down before the monitor. Willy read the description of the watch aloud from the case file.

Spinney started with eBay and began his search, talking as he did so. "There're a bunch of these sites nowadays—dime a dozen—and we may be jumping the gun a little, but it can't hurt."

He wasn't successful at the first three sites, and I could sense Willy's restlessness escalating. He was not a man given to hands-off police work.

Lester suddenly sat back in his chair with a satisfied grunt. "Talk about lucky. The seller even put up a photograph of it." He hit a button on the screen and popped up a picture of a gaudy, oversize diving watch, complete with gold inlay and small diamonds.

"That it?"

Willy pulled out William Manning's picture of the watch. "No shit."

Lester began manipulating the computer mouse. "Okay, now we backtrack it to the seller and keep our fingers crossed he has more than just an e-mail address. And . . ." he paused a moment for the information to appear, "there you go: Walter Skottick, Old Route 5, Putney, Vermont—complete with phone number."

There was a telling moment of silence while everyone except Lester digested the ease with which he'd just conjured up the watch's location.

Willy was the first to break the spell. "Let me have that number."

He reached for Lester's phone, tucked the receiver under his chin, and dialed.

"Mr. Skottick?" he asked in a theatrical upper-class accent. "W. Graham Morrison here. Are you the person selling that marvelous timepiece on the Internet?"

He paused and elaborated, "That's correct, I did mean the *watch*. Well, believe it or not, you and I are almost neighbors—quite unusual, all things considered. I live in

Boston, so I was wondering if I might take a look at it in person. It's so much more compelling than seeing just a photograph."

He listened for a minute before adding, "Not at all. I'll place my bids along with everyone else. I'm not asking to subvert the system, but since fate has placed me so nearby, I just had to ask for a closer examination, especially given how much I might be willing to pay."

He waited a little more, and finally said, "Excellent. Isn't that spiffy? I'll come by in a few hours."

He hung up with a smile. "That ought to give us time for a warrant."

Sammie shook her head and stared at him in wonder. "Spiffy?"

Willy raised an eyebrow. "Whatever."

North of Putney village, Old Route 5 turns from a paved road to dirt and then vanishes altogether over a very short distance, a victim of Interstate 91, which was traced across the map in the 1960s with the subtlety of a broad-tipped magic marker, cutting off or obliterating dozens of ancient meandering country roads that had taken their cues from a host of preceding Indian trails, cow paths, and wagon tracks.

Old Route 5 also is just north of a settlement that future scientists will ponder at length, and about which—I dearly hope—they will reach some truly bizarre conclusions about Vermont's overall placement on the national oddball scale.

Santa's Land is a tiny petting zoo and theme park given over to a menagerie of approachable, photogenic beasts, corralled among a startling collection of Swiss huts, elves' workshops, and cement igloos, some with paint jobs as garish as a punk rocker's toenails.

Every time I drive by it, fantasizing about what those scholars will make of it, my pleasure is heightened because it also happens to be located in a village famous for its political correctness and artistic high breeding. Such jarring juxtapositions are one of the regular aspects of this state I find most appealing.

The residents of Old Route 5 occupy a standard sliding scale for rural Vermont, from houses plucked from a frugal and practical contractor's imagination, to mobile homes that were rolled into place so many years ago that the trees now surrounding them make all notion of mobility inconceivable. That quixotic and contradictory sense of humanity's imprint mingling with signs of its own impermanence is driven home by the steady rumble from the unseen interstate nearby: a siren call to progress and the restless.

Walter Skottick had staked out a middle ground between these extremes, living in a cobbled-together wooden house that had begun enthusiastically years ago, complete with siding and an asphalt roof, only to settle eventually for a series of plywood, barn wood, or plain tar paper extensions, all clearly designed for some specific purpose, and all stamped with the homeowner's ever lessening standards.

Willy and I left my car and surrendered to the cold-nosed nuzzling of four friendly dogs, their combined nostrils producing a fog machine's worth of condensed air.

The front door to the ramshackle house burst open, and a large, bearded, friendly man waved a meaty hand at us.

"Hi, there. Sorry about the dogs—should've warned you. *Boys . . . Guys . . . Here.*"

The dogs totally ignored him and made our perilous trip from car to house even more challenging than it would have been otherwise. There are two ways of attacking a snow-clogged walkway in this country: The compulsive among us shovel diligently down to the frozen earth every time it's called for, neatness and a sprinkling of salt counting for extra points. The more casual merely let their guests beat an ever thickening, increasingly slippery path to their doors. Mr. Skottick was one of the latter, making Willy and me, aided by the gamboling dogs, look like a couple a drunks.

Skottick stepped back as we drew nearer. "I really am sorry. Never got around to training them. Is one of you Mr. Morrison?"

Willy, having almost fallen three times, testily fished out his badge. "I lied. We're cops."

"Vermont Bureau of Investigation, Mr. Skottick," I explained, irritated at having our cover blown prematurely. It would have been nice to at least see the watch before announcing ourselves. "We apologize for the subterfuge, but we need to talk to you about that watch."

Of the various reactions available to him, Skottick took the one I was coming to dislike the most, exacerbating my mood. "The Vermont *what*?"

Willy shared my feelings. "Bureau of Investigation. It's like the FBI, but with shit on their shoes. Where's the watch?"

Skottick understandably took offense. "Just a minute. I don't understand."

I took the warrant from my pocket, giving Willy a hard

look. "Mr. Skottick, we have reason to believe the watch you have for sale was recently stolen. We're here to take possession of it and anything else that was stolen along with it, and we'd also like to hear your side of the story."

His face above the beard went pale and then flushed red. "That son of bitch."

"This oughta be good," Willy muttered, ignoring me and entering the house uninvited.

"Who're you talking about?" I asked as I followed suit, forcing Skottick to join us.

"Marty Gagnon. He's the one who gave me the watch. I sold him a car, he didn't have what he owed, so he gave me the watch. Told me it was a family heirloom."

"And you swallowed that?" Willy asked from an interior room. "Why would he need a car from you if he had a watch like that?"

"Better get it for us," I said gently.

His shoulders slumped, Skottick eased past Willy into a cluttered workroom. "I didn't know anything about this. I swear to God. Maybe I was stupid, but I knew I wouldn't get the money out of him any other way."

He rummaged around in a desk drawer and withdrew the watch, which glittered in the light through the window. "I thought it was fake, to be honest. I mean, it looks like a Christmas ornament. That's why I put it on the Net instead of just selling it to a jeweler. I figured the diamonds were phony."

"They're not," Willy said shortly, taking the watch and working it into an evidence envelope with one hand.

"What else did Marty Gagnon give you?" I asked.

"That was it. I promise. You can search the place, if you want."

I turned to Willy. "You want to look around a little? I'll talk to Mr. Skottick in the living room."

Willy nodded and the two of us left him alone. Skottick sat heavily in an old armchair like a bear at the end of a long day, his paws dangling between his knees.

"Tell me about Gagnon," I told him.

"Not much to tell. I advertised a car in the paper about a month ago. He came by right off, paid me half in cash and promised the rest later. Said he hadn't gotten his paycheck yet. I trusted him. A couple of weeks later, I called him and he told me he got fired. He didn't have the money but he'd get it soon. I was angry—threatened to put the cops on him—so he told me he'd take care of me some other way. It would just take a little more time. Finally, he called and said he had better than cash. He'd had a relative die and he'd inherited some stuff and had a watch that was worth a lot more than the balance he owed me. Maybe it was dumb, but I cut him some slack. I was getting sick of it. He came right over, gave me the watch, and that was that."

"This all happened when?"

"He gave me the watch yesterday."

"You moved pretty fast to put it on the Net."

"I sell a lot of things that way. Been doing it for years."

"You still have that phone number?" I asked.

He shifted his bulk to reach into his back pocket, pulled out a ratty wallet, and removed a small, soiled scrap of paper, which he handed over. "Am I under arrest?"

I looked at the number. It was a Brattleboro exchange. "No. Did he give you an address?"

He shook his head.

"How 'bout a bill of sale or the registration transfer info? That would have it."

As if snapping out of a dream, he blinked once and dug into the wallet again, producing what I was after. "What's going to happen to me?"

"If you're telling the truth, nothing. This says it was an '88 Subaru. What did it look like?"

"Dark blue where it wasn't rust. I was asking five hundred for it. I'm really sorry about this. I didn't mean any harm."

"Don't worry about it," I said reassuringly, all but convinced by now that he was telling the truth. "At worst, you're out a car and some money, and if we get lucky— and you don't hold your breath—maybe you'll even get the car back."

I took a business card from my pocket and gave it to him. "Now that you know what's up, give it some more thought. Anything comes to mind, even something trivial, call me or leave a message." I held up my index finger for emphasis. "Keep one thing in mind, though, okay?"

After a pause, he asked, "What's that?"

"I've cut you some serious slack here, taking you at your word. If I find out that was a mistake or that you've been spreading the word about our visit today, especially to Marty, I'll be a lot less pleasant the next time. Understand?"

His eyes widened at the threat. "I won't say nuthin'. Promise."

There was a thud from the other room, followed by a curse.

"I'll get him out of here," I added.

CHAPTER FOUR

DAMN, BOSS, YOU COULD'VE GOTTEN US A HEATED LOOKout." Lester Spinney rose from the chair by the window and walked around the bare, shadowy room, thrashing his sides with his arms like a penguin doing aerobics.

I kept my eyes on the darkened apartment across the street. "I told you to dress warmly."

"I am. I did—to cross the street or something, not stand around inside a freezer."

"Oh-one from oh-two," Sammie's voice came over the portable radio.

I picked it up and keyed the mike. "Go ahead."

"Anything?"

I sympathized with everyone's boredom. We'd been there for six hours already. I only hoped Willy wouldn't chime in from his position—I doubted he'd be so gentle. "Nope."

She didn't respond. I replaced the radio on the windowsill and resumed watching Marty Gagnon's windows, curtainless and as blank as they'd been all night.

We were on Main Street, downtown Brattleboro, Spinney and I on the west side, above the pharmacy, Willy bundled up and dressed like a bum at the back of the alley, near the back door of Gagnon's building, and Sammie, the only warm one among us, holding tight in an apartment directly above the suspect's. And none of us with anything to look at.

We'd been like this since suppertime, hoping Marty Gagnon would reward us by coming home. Following our visit to Walter Skottick's, we'd discreetly dropped by Gagnon's place and found the rusty Subaru in a parking space by the railroad tracks nearby, but no Marty.

The choices after that had been several: a canvass of his neighbors, friends, and family; a sit tight approach, waiting for a reaction to the bulletins we'd sent around; a combination of both; or—the most expensive alternative—a stakeout.

I'd opted for the last, to universal groans.

My explanation was that, according to Marty Gagnon's records, we were dealing with a man as prone to flight as a cat in a dog fight. He had a history of running off worse than anyone I'd seen. He'd skipped on court appearances, parole meetings, counseling sessions, and everything else for which he'd ever been held accountable. It had therefore seemed more cost-effective to me to blow a single night's overtime and nab him fast than to tip him off through routine inquiries and then waste days chasing him down.

What I hadn't admitted to the others was the additional juvenile appeal of handing this case gift wrapped back to Snuffy Dawson only forty-eight hours after inheriting it.

Which was just as well, since now it was looking as if

I'd blown my budget solely to create three cranky colleagues and a skeptical boss at headquarters.

The cell phone in my breast pocket began vibrating silently against my ribs.

"Gunther."

"This is Dispatch. We just got a call from a Walter Skottick. He was assaulted at his home by someone looking for Marty Gagnon."

"He okay?"

"Didn't sound it. I sent the ambulance to pick him up. They should be at the hospital in about half an hour. He wanted me to tell you specifically that he didn't talk to anybody. That make sense?"

"Yeah." I put the cell phone away and keyed the radio again. "It's a wrap, everybody. I think our target's already long gone."

Sammie Martens stood in the ER waiting room, her head tilted back, staring at the television set mounted high on the wall. On screen, a couple was visibly screaming at each other from opposing chairs, an interviewer with a microphone trying to walk a fine line between verbal abuse and furniture tossing—but the sound was off, making the whole drama a pantomime. A caption at the bottom of the screen read, "Men who slept with their sisters."

"What do you think happened?" Sammie asked the TV.

I understood the oblique reference. "Skottick will have to confirm it, but my bet is whoever beat him up did what we did in reverse, looking for Marty Gagnon, asking a lot of questions, until he finally ended up at Skottick's place, giving Marty the heads up in the process. That would explain why Marty never came home."

She didn't move. "Makes you wonder if this person is looking for him for the same reason we are."

Walter Skottick seemed in pretty rough shape when he was rolled into the ER on a backboard, his face bandaged, his neck in a brace, and two IVs running into his arms.

Sammie and I waited in the hallway while the nurses and technicians went through their routine and the on-call doc finally arrived to survey what was left.

Luckily, that doc turned out to be James Franklin, the hospital's best general surgeon and a man I had known for years.

"Jim," I asked him on one of his trips out of the treatment room. "He going to make it?"

Franklin stopped in his tracks and laughed. "If we don't kill him. You read that article on how many people die in hospitals every year through negligence? It's amazing. Hi, Sammie. Walk with me, I gotta get something to help out with his lung. How've you guys been? Haven't seen you since that gunshot wound to the heart. Remember that, Joe? Hell of a deal. At least I didn't do *that* guy in. Miracle I saw him at all. Shoulda been DOA. Still, you know, I keep thinking about that case, wondering if there mightn't have been some way . . . Remember, Joe? I had my finger right in the hole . . ."

He finally paused long enough to notice neither one of us had said a word. This was typical James Franklin.

"Sorry. Right . . . This guy has a concussion, facial fractures, a few missing teeth, four broken ribs, and a collapsed lung. Basically, beaten to a pulp. But he'll live. That answer your question?"

"One of them. Will I be able to talk to him?"

Franklin grabbed a sealed package from the shelf of the supply room we'd escorted him to. "Fine with me, but it's up to him."

Walter Skottick would have looked like a movie mummy if it hadn't been for the oxygen tubing up his nose and the tufts of beard poking out from between the bandaging. He was so still, I wasn't sure he was breathing. Sammie and I stood at the foot of his bed for a moment, I toying with the fanciful notion that the hospital staff would soon discover their patient had died unnoticed under all their packaging.

"Mr. Skottick?" I said gently.

The one nonswollen eye opened. The voice barely emanating from the dressings managed to say, "Wha?"

"It's Joe Gunther, Mr. Skottick. We met earlier—about Marty Gagnon."

One hand flapped anemically on the bed sheet. "Wha' the hell you do to me?"

Sammie furrowed her brow, not having been at that first meeting. "What do you mean?"

"Fine till you came," he answered, and then stopped to gasp for breath.

"Mr. Skottick," I said. "I know you feel lousy, but we need to ask you some questions if we're going to get the person responsible for this."

"Didn't see."

"Was he wearing a mask?"

"Yeah."

"How did he get in? You were inside, right?"

He nodded weakly. "TV. Behind me."

"He came up behind you?"

"Yeah."

"And he was looking for Marty Gagnon. What did he say, exactly?"

"Just where—'gain an' 'gain—where, where, where."

"But he didn't say why?"

"No."

"Why did he keep beating you? You put up a fight?"

"At first . . . not much. I didn't know. I told him cops came."

"You told him about our visit?"

"Yeah."

"Did you get any other calls about that watch, besides ours?"

"No."

"Okay, Mr. Skottick. One last thing, and please don't take offense, 'cause you may not like it. But are you being totally straight with us? About the watch and this attack, both?"

The man's entire body shifted with frustration under the sheets. His hands balled up into fists. "Shit. I wanted . . . sell . . . car—that's all."

"All right, all right," I tried soothing him. "I had to ask. We'll get this guy. You just work on getting better."

Sammie and I stepped out into the hallway.

"You think he's telling the truth?" she asked.

I waggled my hand back and forth equivocally. "Could be. Dumber things have happened. What's interesting to me is how his attacker found out about him. If he did chase down some of Marty's friends first, like I'm thinking, then Skottick may be just the latest of a string of such interviews. I'd like to know what Marty did or didn't do, saw or didn't see, that got whoever this is so interested in finding him. And does the stealing of the watch, or anything else from the Manning house, have anything to do with it?"

Sammie knew better than to respond.

"Since the cat's obviously out of the bag," I continued, "we might as well go after Marty's known playmates."

Marty Gagnon's criminal record was as stuffed as a phone book with names and addresses of promising "past-known associates," many of which we got from our erstwhile colleagues at the Brattleboro Police Department. Ron Klesczewski, part of our old squad, was still there, along with J. P. Tyler, who'd been our forensics man, and it was Ron who came upstairs to our office early the next morning with the PD's internal file on Gagnon—those investigative tidbits that didn't merit being injected into the state or national data banks.

So, allowing Sammie to sleep late and letting Lester work on his caseload, I had Ron and Willy help me compile a contact list of the most promising among Marty's circle. As soon as he saw the name Don Matthews, however, Willy put him at the top of the heap.

"Of all these losers," he explained with the sure-footedness of a museum curator, "Don's the best at handling hot property. I'd start with him."

"He still around?" I asked Ron.

"Around and off the leash. He finished his parole three months ago. Got a job up in Springfield at the battery plant."

Sitting next to me in my car several hours later, Willy stretched his right arm out straight and checked his wristwatch. "Matthews is on the graveyard shift, so he should be at home catching Z's by now. I called his supervisor, and he told me odds and ends have been going missing ever since Don started working there, mostly from the locker room. No proof—surprise, surprise—but I figured we could use that to squeeze his nuts a little."

We finished our meal of greasy offerings from a fast food place in Springfield, Vermont (about forty minutes north of Brattleboro), and drove a few blocks north, past a near-derelict shopping mall with half its parking lot unplowed, and into a neighborhood of two-story apartment buildings lined up like shoeboxes left too long in the rain. Both sides of the narrow street were dotted with rusting cars and dirty snow. Many of the windows were boarded up or covered with plastic sheeting, and the top edges of several of them had been licked with black soot from past fires, both arson and freebasing being popular time killers here.

"What number?" I asked.

Willy merely pointed through the windshield at the next address, and said, "Apartment one-fourteen. Rear."

"There a back door?"

He nodded, pulling into a parking place in front of a pickup with three wheels. "There's a fire escape, according to my source. You want me to cover it?"

"Sure," I said, surprised by the offer. Willy normally prided himself on kicking in doors.

He swung out into the sharp cold air in one graceful movement. "You got it. Give me five minutes to set up."

I stood by the car as he strode off, the odd asymmetry

of his gait as familiar to me as my own brother's. Despite the bureaucratic hassles I continued to take on to keep this man employed, I still enjoyed seeing him in action. Under his thick, hard-boiled exterior was a passion rarely seen in a veteran of any job—one which found outlets in old-fashioned justice, a reserved but endearing affection for Sammie, and even—I'd discovered once but was angrily sworn never to reveal—a remarkable ability to pencil sketch, something he indulged in while sitting alone on stakeouts.

I checked the time. Five minutes. I crossed the uneven sidewalk, went up the path to the scratched glass lobby door, and entered the building.

The heat was instantly unbearable: arid and rancid with the stench of unwashed bodies. I could hear people muttering through the thin walls around me, yelling, playing music or the TV, all in the middle of a weekday, like worker bees laboring in a hive. Except that they weren't producing anything—at least nothing legal.

I took the stairs, having learned the hard way about the reliability of elevators in such buildings, and opened my coat wide, both to cool off and to give me better access to my gun.

At the second-floor landing, I came to a T-junction of poorly lit hallways and took the one heading straight back, reading what numbers there were off the battered hollow-core doors. One-fourteen was the last one on the left.

I knocked loudly. Willy had described Don Matthews as tall, nervous, skinny, and wearing a ponytail, not at all like the hairless round runt who opened the door after the third pounding. So much for Matthews's catching some sleep after a factory shift.

I showed this man my shield. "Police. Who're you?"

His thin, unshaven face paled. "What?"

"You're not Don Matthews, so who are you?"

He groped for an answer. "Ah . . . Ted . . . Smith."

"I need to talk to Don—right now."

His eyes darted over my shoulder, checking the hallway. "Oh . . . Yeah. Well, he's kind of busy right now."

"Let me in. I'll wait."

He looked slightly alarmed. "Hey, no. I mean, he's in the bathroom . . . Look, it's not my place, like you said, so I can't really let people in uninvited. It may not be legal or something, right?"

"You got something in there you don't want me to see?" I asked.

He licked his lips. "I don't got nuthin'. It's just private property, is all."

There was a sudden sound of glass breaking behind him. Startled, Smith turned to look, inadvertently opening the door wide enough for me to see a man standing on a table against the far wall, his hand halfway through the window he'd been trying to open. His description fit Don Matthews.

"Don't move," I yelled. "Police."

I might as well have fired a starter's pistol. The man on the table threw himself at the window, falling outside, while Ted Smith made a feeble attempt to push me across the hallway. I pushed him back as I entered the room but tripped over his legs when he stumbled before me. I fell to my knees and felt his hands groping for the gun under my coat. I twisted around, rolled onto my back, and planted a heel between his eyes, stunning him like a cow.

"You son of a bitch," I snarled, "consider yourself busted." I then regained my feet, ran to the now empty window, and yelled outside, "Willy—he's coming down the fire escape."

A noise behind me made me spin on my heel, my gun out, in time to see Smith crawling out the door. "Don't move, Ted, or I'll shoot your ass off."

He froze, his upper body already out in the hall. I pulled out my handcuffs, dragged him back inside, and attached him to a water pipe running up the wall. "Stay there. I'll be back."

I returned to the window, being careful of the broken shards, and climbed out onto the wooden fire escape, leaning over the railing to see the alley below. Willy's thin, pale face was staring up at me.

"You got him?" I shouted.

"Almost," he answered calmly, and then gestured with his arm as if directing traffic. "Come to Poppa, Don."

I started down the rickety stairs through the opening in the landing and almost immediately saw our quarry poised on the next level between me and Willy below— gaunt, hollow-eyed, his ponytail almost reaching his waist.

I pointed my gun at him. "Stay where you are. We're police officers."

But he obviously knew I wouldn't shoot unless he threatened me, and he had other things in mind than fighting. Instead, he jumped up onto the railing, positioned himself like a diver as I came off the stairs to stop him, and threw himself into the void, sailing over both

Willy's head and a sagging chain-link fence cutting the alleyway in two, and landing with a crash onto the roof of a parked car, blowing out its windshield in the process.

Willy stared helplessly through the fence. The man on the other side rolled off the roof, landed in the snow on the car's far side, and scrambled to his feet to race down the alley for a clean getaway.

"Get the car, Willy," I yelled as I continued down the fire escape as fast as I could, opting against the airborne route.

Instantly accepting his inability to climb the fence with just one arm, Willy took off in the other direction as I struggled with the wobbly chain link, landing in an untidy but intact pile on the same semidestroyed car.

I still had our man in sight, his greasy hair swinging like a horse's tail behind him. He was as scrawny as a scarecrow, and from the quick glance I'd gotten, seemed nearly as fit. If I managed not to lose him, I figured even I could wear him out. There was no way this clown would last too long on adrenaline alone. I hoped.

Unfortunately, his athletic prowess wasn't put to the test. After rounding the corner at the alley's mouth, I found myself staring at an empty sidewalk.

"Shit," I muttered under my breath.

I saw a man across the street, sitting on a bus stop bench, looking up from his reading, staring at a spot only thirty feet ahead of me, as if he'd just seen something interesting. It was all I needed. As the spectator returned to his newspaper, I jogged to the spot, found a door between two businesses, and waited until Willy drove into view a block away. I waved at him, pointed to the door, and entered.

I was in a lobby facing a broad set of stairs heading up to the second floor. Unlike the apartment building I'd just left, this place was quiet, odorless, and except for the fluorescent lighting humming overhead, seemingly abandoned.

I unholstered my gun again. Wisdom dictated waiting for backup. Experience suggested my quarry would take that time to disappear entirely.

I headed upstairs.

On the landing, I found four doors, all labeled, three with business names—a lawyer, a barber, and an accountant—and the last a rest room. Apparently, business was bad enough that either everyone had gone home or had simply died at their desks years back. I could hear no phones, no keyboard tapping, nothing except the lighting and the same muted mechanical murmur that all commercial buildings seem to exude, like a person's breathing.

Logic suggested the bathroom. It was possible the guy went to a friend's office or was behind one of those doors holding the occupants hostage, but more likely, he'd holed up where he felt more at ease, around a bunch of toilets.

Unless he'd gone in there to use another window.

I decided not to take the chance. I approached the door, planning to open it from the knob side, so as not to be in its way when it swung back, when it suddenly did just that. The door hit my foot and threw me off balance, and the long-haired man came barreling out, slamming into me like a linebacker on his way back down the stairs. I went flying against the opposite wall, my gun clattering across the floor, and felt the wind get knocked out of me by the impact.

"Damn," I swore, by now seriously angry. I staggered to my feet, lurched to the top of the stairs, ripped a fire extinguisher off its wall bracket, and threw it with all my strength at the man about halfway to the ground floor.

It caught him behind the knees and sent him sailing head first into the lobby, where he landed with a terrific crash.

I quickly retrieved my gun at the far end of the landing. When I reappeared on the stairs, however, Matthews was no longer alone. Standing over him, smiling, was Willy Kunkle, a pair of handcuffs in his hand.

"He still alive?" I asked him.

Willy chuckled and leaned over to apply the cuffs. "Not happily, but yeah. Are you?"

CHAPTER FIVE

DON MATTHEWS EYED ME WARILY FROM HIS HOSPITAL BED. "You gonna read me my rights?"

"I hate to tell you this, Don, after all you've been through, but we weren't there to arrest you. We just wanted to ask you a few questions."

He gingerly touched the bandage encircling his head, looking like a CliffsNotes version of Walter Skottick. "You're shitting me. I should sue you guys."

I narrowed my eyes. "You can try, after I bust you for unlawful flight, assault on a police officer, destruction of private property, and knowingly selling stolen property. The fat little weasel you were doing business with when we dropped by is talking his head off. With your record, that'll all weigh more than you want to carry, believe me."

He seemed to agree after a moment's thought, because his next question was, "What did you want to ask me?"

"We're looking for Marty Gagnon. You seen him?"

Matthews laughed in surprise and then winced with pain. "That's what this was all about? Jesus. No, not in weeks."

I looked at him for a long moment, as if contemplating his fate. "You know, Don, maybe I'll drop the hammer on you, anyhow. The more I remember our little foot race, the more pissed off I get."

His mouth fell open. "Oh, come on. I guess I came out worse than you did. Look at me, for Christ's sake—you totaled me."

"I can add to the damage. I'm the good guys, remember? What's the problem, anyway? Just give me an address and I'm out of your hair."

He stared at me sullenly.

"Or," I added, "I can start digging into your life history even deeper to find out why you're holding back. You up to something with Marty you don't want me to know about?"

Matthews made a disgusted face. "It's a pride thing."

I hid my amusement at this curiously honest admission. "At any price?"

"No," he conceded, as if finally concluding a social obligation he hadn't believed in from the start. When he resumed, his voice was more confiding. "Okay, this is straight. It's all I know. Marty was feeling some heat— not you, somebody else—I don't know who. But he figured he'd lay low for a while."

"You know he'd just pulled a job?"

"At Tucker Peak? Yeah. He was going to show me some stuff, but we never got around to it. He didn't call like he was supposed to."

"Was the heat turned on after that job? It was only a couple of days ago."

"I guess," he conceded. "Whoever this was came down

hard. Started rousting all Marty's friends like he'd had a lot of practice."

"You, too?" I asked, surprised.

"That's why I ran when you came to my place. I was a little gun shy after the last visit."

"You saw this man?"

He shook his head. "Don't I wish. He found me last night, outside in the dark, on Flat Street. Came up behind me, shoved me against the wall, stuck a knife in my ear, and asked me about Marty."

"And you told him where he was?"

Don Matthews smiled. "I told him squat. I gave him a phony address."

"Pretty risky."

The smile broadened with the implied flattery. Matthews might not have told the truth to the man with the knife, but his ego demanded he share his secret with some appreciative audience. For those scant few minutes, he and I were bonded.

"Like I said. It's a pride thing. But it did make me twitchy."

"You call Marty to warn him?"

"I left a message."

The next question was a given. "How do I do the same thing?"

"Talk to Jorja Duval. She lives in Bratt, on Baker."

Baker Street is just a block beyond one of Brattleboro's busier, four-way intersections. The other three streets either lead downtown or to shortcuts to the south side. But the extension feeding into Baker falls off a slight embankment and is part of a closed loop bordering a large, empty field near the Whetstone Brook—out of sight and largely out of mind.

The buildings along it run from decrepit to slightly better, in varying stages. The address Don Matthews had given me was a two-story apartment building, once a home, now cut into four small, dark sections, each one neglected, stagnant, but cheap. The windows were all covered with familiar brittle and tattered plastic wrap, once put up to help stop the freezing air from whistling through the gaps but left to age through all four seasons, year after year, until its only remaining effectiveness was to proclaim the hopelessness of those inadequately sheltered behind it.

Willy and I had decided on a quiet approach, parking up the street and coming around the corner on foot. The weather was good—clear, sharp, and cold enough to make your nose hairs tingle—and I didn't mind the chance, however oddly presented, to be outside and away from the stifling indoor heat most people found comforting during the winter.

We walked down the middle of the street. There was no traffic, and the sidewalks had been left to reemerge in the spring, as usual in most of the town's less stringently tidy neighborhoods.

"Anything we should know about Jorja Duval?" I asked Willy as the house loomed nearer.

"Nothing you couldn't guess," he said. "On welfare, on drugs, small history of dealing, tricking, and petty theft. Featured in a few domestics, according to Bratt PD, always as the punching bag. I knew her father back in the old days. Always figured he was banging her, although no charges were ever brought. He's at St. Albans now on a manslaughter charge. Jorja had a brother, too, but he OD'd about five years ago."

"How old is she?"

Willy hesitated. "Twenty-five? Maybe younger."

We drew abreast of the house, took it in quickly with a practiced eye, and then struggled our way up a pathway that had been cleared in the Walter Skottick fashion—not at all.

The peeling front door sported four rusty mailboxes by its side, none of them labeled. There were also no doorbells. I raised an inquiring eye at Willy.

He pointed to the window above us and to the right. "That one," he said softly, and twisted the doorknob.

The door swung back to reveal a gloomy, barefloored hallway with a set of stairs heading up. The odorous fog that crept out to envelop us was rancid and flavored with mildew and a smell of humanity reminiscent of an overripe diaper pail. Neither one of us reacted, since as working environments went, this was pretty standard fare.

We both paused for a moment, watching and listening, taking nothing for granted, knowing full well that inhabitants of such places were capable of anything.

Hearing nothing, we headed upstairs. There was an extra stillness to the cold air I didn't like, though, and I could sense Willy felt the same way. He unbuttoned his coat and removed his gun from its holster.

Walking on the balls of our feet to partially muffle our shoes and the squeaking of old floorboards, we moved to either side of Jorja Duval's apartment door and paused once again, listening to nothing but our own breathing.

I finally reached out and rapped on the door, looking up and down the hallway as I did so for any movement from the other two apartments on the landing. "Jorja Duval? This is the police. Open up."

The response was immediate, otherworldly, and psychologically chilling. From inside, we heard a single, high-pitched animal howl, followed by a series of thuds, crashes, and the sound of claws scrabbling across bare wood at high speed. It was as if my knock had unleashed some demonic pinball that was now smacking off every wall and obstacle inside the apartment.

"What the hell?" I muttered, and grasped the door knob, twisting it slowly.

The door opened and a tabby cat flew out and froze for a split second at the sight of us, its hair on end, before shooting off like a rocket down the stairs. But not before I'd seen that all four of its paws were crusty with dried blood.

"Jesus," Willy burst out.

Still recovering from the surprise, I chanced a fast glance around the corner, my own gun out as well. Pulling my head back, I described what I'd seen to Willy. "Short hall, two closed doors opposite each other. Big room beyond. All I could see there were two legs sticking into the middle of a big bloodstain, and red paw prints all over the place."

"We call for backup?" he asked.

I paused, thinking of the eerie stillness I'd noticed earlier. "No time. Ready on three?"

I held up three fingers, one at a time, and the two of us entered the small hallway as one, covering both the distant room and the two closed doors.

The precautions proved unnecessary. The place was empty except for the dead woman in the middle of the floor, lying faceup, spread-eagle, with her throat cut wide. The room was dingy, dark, barely furnished, splotched with blood, and seemed far less comfortable than the average coffin.

"This Jorja Duval?" I asked Willy.

He holstered his weapon. "Was."

I opened the back of the Brattleboro Police Department's converted ambulance and hauled myself inside. Used for everything from carrying their special reaction team to serving as a mobile command vehicle, it was now parked outside Jorja Duval's apartment house primarily to give us all a warm place to confer. The landlord had still not been located, so no one had found a way to turn up the heat in the building, which was now crawling with state crime lab technicians in any case, clad in puffy white overalls and booties, like scientists escaped from a movie lot.

Inside the van were Ron Klesczewski, Sammie Martens, a couple of Brattleboro cops taking advantage of the portable coffee urn, and a woman I'd never met but knew to be the head of the forensics team. We'd all been here for five hours by now, following the standard protocol for the discovery of a homicide, and were processing the apartment, interviewing the other residents, and canvassing the neighborhood.

I found a spot on the bench running the length of the van's side and slipped off my coat, greeting the others as I did so. I'd just returned from the office, where'd I been making more inquiries into Marty Gagnon and his known contacts.

The lab tech was a tall, striking woman named Robin Leonard, who introduced herself with a firm handshake and a no-nonsense manner.

"Okay," I asked them all, after that introduction was over, "where do we stand?"

Sammie had been in charge during my absence, and while not prone to sitting back in most cases, she knew better than to speak first right now. In exchange for its elite status, or because of it, VBI had drummed into its ranks an instinct for diplomacy, Willy notwithstanding. We didn't need the FBI's reputation for stepping on toes. Sammie kept her peace, looking directly at Ron instead.

It was a familiar scenario. When the three of us had worked together in the old days, both the pecking order and the interaction had been similar. I'd been the lieutenant, Sammie the eager up-and-comer, and Ron the thoughtful introvert, hard-working but self-conscious, always doubtful of his true worth. Now, by simple attrition, he was head of that same detective squad, and I knew he'd been struggling with the trappings of the job. I'd always believed he had the makings of what he'd finally become. I'd even made him my second-in-command in preparation once, prematurely, as it turned out. But he was also his own worst obstacle, and could be frustrating to watch in action.

Not now, though. The pressure, while real, was still predictable this time, so after a moment's hesitation, and the stimulus supplied by Sammie's telling look, Ron cleared his throat.

"Right now, from our perspective, things aren't looking too good," he admitted. "We still have to chase down a few residents who aren't in right now, who might've seen something at the time, and we need to find out if anything like the mailman or any service trucks were in the area when we think the victim was killed, but so far, we have nothing—no unusual activities or sounds, no interruptions to the neighborhood's normal patterns. And no one has anything to say about Jorja Duval, Marty Gagnon, or anyone else who might've been in that apartment."

"Meaning they never even saw them?" I asked.

"The woman across the landing and the guy who lives downstairs admit they knew Duval. Saw her coming and going. But they never talked to her, and they deny she ever had guests or caused any disturbances. To hear them, she might have been a ghost."

"Meaning they're lying," Sammie softly echoed my thoughts.

"Maybe," Ron agreed, "but we can't prove it. Not yet."

"What *was* the time of death?" I asked.

Robin Leonard spoke up. "I asked the assistant medical examiner that when he was packing her up for transport. After the usual disclaimers, he guessed sometime last night."

"And the neighbors were in?"

Ron nodded. "Supposedly."

One of the cops spoke up unexpectedly, no doubt hoping to impress Leonard. "You'll probably find some dandruff or something that'll nail the guy. I read somewhere you folks can even pick out individual cat hairs. Maybe the tabby'll help you out."

Leonard glanced at the man for a moment, forcing him to look away. When she responded, however, it was as if his comment had been purely professional. "I'm not that hopeful. I was told she'd only been living there a few weeks, and that the apartment has seen a half-dozen occupants in the last year. My guess is we'll end up collecting as many samples as we'd find in the average bus station, half of which we'll never connect to anyone."

"So, you don't have anything hot right now?" I asked. "Like the proverbial bloody footprint?"

She smiled and pointed to the cop, in part, I guessed, to ease him off the hook. "Just the tabby cat's, and we have a few thousand of those."

I turned to Sammie. "Robin's people let you poke around, too, right? You find any documents or clothing or personal items that might have belonged to anyone other than Duval?"

"Hard to say," she answered. "The clothes she was killed in were men's, as were half the rags in her closet. Looks like she wore whatever she could get her hands on. There's nothing obvious belonging to somebody else, and the only documents I've found so far are pretty routine: mostly welfare or parole related, along with some junk mail."

"Did I notice a phone up there? Seems like a luxury for someone living at rock bottom."

Sammie tried to hide her embarrassment at not having made the same observation, a reaction that was typical of the high standards she set for herself. "Yeah. I'll get a warrant for the records."

"What about Marty's car?" I asked Ron. "Anyone ever see it around here?"

He shook his head. "Not that we know so far."

"You check if he got any tickets recently? According to Skottick, he's been driving it for a month or so. Probably won't help us even if he did get one, but you never know."

"Will do," Ron answered neutrally, possibly thinking I was grasping at straws.

"I assigned a couple of people to search the car like you asked, by the way," Robin Leonard said. "Haven't heard anything back yet. I wanted to wait for the full crew to be finished here before we tackle his apartment."

I checked a list I'd taken from my pocket. "Thanks. You put a guard there, Ron?"

"'Round the clock. I also made sure all our guys have been briefed to keep a lookout for Gagnon. What did you get out of the computer?"

"Not much," I admitted. "I went downstairs to check your in-house files, too. I was hoping if I ran checks on both Duval and Gagnon, I might get some overlaps, some common ground to cover. But nothing came up. I just got more people to look for. I'm afraid we're all going to be knocking on a lot of doors."

In the slight pause following that, Sammie asked, "You think Marty killed her?"

"I have no reason to think he didn't. It's more likely that the guy who punched out Skottick killed her trying to find Marty, but who can tell? Whoever did it, Marty seems to be the key. And," I added, "if nothing else, at least we know what he looks like."

Sammie let out a sigh. "Assuming he isn't dead, too."

*   *   *

The next several days were spent coordinating dozens of separate activities, all dedicated to locating Marty Gagnon. His apartment and car were disassembled, everyone we could find who knew him or Jorja Duval was interviewed, as were—again—Walter Skottick and Don Matthews. We even called William Manning in New York for more details, and gave his background extra scrutiny. Neighbors were questioned, regular delivery people stopped and quizzed, and every scrap of paper found in our searches was analyzed for any lead at all. The medical examiner in Burlington was asked to conduct an especially thorough autopsy, which request stimulated both a frosty reaction and the simple result that Jorja Duval had died of a single cut to the neck—no defense wounds, and only slight bruising to the upper arms.

We had cooperation in all this from the Brattleboro cops, the local state police barracks, and for outlying addresses, various deputy sheriffs. We also issued a BOL, or Be On the Lookout bulletin, nationally for Marty Gagnon.

None of it led to anything beyond finding a few more people who, like Don Matthews, had been approached by a man they didn't see, and asked about Marty's whereabouts. But Gagnon himself remained invisible, as did the man who'd assaulted Skottick, threatened Marty's friends, and possibly murdered Duval, and we didn't get a single hit on any of the notices we'd sent out over the wire.

At least, we didn't until Sammie Martens walked into

the office one afternoon brandishing a single piece of paper and a smile on her face.

"What's that?" I asked, hanging up the phone.

She laid it down before me. "Maybe nothing. I got a court order for Jorja's phone, like you suggested. I think you'll get a kick out of what we got."

She placed a fingertip opposite the only long distance number on the document. "That call was made two days before the Manning place was ripped off—to a pay phone in the employee locker room at Tucker Peak."

CHAPTER SIX

BILL ALLARD SAT BACK IN HIS CHAIR AND PENSIVELY cupped his cheek in his hand. "God, Joe, it seems awfully thin. Don't you have anything more linking Marty Gagnon to Tucker Peak than a single call made from his girlfriend's phone?"

"There's a speeding ticket he got on the access road," I told him, hoping to stoke his enthusiasm slowly, using the little I had to its best advantage.

The two of us were in Allard's office on the top floor of the Department of Public Safety building (also the headquarters of the Vermont State Police) in Waterbury, a conveniently short drive away from the state capitol building, the legislature, and those who controlled the purse strings.

Allard didn't respond to my comment about the ticket. He was the head of VBI and an ex-trooper from downstairs, a lineage which, given the state police's sensitivity about us, had made his selection about as politically subtle as choosing a union head to be shop foreman. But he was highly regarded by everyone in the profession and someone I had instinctively liked from the start, which was just as well, since he was my immediate boss.

Now, however, I could tell he was having problems with my latest scheme. Politics were as important to him as they'd been to the people who'd chosen him. They, especially the commissioner of public safety, were watching the entire VBI experiment as something from which the plug could be pulled at a moment's notice. It was Bill Allard's job, therefore, to not only manage the budget and the Bureau's nascent needs but also to make sure the assignments it took on made it indispensable and not too pushy.

I was proposing that both Sammie Martens and I go undercover as employees of Tucker Peak, while Willy and Lester worked the string of burglaries we suspected Marty Gagnon had been running before his disappearance.

Bill began with a question I'd pondered earlier: "Isn't there a pretty good chance you'll be recognized? You've been a cop a long time—a lot of people know you."

"I have a fast-growing beard, and I'll dye and change the way I comb my hair. Shouldn't be a week before I look pretty different."

He switched to a more diplomatic concern. "What did Snuffy have to say about it?"

"It's a win-win for him. He gets extra police presence on the mountain, a specific focus on his biggest current problem, all the credit if we're successful, and he doesn't have to pay for any of it."

"But why not a conventional investigation? The burglaries are common knowledge. People know the cops are looking into them. Seems to me it would be a lot simpler—and cheaper."

"Simpler, maybe, but higher risk, too. The Tucker Peak crowd might know about the burglaries. They don't know a murder may be connected to them. If we do this in the open, that's bound to get out and make our job harder, with the greater chance that we'll fail and end up with a black eye. But if we let whoever killed Jorja Duval think we've hit a brick wall while we're actually poking around from the inside, it gives us an advantage."

"Except that you have no idea who killed Duval, or if it's connected to Marty Gagnon or Tucker Peak or any burglaries anywhere. Going undercover seems pretty fancy for what amounts to a gut instinct. I'd be happier if you had a single, solid lead."

"In the absence of anything else," I answered him, "what we have *is* a lead."

"A single phone call."

"To an employee, lasting twelve minutes, just a few days before the Manning place was robbed." Then, feeling like a trial lawyer pulling his prize witness out of a hat, I removed a sheet of paper from my jacket pocket and slid it onto his desk.

"A pattern we found repeated three more times on his home phone bill."

Allard gave me a sour look, knowing full well I'd been working him like a game fish. "Now he tells me."

"Each time," I continued, "according to Snuffy's records, a burglary was committed at Tucker Peak several days after Marty called that same number. And each call lasted about as long."

Allard was studying Gagnon's phone record. "And

each call was made about the same time of day," he murmured.

"Yeah, the shift change between the day and night crews, meaning the recipient could've been from either."

Bill Allard sat back and gazed at me thoughtfully. "Bottom line, Joe—you really think this is the way to go?"

I answered him as truthfully as I could. "It is a gut feeling—you're right there—but, yeah, that's what I think."

"All right," he finally gave in. "But short term, okay? You and Sammie do your sniffing around fast. One month tops unless you get something hot."

Gail Zigman poured herself a glass of red wine and joined me on the couch, where I was already sipping coffee. We were in her condo just outside of Montpelier, a slightly sterile corner of an apartment complex she'd gotten for the panoramic view of the valley below, which right now amounted to a scattering of lights in the night, hovering like small, pale moths around the spotlighted golden dome of the capitol building far in the distance.

"Undercover? Sounds dangerous."

I'd been there for over an hour already, but we'd only begun getting conversational. One aspect of living far apart, we'd discovered, was that when we did meet up, we wasted no time taking our clothes off. From the couch, in fact, I could still see a trail of shirts, pants, and socks trailing off toward the bedroom. Only now had I told her why I was in the neighborhood.

I waited until she was comfortably settled against several fat pillows, her legs tucked up underneath her thick terry cloth robe.

"The biggest danger so far was getting the go-ahead. We don't actually have a lot to work with."

"This connected to the dead girl I read about in the paper?" Gail asked.

"Yup, but I'll be focusing on Tucker Peak. That's our only lead right now."

Her eyes widened. "Tucker Peak? You're kidding. I'll guarantee you *some* activity, even if it's not what you're expecting."

"What do you mean?"

"We were just given the heads-up on a protest there. A bunch of people are unhappy with Tucker's plans to build a hotel, cut more trails, and tap into a nearby lake for their snowmaking guns. They're saying it'll be bad for the land, the fish, and the local bears, among other things."

I remembered the placard-wielding group Willy and I had passed on our way to Manning's house—one of the reasons Snuffy was short of help and had brought us in. "Who are they?"

"They call themselves the Tucker Protection League— TPL for short."

VermontGreen, the firm Gail worked for, often acted as a clearinghouse for such protests, approached by smaller organizations hoping for their blessing, their backing, and their expertise, in that ascending order.

"Are you going to help them out?" I asked.

She paused to take a sip before answering indirectly. "The resort jumped through all the regulatory hoops, and we were watching closely during the entire two-year process. We had a few objections along the way, but Phil McNally took care of them, including the land, fish, and bears."

"McNally's the boss?"

"The CEO. I suppose the board's the boss, technically, but he's the one we dealt with. Very helpful, unlike some of his counterparts at other mountains. He's actually co-operating with TPL, giving them space to demonstrate."

"So why the protest, if everything's so squeaky clean?"

"Well, that's always the question, isn't it?" she mused. "What exactly is squeaky clean? The regulations were put together by politicians, after all. You know how screwy that can get. McNally and his crew, as accommodating as they've been, are still corporate types, known to say one thing and do another. And then there's the science. We all rely on naturalists to give us the straight and narrow, but we're dealing with human beings on the one hand and Mother Nature on the other. There may not be a straight and narrow. The people bitching now might be right. They might know something the rest of us missed."

"And they didn't get around to mentioning it till now?" I couldn't keep the incredulity from my voice. "I thought this rigmarole took years to reach this stage."

She laughed. "Okay. I'll admit they may not be overly organized, but that doesn't mean they're not right. They weren't allowed party status during the regulatory process—in answer to your question—and now that it's almost a done deal, TPL's claiming major environmental obstacles were swept under the rug for the sake of big business."

"But I thought VermontGreen had party status."

She pursed her lips regretfully. "We did, and we signed off on the project. TPL is calling us traitors because of it."

I raised my eyebrows, suddenly understanding her earlier hesitation. "Oh. That makes it awkward."

She put her glass down on the coffee table beside her and crossed her arms. "Yeah. I feel a little funny about it. VermontGreen's supposed to be the environment's protective mother ship. I try to be objective about it—I'm a big girl, a lawyer, pretty good at swimming with the sharks—but I used to be in the trenches, too, looking at people like me and thinking they'd sold out. It's kind of odd. I don't want them to be right."

For all her efforts to help the downtrodden, Gail wasn't an overly sentimental woman. She had a pragmatist's way of dealing with adversity and could make a deal if it helped her cause. But she held her integrity dear, and her doubts right now made me want to find out more, especially since her protesters and I were going to be sharing the same neighborhood.

"Who are these folks, anyway? They part of a bigger group?"

"Some of them are locals, others are part of the crowd that jump on every passing bandwagon. They don't have an organization per se, but they do have a steering committee headed by a guy named Roger Betts, who every time you talk to him says he's not their leader. He's a good man, pushing ninety, an old-time socialist type from the Woody Guthrie school, I guess. He's lived near Tucker Peak for decades, and I've known him almost since I got here. He's one of the true gatekeepers of Vermont's environment, writing articles and giving workshops—taught high school for a living. A sweet man with a powerful moral sense. He's actually the primary reason I'm worried we may have missed something. Roger's not prone to tilting at windmills."

"Except that this one's in his own backyard. That may

have made him less objective. How come I've never heard of him?"

She picked up her wine again and took another sip. "You don't exactly pursue the same interests. Plus, he's normally pretty self-effacing. This is the highest-profile I've seen him, which probably ties in to what you just said. And you could be right. Proximity may've colored his thinking. That's another reason I'm wobbling. I can't make up my mind."

"What exactly are they accusing Tucker of?"

"Cooking the research, paying off a naturalist or two, keeping crucial facts off the books. The idea of laying a pipeline into a lake and drawing water to make snow isn't so bad all by itself. There's hardly a mountain around that doesn't do something like that. Tucker did it about twelve years ago themselves, when they tapped into their current pond. But it's how many gallons and the rate of extraction and how many times a day or week this new lake will be used that only the mountain will know about. There's monitoring equipment and on-site inspectors to keep people honest, but who's kidding who? In a state like Vermont, there aren't the resources for that to mean much. Machines can be fooled, and there aren't enough inspectors to go around. And that doesn't even touch the hotel and the new chairlift and the extra planned trails, all of which will leave footprints on the environment."

"I thought you said Phil McNally was playing ball," I reminded her.

Gail made her eyes wide as if she were going nuts and jerked her head around in pantomime. "*I know*," she burst out. "That's my problem. McNally's a good guy, Betts is a saint, the corporation's done all the right things. Which only means TPL is either a bunch of cranks led by a sentimental old man, or right on the money and occupying the last line of defense, with VermontGreen as one of the enemy. It's driving me crazy."

She paused, relaxed a little, and added, "And it'll add spice to your life, too, even though you've got nothing to do with it." She suddenly studied me more closely. "Unless you do. You never told me why you're going undercover. Is it connected to all this?"

"No, we think the girl's murder may have had something to do with a string of burglaries up there. But what is TPL planning to do? They really going to create havoc?"

She looked unhappy again. "I'm on the suspect list, remember? They wouldn't tell me. But assuming they fit the model, they'll try to undermine McNally's hospitality, mess up the mountain's day-to-day business, block traffic, slow the lift lines, and be loud and obnoxious. Basically do the civil disobedience thing until the cops run them in and make them front page martyrs. It might actually turn out to be handy for you. Maybe you can use the chaos to flush out whoever you're after."

I had my doubts about that. It sounded like the goal was to fill the resort with protester-busting cops, which was hardly the low-key scenario I'd been hoping for.

I gazed out the dark window at the distant lights and answered her vaguely. "I guess I'll find out soon enough."

The next morning, I ran into Sammie Martens as I climbed the stairs to the top floor of the Municipal Building. She was headed down, dressed for the outdoors.

"You get the go-ahead from the chief?" she asked.

"I had to wear him down," I told her. "And he said if we don't get something in four weeks, he'll shut us down."

That didn't seem to bother her. "Good. I was hoping he'd bite. I was thinking last night we ought to find someone who used to work at Tucker Peak—to maybe educate us a little—when I suddenly remembered one of Snuffy's men moonlighted in security. I was going to chat with him, if that's okay."

"Is he the one Manning said was crooked?"

"One and the same. I read the internal report about that, though. Clean as a whistle."

She checked her watch. "And he's due at his office in ten minutes."

"But he doesn't know we're coming?"

She smiled. "I thought I'd use the personal approach right off, given our reputation."

I saw her point and changed directions. "Lead the way."

Forty minutes later, Sammie and I pulled into the parking lot of a converted, two-story family home with a sign outside advertising the county sheriff. Unlike state police barracks buildings all across Vermont, which suffered from a uniform architectural blandness that only made you pity the inhabitants, sheriffs occupied a broader spectrum, which also unfortunately included the odd, windowless municipal basement. Snuffy had been luckier than most.

We walked up the handicap ramp to the front door, and into the tiny lobby. Sammie showed her badge to the woman behind the thick pane of glass overlooking the entryway. "Hi, is Tom Newell here yet?"

The woman leaned forward slightly to study the badge more closely. "What's that say?"

Sammie snapped the case shut and put it back in her pocket, fighting her irritation. "VBI. We're working on a case with your department. Could you tell him Agents Martens and Gunther are here to talk to him?"

The woman smiled slightly and picked up a phone. I couldn't tell if she'd consciously pulled Sammie's chain or was simply amused by the reaction she'd received. Sammie's vote, on the other hand, had clearly been cast. Having been skeptical about VBI myself, when it was staggering to fruition through last year's legislature, I could sympathize with those who needed proof of its legitimacy. Sammie, however, was younger, prone to forming strong allegiances, and quicker to judge those she deemed were judging her. To her way of thinking, to regard the Vermont Bureau of Investigation with anything other than respect was to be an idiot.

Two minutes later, the far door opened and a tall, slim, broad-shouldered man dressed in the gray pants and dark blue uniform shirt of sheriff's departments all across the state stepped into the lobby. His expression was markedly wary.

To give her credit, Sammie opened with a wide smile and an extended hand. "Tom Newell? I'm Sammie Martens. This is Joe Gunther. We're from VBI—wondering if you could help us out with something."

His face didn't change as he shook both our hands, but he looked at me closely. "I heard the sheriff'd brought you on board. You used to head up the plainclothes unit at the PD, right?"

"Yup." I glanced at the year stamped under his name tag, identifying that he'd become a cop five years earlier. "Did we ever meet? I'm sorry I don't remember."

"Nope. You want to come on back?"

He led the way through the far door into a narrow, dark hallway, at the end of which was a large room used for everything from lunch breaks to staff meetings to general storage. We sat around a long folding table, Newell on one side, Sammie and I on the other. Given his body language, I felt like launching into a speech about how our two countries were destined to become friends, but I didn't think he'd see the humor. It made me wonder if he thought we might be following up on the accusation that he'd been in on the burglaries.

"What can I help you with?" he asked.

"We heard you work at Tucker Peak," Sammie said.

He frowned. "Not anymore. I quit."

I spoke up then, beating Sammie to it, wanting to set a softer, more conciliatory tone. "Sorry to hear that. Snuffy Dawson's asked us to do a little digging around for him there. We were hoping you could give us the lay of the land. Who's who, how the politics work, stuff like that."

His eyes narrowed slightly, and I realized my instincts had been right. "That's all?"

"That's it," I told him honestly. "Snuffy mentioned Manning's allegation early on. He also said it was a crock. That was good enough for me."

A silence fell among us, which Sammie filled encouragingly, having taken my cue. "So, can you help us out?"

He hesitated, and I could tell he was debating whether

or not to tell us to pound sand—since this visit was clearly unofficial—or give us the assistance that all cops were supposed to give colleagues without a second's thought, but often did only grudgingly.

Happily, he opted for the second, while maintaining his deadpan expression. "Ask away. I can't guarantee how much good I'll be, though. I was mostly outside, on patrol. A lot went on I don't know anything about."

"That's okay," I told him. "We're just looking for an overview, enough to give us a jump start, maybe."

Despite harbored suspicions, he finally opened up. "All right. Stop me if I'm going where you don't want to go. If you're talking flow chart, there's a top man, the CEO, which used to be just 'general manager' till somebody figured CEO sounds better. That's Phil McNally. He works with a CFO named Conan Gorenstein, if you can believe that—a mousy little guy nobody sees much. Then there's a mountain manager. She's a hot ticket named Linda Bettina. The only female mountain manager in the business, far as I know—good people, pretty tough, and not so into the women's lib thing that she can't yuk it up with the boys."

He was watching Sammie when he said this, presumably hoping for a reaction. She stuck to taking notes.

Disappointed, he continued, "After that, it spreads out. You have a food and beverage manager, a personnel manager, marketing manager . . . brass hats like that, and each of them has a bunch of people under them that swells or fades depending on the season."

"Anyone run the CEO?" I asked.

"Oh, yeah. There's a board of directors. They're basically invisible except when they use their gold passes to cut to the head of a lift line. I don't know when they meet or what they do, but none of us ever heard about them. It was all the CEO or CFO on down, and for the operational types, mostly Linda and the individual department managers."

"What's McNally like?" Sammie asked, not looking up from her notes.

"He cruises around like the captain of the Love Boat, trying to make everybody feel good—just the opposite of Gorenstein. No one who works there has much time for him, since he didn't really know anything except how to dress good and play politics, but I guess they needed all of that they could stand."

"Why?"

"I worked other mountains when I was younger, mostly as a garage mechanic. That's actually how I started at Tucker, before the security job opened up. The pressure's about the same everywhere, but some are run well, with the employees taken care of and the equipment kept up, and others are pretty fly-by-night. Like Tucker. So McNally had to sound and look happier than maybe he was. He's a good enough shit. I mean, I liked the guy, 'cause I knew he was in a jam. He never showed it, though. Always acted glad to see you—and remembered names, too."

"I heard they were getting ready to spend a fortune," I said. "Really fix it up."

Newell looked unimpressed. "Yeah, well, whatever. It would take a fortune just to bring the dump up to code, if you ask me . . . Not that you are."

"What about the resort generally? The nightclub and

condos, the owners versus the day skiers, the full-timers and the seasonal workers. What's it like as a society?"

He paused thoughtfully before answering, "It's a company town—lives and dies with the resort. That makes it like a soap opera, with everybody angling for position and every clubby little group pissing on the other. And there's a real pecking order. The lifties—that's the lift operators—they're probably at the bottom of the heap. Some of them, especially the loaders who just make sure people get seated without killing themselves, they're barely conscious half the time. Long hair, tattoos, body piercing, into drugs. Not all of 'em, of course, but a bunch.

"At the other extreme, not counting the management types, the ski patrol, and the instructors, you got the snowmakers. They have as many misfits, but they're big on the job, you know? They get off on making snow, like it was an art form. And they see themselves as Navy SEALs or something—the elite. They tear around on snowmobiles like Harley riders, strut their stuff, pretty much keep to themselves as a group. If ever some employees get into a bar fight or have a run-in with the police, they're probably snowmakers."

He'd loosened up during all this, his face relaxing and his hands becoming more expressive. There was something about being part of this culture that clearly captured his imagination. Cops tend to find comfort in a regulated world with rules and parameters and clearly defined social structures, but they're also tribal by nature. It sounded like Tucker Peak and its brethren offered a perfect mixture of both.

"From what I've heard," he continued, "the mountain's

more like a traveling circus as far as personalities go. People are real loyal to it, even with the shitty pay. They come back year after year—guys like home builders and roofers and others who can't do their regular work in the winter. And some of the instructors and snowmakers are like gypsies—when we got our summer up here, it's winter in Australia or New Zealand or South America, south of the equator, so they go and work for resorts down there, skiing year 'round."

He paused, staring at the tabletop. "'Course, that's all changing, too. Money's tight, management's looking for cheap labor. A lot of the older hands have moved on to better mountains. I got sick of all the deadheads they were hiring, who basically sign up to ski for free and fuck up the equipment. Real foolish, if you ask me. That's why I quit." He looked suddenly belligerent. "Not 'cause of that prick Manning."

"Were you aware of much criminal activity going on?" I asked, blandly ignoring the reference.

He smiled broadly for the first time. "I don't guess I'm the best one to answer that. Everyone knew I was a cop, or that I wanted to be one in the early days. So, they didn't brag much around me. But look at what you got—bunch of bums, basically, wandering from place to place, leading a hard life with weird hours. You're going to get some criminals mixed in, and some dopers, guaranteed. Hell, I used to get high just walking through the locker room at shift change, the air was so full of dope."

"But nothing like a ring."

He laughed. "Too organized—those people're way too flaky for that. Anything's possible, I guess, but I don't see it. A few tickets would be ripped off, or a till would go light at the end of the day, but I don't see a gang operating there. I said it was like a separate world, but a small one, too: Everybody knows what everybody else is doing."

He paused and scratched his cheek. "'Course, on the burglaries, if there were only two guys, maybe—one inside, one out—I could see that."

"Any candidate you can think of that still works there?" I asked him.

He shrugged. "I'd look at the newcomers, the ones without the loyalty. Tucker Peak may be on the skids, but there's still a shit-load of money on that mountain. Given the caliber of some of those employees, I'd say that's a hot combination."

Chapter Seven

Two weeks later, near midnight, I stepped outside the one bar that catered almost exclusively to Tucker Peak employees. It was on the highway feeding the access road, two miles from Lifton, located in a no-man's-land among a small cluster of commercial buildings that survived like mollusks on the hull of a ship: a general store, a gas station, a ski equipment and rental place, a motel, and a couple of nondescript storage buildings. The bar was named the Butte, either out of some Far West nostalgia or by someone who couldn't spell. I'd been coming here almost nightly since being hired as a carpenter the week before, eavesdropping, striking up friendships, and sporting the new hair color and beard I'd been growing since my meeting with Allard.

I breathed in the hard freezing night air to cleanse my lungs of the smoke and stench I'd just left, the blackness around me as silent as a tomb in comparison with the din of the bar.

I began walking toward the gas station a hundred yards down the road. There wasn't much light, just the sign ahead of me and the muted neon of the Butte. Both stores were closed and dark, and the motel didn't brag much. I almost needed a flashlight to see.

About halfway to the station, I paused by one of the storage buildings, looked around carefully, slipped into the shadow, and then walked quietly down the rutted alleyway to the back. I heard a metallic click ahead of me, and the sound of a van door sliding open.

A soft voice called out, "Joe?"

"Yeah."

A pinpoint of light appeared in the utter gloom, guiding me to a parked van. "Nice bush you got going," Lester Spinney said, moving out of the way and letting me inside. The warmth that greeted me was welcome, even after so short a walk. "You look like a young Ernest Hemingway."

Lester slid the door shut and hit a switch on the wall. The interior was suddenly washed with the muted glow from a battery-powered safelight, much like a darkroom's, barely bright enough to reveal Willy and Sammie also sitting there, waiting.

The van's windows were opaque, and a curtain separated the back from the driver's compartment.

I found a seat and removed my coat. "You been here long?"

"Half the goddamned night," Willy complained.

"Twenty minutes," Lester said.

This was the first meeting we'd had as a group since Sammie and I had gone undercover. As far as I knew, nothing had occurred as a result of our digging, but I'd wanted to compare notes anyhow. Sammie and I had taken advantage of Tucker Peak's tenement-style em-

ployee housing to immerse ourselves in the local culture
and put our time to the best use, but the tradeoff had been
a news blackout from the outside.

"What've we got on the Jorja Duval killing?" was the
first thing I wanted to know.

Willy shook his head disgustedly. "Zip."

Lester was more generous. "The autopsy didn't give us
much more than what we saw, including the bruising on
her arms and shoulders that suggests she was manhan-
dled just prior to death. The crime lab guys went through
all the trace evidence they collected and figure it came
from about two dozen different people, which, given that
place, probably amounts to two weeks' worth of renters."

"I think she talked," Willy interjected. "That's why she
wasn't beat up worse *and* why she was killed."

"Could be," I agreed, struck by the irony of options.

"Marty's still making like Casper, of course," Lester
resumed, "probably lurking around till the dust settles.
His car and apartment have been minor gold mines,
though. Klesczewski and his bunch are having a field
day. Turns out Tucker Peak wasn't an exclusive target.
Marty's been ripping off cars and homes all over Bratt for
over a year. Weird part is, he kept most of the stuff, which
makes you wonder why he bothered stealing it in the first
place. Ron's backtracking from the loot to whatever owners he can find, but it's still not leading him anywhere."

"What about the burglaries here?" Sammie asked. She
was wearing faded jeans and an old pair of boots, but
with her red ski instructor's parka and freshly dyed blond
hair, she was looking quite exotic. She knew it, too.
She'd taken the name Greta Novak for her cover—a dou-

ble Hollywood homage. I'd settled for the far more mundane Max Lambert, which I'd made up out of thin air.

Spinney pursed his lips. "We got the Manning stuff, of course. And we found a storage unit Marty rents. That's where he kept most of it, and where Ron's having his second Christmas for the year, but there were only a few pieces from Tucker Peak. No explanation for the discrepancy. Maybe Marty's inside man kept most of what they stole. I reinterviewed Don Matthews and he confirmed that Marty usually took his time before fencing his goods, so that might fit. In any case, Willy and I're thinking our best bet is going to be sticking to Tucker Peak and working things from this end with you guys. Ron'll feed us anything useful if and when he finds it."

"Which is doubtful," Willy added. He and Ron hadn't gotten along when they'd both been detectives, being so different in nature as to be classified separate species. His comment just now was as clear an indicator as any of Willy's turmoiled outlook on life; with no one else I knew could a person as decent, hardworking, and self-effacing as Ron Klesczewski evoke and maintain such rancor.

Spinney paid no attention. "What we're doing now is taking all the burglaries we think Marty pulled on the mountain and breaking each one into its component parts: timing, location, day of the week, season, weather, target, MO, items stolen, follow-up police data, and victim background. We're also checking into who was insured and who wasn't, and for how much, and the patterns of custodial visits, mail deliveries, service calls, and the rest."

"How many houses are we talking about?"

"Eight," Willy answered. He looked at Sammie. "What've you been up to, besides catching rays?"

Having been hired after me just a few days ago, Sammie was already sporting a noticeable tan. I realized that her striking appearance was getting under Willy's skin—never a hard reach at the best of times.

"Mostly just figuring out who's who and what's what." She returned Willy's stare. "Joining the ski instructors turned out to be a lucky choice. They have a fuller run of the place than almost anyone, including going to the nightclub. Everybody's happy to see them coming except the ski patrollers and the snowmaking and maintenance bunch. The first because of some weird rivalry thing, and the second because they treat everybody like shit. So, once I get past being the new guy, I should have a pretty good vantage point."

"Carpenters have the same leeway," I added. "We don't do the social circuit, but we're almost invisible so long as we're carrying tools. We're also loaned out to the condo management division to do repairs outside the lodge and summit buildings, so I might be able to gain access there if we need it."

"Any ideas yet on who we can trust and who we can't?" Lester asked.

"I bet Linda Bettina'll pan out in the long run," Sammie suggested. "Everyone thinks pretty highly of her."

"Oh, hell, Sam," Willy growled. "They just want to get into her pants. It's a Wonder Woman fetish."

Sammie shook her head and said, mostly to herself, "You're such an asshole."

"She's been a big help to me, checking employee

records," Spinney volunteered, which earned him a silent, dark look from Willy.

"How's that going, by the way?" I asked. "I've been loitering around that phone during shift break, but so far it's been a dead end. Either Marty and his contact are spooked and laying low, or they've got another way of keeping in touch."

Lester didn't look happy. "I hate to admit it, but the best thing might be if they hit another condo while we were here. There're up to twelve hundred employees on this mountain during the peak season, Joe, running the gamut from dropout lawyers to trailer trash that had criminal records in the womb. They come from just down the road and from overseas, and some of them lie about their names. Bettina hasn't held anything back, but their records're almost useless. She says that for the money they pay the lower ranks especially, they don't make much effort checking under the hood." He smiled and added ruefully, "I mean, you two got jobs there, right? How careful can they be?"

"Doesn't that bite them in the butt sometimes?" Sammie asked.

"More now than in the old days," Spinney admitted. "But they're between a rock and a hard place. Recently, they've been putting up with whatever screwy behavior they're handed just to keep the place going. And they don't make a big deal about it when they do get bit, since it might give the resort a bad name. Pretty ironic that you get a bunch of pampered rich folks being catered to by potential crooks, all because you're paying so poorly, you don't want to ask questions you don't want answered."

"Sounds like poetic justice to me," Willy said.

I returned to the original inquiry. "It still doesn't hurt to assume for now that Marty's contact is someone local, or at least someone he knows from the past. Did you compare all the names we've collected from Marty's background to the employee records here?"

Lester nodded. "Yup. And got nothin' yet. Still, Marty Gagnon's no Einstein, and I'll bet money his contact's not, either. They probably started ripping off condos 'cause it seemed like a good idea at the time. We just need to connect the right two dots and hope one or the other sticks his head out of the bushes."

Spinney paused, as if reflecting on his own words, and then asked, "What about the protesters? They something to factor in?"

"I don't think so," I answered him. "At least not yet. So far, all they've done is sit in the road, surround the ticket booth, and hang a banner from the ski lift towline in the middle of the night, which I thought was pretty creative."

"No one's been busted yet?" Spinney asked.

"One or two who went too far, but the resort's still playing nice. From what we heard, McNally, the CEO, is trying to work out a compromise. That's good for us, though. Snuffy's deputies are out in force every day, straining at the leash—you and Willy asking questions and checking backgrounds are fitting right in."

"I don't see why McNally's dicking around with those people," Willy said. "They're a pain in the ass."

"He probably thinks they'd be a bigger pain if he let Snuffy have his way," I suggested. "It would just make for bigger headlines."

There was a slight lull in the conversation, which I ended by grabbing my coat and awkwardly putting it back on in the van's tight confines. "Okay, I guess that's it. Lester, how soon before you think you'll have some names Sammie and I can zero in on?"

"Maybe a couple of days."

"Then we'll do this again in forty-eight hours, unless something breaks before then." I looked over at Sammie. "You drive down here?"

She nodded.

"I'll walk you to your car."

My tone of voice made it clear that this wasn't merely a suggestion—and that nobody else was invited.

Outside, back in the cold and the darkness, we both watched the departing van lumber up the gloomy alley toward the road. Its brake lights flared briefly at the road's edge, and then it vanished with a sudden burst of acceleration, leaving behind a plume of exhaust that lingered like a ghost in the soft glow from the gas station sign down the street.

"You fitting in all right?" I asked Sammie in the sudden silence.

"Yeah. It was easier than I thought. I figured they'd all be Olympic dropouts: super hotshots that would pick me out in a New York minute. Turns out they're too busy trying to get laid to care if I know a ski from a pole. A third of them are amazingly shitty instructors—hate the people they're supposed to be teaching. So, I'm looking pretty good, and the instructing's kind of fun." She smiled at me suddenly. "If the money were better, I'd think about doing it full time."

"Right. I believe that. You pick up anything interesting yet?"

"Not really. I meant what I said in the van. There is one

guy, though—Richie Lane—a real predator. Put the moves on me right off, took the hint, and moved on, like a shark checking out bait. I watched him with a class yesterday. He had his hands all over the women, but talked up the guys, too. Has a fancy watch, expensive clothes, drives a 'Vette, although an old one. Could be he's just a gigolo—he basically lives in the nightclub—but he might be up to something more. Wouldn't be the first time a thief got inside information through a little pillow talk."

"We can tell Lester to put him under the microscope."

We were walking down the same path the van had taken earlier, and now paused in the last of the alleyway's deep shadow.

"It's none of my business except for how it affects the job," I said finally, "but how're things between you and Willy?"

She stayed staring out at the empty road, looking suddenly small, thin, and vulnerable. It wasn't the first time she and I had discussed such a personal subject. There was a father-daughter element to our friendship that encouraged it, and which I used occasionally to check on her well-being. Having been abandoned by her real father at an early age hadn't done her later dealings with men much good.

"They're okay."

"He's not easy to get along with," I prompted.

"No," she admitted.

"Meaning you're having some problems?"

She looked at me then. "Not really, which I guess is good news. I don't know why, but when it's just the two of us, it's incredibly easy. He's peaceful and quiet and supportive—and funny, if you can believe it. But outside of that, he's like Jekyll . . . or Hyde . . . whoever the monster was, and that's when all of a sudden I get the shit end of the stick. Makes it kind of tough to adjust, you know?"

"So, there was nothing to the suntanning crack?"

Her expression showed her doubt. "Ever since I went undercover, dyed my hair, he's been a little weird."

"Jealous?"

She nodded. "Probably. Fits some of the other comments he's made."

"You're an attractive woman, Sam, and you're strutting your stuff right now: tight jeans, nice tan, ski instructor reputation. All of a sudden, you're not one of the guys toting a gun and busting bad guys. It's the first time he's seen you out of context—probably makes him feel vulnerable. I doubt he considers himself a chick magnet, so I don't doubt he's totally amazed that you two have become so close—"

She stuck her lower lip out thoughtfully. "It's too bad."

"You going to do something about it?"

She suddenly smiled and spoke more confidently. "Nope. He'll just have to get with the program. I put up with his crap. He can put up with some of mine."

I patted her shoulder, satisfied for now that her emotions weren't threatening her job. At the moment, hers was hardly the most dangerous of undercover assignments, but as a friend and a boss, I'd have been remiss not to inquire. "Good. Keep me up to date. You better go first." I nodded toward her Jeep, parked in the gas station lot.

She hesitated briefly. "You don't need to worry. You know that, right?"

"Got it," I told her, primarily to keep her happy.

She checked up and down the road, and then jogged into the light toward her vehicle, her blond hair suddenly glowing in the night. Willy Kunkle was a lucky man, I thought—which only made me more confident that I was right about what was bugging him.

It was past one in the morning when I parked outside the maintenance shed out of sight of the base lodge behind a strategically planted screen of evergreens. This was where the tourists weren't supposed to wander—a floodlighted enclosure of oil-stained packed snow and scattered equipment ranging from snowmobiles to grooming machines to bits and pieces of chairlift paraphernalia, all looking like a dented, scarred, and rusting factory graveyard.

As I crossed toward the shed, hoping to fish casually for information from the night creatures inside, I heard the distinct combination of rattling, roaring, and the high-pitched whine of an approaching big groomer. I stopped and watched an enormous Bombardier round the corner, its lights and oversize flashing caterpillar tracks making it look like a mechanical bug from a futuristic nightmare.

Engine still running, the Bombardier stopped outside the building's double bay doors, and a large, heavy, wild-haired man dressed in filthy insulated coveralls and a mustache the size of a horse's tail emerged from the cab above the tracks and swung down onto the ground.

"Hey, Max," he called over to me, using my cover name. "They throw you out of the Butte?"

Bucky Arsenault was one of the chief groomers, a veteran of twenty years or more whom I'd only met a couple of times, and then only briefly, the night and day shifts having different hours and different cultures.

"Threw myself out," I answered him. "Not my kind of crowd."

He nodded. "Know what you mean. I don't even go there no more. What're ya doin' up here?"

I shrugged. "Too early to hit the hay. Thought I'd shoot the shit a little with whoever's in there."

Bucky looked at me doubtfully. "You know those guys?"

"Nope."

"Don't want to. Trust me. Bunch of teenage, dope-smoking losers, if you ask me. You don't seem the type." He hesitated a moment, and then said, "How soon you want to go to bed? Got a few more hours in you?"

"Sure."

He jerked a thumb at his noisy rig. "Climb in, then. I'll show you the real mountain. I just gotta grab something from inside. Won't take me a minute."

The Bombardier's cab was surprisingly new and modern, given Tucker Peak's overall shabbiness. Seated in a comfortable, upholstered chair, surrounded by sound-deadening glass and faced with a console and steering mechanism reminiscent of a space ship, I was forced to take the intergalactic metaphor even further when Bucky drove us out of the compound, up the nearest slope like a rocket gathering speed, and straight into the black void of night. Pressed back in my seat, watching the moonscape of contoured snow unfold before the groomer's powerful lights, I was surprised by how utterly foreign it all looked, how unlike the familiar, placid web of trails

I'd observed the first time I'd driven over the access road and seen the mountain spread out before me.

Crawling across the same geography at night as though in a heated cocoon, I found the impression completely different. The ground was misleadingly at odds with my perception of it, looking flat in places where our machine would lurch into a depression or suddenly attack an incline. Trees, chairlift towers, and spindly snowmaking water hydrants—tall and thin like metallic storks surrounded by nests of heavy collision-dampening bumpers—all sprang out of the blackness like colorless specters and vanished with equal suddenness. And through it all, like an electronic conscience rambling about whatever came to mind, the radio on the dash muttered barely audible, nonstop scraps of dialogue.

"Rumor has it you were here before the mountain was," I said to him, not as loudly as I would have thought necessary, given the roar of the engine outside the cab.

He laughed. "Feels that way."

"Must've seen a lot of changes."

"Oh, yeah." He reached under his seat, pulled out a Styrofoam cup and delicately spat a glob of tobacco juice into it. "Started out, we'd groom with homemade tillers pulled by anything that'd work: caterpillars, tractors, whatever. Dangerous and stupid, I guess, and more hassle than it was worth, if you ask me, but it gave the mountain bragging rights and brought in skiers."

"Bragging about a groomed mountain, you mean?" I asked.

"Yeah. It's always something: the grooming, the number of trails, the snowmaking percentage, the extra-attentive employees. Now it's fast quads for chairs, slope-side condos, and a lot more nonskiing stuff. That's why they built the nightclub and're shootin' for a golf course and that hotel, lucky for you."

"I don't mind the work," I said.

"Well, you'll always get it at a mountain resort, all the way to when they declare bankruptcy. Just how the business works. It's like building a house of cards—you only stop going when the whole thing falls down."

An artificial snowstorm sprang into our lights without warning, sparkling like a meteor shower. Underneath it was a fresh mound of sugary snow as tall as a house. Bucky stopped his machine shy of the actual downpour. He keyed the mike and exchanged a few quiet words with someone. Almost instantly, the snow stopped and a bundled-up, apelike creature in a hard hat and wearing several white reflectors sewed to his clothing appeared on a snowmobile—a "sled" to its users—and careened recklessly in our direction, coming to a halt beside Bucky's door.

He opened it up to the cold night air and waited for the man to clamber up onto the treads beside him. Wind and noise filled the small cabin.

"Thought you were supposed to be done up here," Bucky said.

Only by the cab's interior light could I see that the white reflective tape on the snowmaker's uniform was actually bright yellow, yet another illusion created by the Bombardier's harsh lighting.

"Don't get your shorts in a twist," he answered. "You can have at it right now. Goddamn cheap piece of shit nozzle froze up on me. Screwed up my schedule all to hell. It ain't as much as the boss wanted, but she can fuck herself if she can figure out how."

Bucky laughed. "Linda's the best boss you'll ever have, man or woman. You just don't know what you're doing out here."

The man swatted him on the arm. "Fuck you and this bucket of bolts. Some of us're doing men's work out here, not running a taxi service. Who's your fare?"

Arsenault didn't even look at me. "Lambert—carpenter—new guy. I'm showing him the scenery from the best seat in the house."

The snowmaker leaned across and spoke to me directly. "Anytime you want to get away from this bunch of pussies, let me know. You won't know mountain work till you spend a night with us."

I gave him a thumbs-up. "You got a deal."

The man jumped down, fired his sled up, and raced away. Moments later, dragging a snow gun still attached to its length of hose, which whipped back and forth like a lassoed anaconda, both man and machine slithered into the night, the sound of his machine's high scream drowned out by the Bombardier's steady rumble.

Bucky dropped the wide plow ahead of us and began the complex task of spreading out the enormous pile of artificial snow, talking all the while.

"Very crude bunch, snowmakers. You might want to watch out before you accept that invitation."

I studied his profile, unable to read his expression under the huge mustache, and then decided to take a chance. "Isn't that where you started out?"

He laughed. "We were all gentlemen back then. Never used such language."

"Oh, right. I really believe that."

"Yeah," he conceded, laughing. "I'm too old to make snow now, but I did love it. Almost makes you feel like God."

I let a moment's silence elapse before asking him, "You said the resort's doing more and more nonskiing stuff. Any resentment there from the employees—against all the fat cats moving in with their toys and money?"

He cut me a quick look. "You writing a book?"

I realized my mistake. "Maybe just talking about myself," I said to cover. "I been out of work for months. I come in here, see all the fancy cars, condos, and cash being kicked around. Kind of pissed me off."

Again, it was the wrong choice of words. His expression displayed a deepening suspicion. I began thinking I was more tired than I'd thought.

"What d'ya want?" he asked me. "You're gettin' some of it. I pick up a communist or something?"

I ducked in another direction, feeling increasingly off balance. "Shit, no. But I heard cops were asking about a bunch of burglaries—talk they might've been inside jobs. Made me wonder what was up."

Luckily, he followed my lead and got me out of trouble. His voice became sad and his demeanor philosophical. "Yeah, you're right," he conceded. "Shouldn't be so sensitive. Old guy like me lives in the past too much." He waved a hand at the void around us. "All this used to be about skiing, and maybe breaking even, if you didn't pay yourself much. I don't know where you're from originally, but I was born in New Jersey. Came up here as a kid whenever I could, did anything they asked me just so I could ski. We were all like that—ski bums working for peanuts and day passes. You ate, slept, skied, got laid if you were lucky, worked when you had to, and skied again as soon as you could."

He shook his head, repeating, "But you're right. That's all gone and buried. Now it's a rat race like any other, maybe worse since this is a one-company town, like the lumber camps a hundred years ago. I heard about those burglaries—made me sick. That's why I snapped at you just now, all that bullshit about us against them. But that's the way it really is. I'm just kidding myself— maybe some of the employees *are* ripping off the condos." He paused before adding, "Everything's gotten upside down, like with those protesters that've been jumpin' our bones the last few days. We used to be the ones wearing the white hat—good for the economy, good for unemployment. Back then, people knew that cutting ski trails opened up a more diversified environment. All sorts of animals started campin' out here because of that combination of slope and forest. Now we're just nature killers."

Throughout all this, we'd been crisscrossing the wide trail, spreading the proud snowmaker's artificial product as if it had suddenly appeared from heaven. The ironies and contradictions of Bucky's dilemma were just as palpable and confusing.

"Not that I think they're totally off base," he added as if I'd challenged him. "It's gone way beyond cutting down a few trees. I can't say the TPL, or whatever, are wrong about using water the way we do. It looks okay to us, but what do we know? Or care? We're not talking skiing anymore. It's just about money."

He abruptly stopped his machine and twisted around in his seat to stare at me. "I changed my mind. You're not a writer. You're a goddamn shrink. How'd you get me to say all this shit, anyhow? I was a happy man before I met you."

I looked at him, slightly at a loss. He was right about my being subversive, after all, even if he had my profession wrong. It made me feel like I'd robbed him of something irreplaceable.

Happily, he then reached across and punched my shoulder. "Lucky thing I don't give a good goddamn, huh?" And he burst out laughing.

But I wasn't so sure. What he had laid out in his rambling, curiously effective way had struck me as a parable for many of society's ills, far beyond this small, struggling commercial enclave. And his final ambiguity about what it all meant and where it might be heading struck a deep, resounding chord.

CHAPTER EIGHT

ONE OF THE MANY DISADVANTAGES OF LIVING IN TUCKER Peak's employee housing was that I'd been given a roommate, a concept I hadn't thought possible for several decades, aside from having briefly lived with Gail. Fortunately, he was an older man, a kitchen worker named Fred who didn't favor loud music, didn't snore too loudly, and wasn't too much of a slob. He did come from the old school, though, that dictated regular bathing to be antithetical to proper thermal insulation during the winter. As a result, he smelled bad enough to make my eyes water.

He wasn't in the room much, however, and was already gone when I woke up from only four hours of sleep the next morning.

But not for long. He came banging through the door just as I was pulling on my pants. "Max, come outside. You gotta see this."

I looked at his wide, excited, bloodshot eyes and decided not to argue, pulling my boots on without socks and my coat without a shirt, all while Fred stood before me, literally dancing from foot to foot, chanting, "You won't believe it, you won't believe it."

It was, admittedly, a sight to behold. Standing at the edge of the employee parking lot, the only vantage point from which the mountain was visible around the bulk of the "Mountain Ops" building, were most of the dorm's inhabitants, many of them half dressed as I was, and all of them staring at a pop artist's dream from the 1960s. Blotching the mountainside across several of its broad trails were a series of large yellow stains, looking exactly like oversize urine deposits. The very snow Bucky and I had been pushing around last night, but whose color we couldn't discern in the artificial light.

"Ain't that too much?" Fred asked, pounding me on the back. "That marketing bunch must be smokin' something harsh."

The marketing bunch, of course, were fit to be tied, which is exactly what the Tucker Protection League protesters had intended when they'd drilled holes through the ice of the existing snowmakers' source pond the night before and injected untold gallons of nontoxic yellow dye. Not only did the end-result supply its own highly suggestive message but also if the mountain managers wished to continue making snow (since the pipeline to the second pond hadn't yet been laid), they'd have to live with its being yellow until the water's spring-fed source diluted it back to normal.

Not that alternatives weren't quasi-hysterically considered. As I walked around the base lodge—and the glassed-in, futuristic scale model fantasy of itself that sat smack in the middle of the lobby like a wedding cake—I overheard heated discussions ranging from adding another color to the yellow to make it more attractive, to importing snow from other places until the crisis passed, and finally—the winner—to making the best of a bad situation by using the camera crews the protesters had already summoned to launch a reverse-spin publicity spiel about being the most colorful resort in Vermont. A contest was even suggested in which people would be issued additional dye of all colors with which to paint the mountain psychedelically from top to bottom.

The fevered pitch of the debate was such that not only was I totally ignored as I moved along the executive hallway with my bag of tools but also I finally got to see Conan Gorenstein, the reclusive CFO, step out of his enclave to join in some of the chatter. A pale, bald, retiring looking man, he didn't last long and disappeared after offering a few totally ignored suggestions.

Through it all, the TPL protesters, whom Phil McNally was still reluctant to forcibly evict, chanted with renewed enthusiasm, their ranks temporarily swollen, and marched around with banners and picket signs, otherwise adding to the carnival atmosphere. Privately, I had to hand it to McNally. Any other CEO would've called for the National Guard. Instead, he stood before the cameras, merely asked that the TPL be respectful of everyone's rights, and closed by offering his critics free food and ski passes, much to their obvious disgust and frustration. Shortly thereafter, in an additional display of one-upmanship, he dressed a few of his employees like protesters on the sly, complete with signs, and had them photographed riding the primary, western chairlift and enjoying his proffered amenities.

It all made me think back to the mountain's overall beleaguered state, and of McNally's reputed canniness in dealing with it. If this resort had any chance at survival, it seemed to me this man would be responsible for it.

I got a bird's-eye view of the evening's dye job later on, when I was told to go to the summit building to put in some trim work. Traditionally, that meant hitching a ride on one of the snow vehicles that regularly traveled the mountain carrying workers, supplies, or occasionally wounded skiers. But the option was ours, more or less, so I took the opening ride on the eastern lift to soak up the morning sun and enjoy the scenery. One odd aspect of undercover work is that a good deal of the time, in order to maintain cover, you simply have to play the role you've assumed, asking no questions and practicing no subversion.

And at moments like that one, such sacrifices are easily borne. The air was clear and sharp, the breeze nonexistent, and the sky a cobalt blue hard enough to hurt the eye. As the chair slowly slid up the multihued slope below, the lower mountains of the bowl, through which the access road had been cut, dropped away and allowed for an ever expanding panorama of the landscape outside this enclosed and introverted community. The Green Mountains spread out to the horizon, snow-capped, bristling with conifers and naked hardwoods, and shaded in subtle grades of heather, gray, light brown, and purple. Ahead of me, still high overhead, was the row of surreal windmills, twirling in the apparent calm, looking like whirligigs, their long, slender blades flashing in the sun.

I had just twisted around in my chair to admire the fake Swiss village look of the base lodge, when I heard a woman shout in alarm down the line. An empty chair, just beyond the one below me, was gathering speed as it began slipping backward toward a woman and her child, helplessly trapped, their eyes wide with panic. Their legs weighted down with skis, only a flimsy bar separating them from several hundred pounds of metal, the woman and her daughter began to scream.

Until the chairs collided.

Following a solid smash and a small, thin wail, there was total silence.

The remaining chair between us carried a frightened teenage boy with a snowboard dangling from one foot.

"Oh, man. Oh, Jesus. Holy shit . . ."

"Can you see how they're doing?" I shouted down to him.

"It's bad. Shit. She's like bleeding, man."

"What's your name?"

He stared at me, open-mouthed. "What?"

"Your name."

"Spike. People call me Spike. It's not my real name, but . . ."

"Spike's fine," I interrupted. "I need you to get real focused here, Spike. You need to help me help those two people, okay?"

"Yeah, yeah. Whatever."

"Tell me how they're doing."

He glanced back over his shoulder before reporting, "The little girl looks okay—mostly scared. But the mom's bleeding bad. It's dripping off her boot and she's like unconscious or something."

"Is she staying put in her chair or does it look like she might fall out?"

He didn't have to double-check this time. "She's real wobbly, man, slumped over and kind of sliding, maybe."

The lift had stopped moving, the accident having triggered an automatic shut-off, and the chairs were swinging peacefully, silently. I tucked my legs up, swung around in my chair, and stood up. I could just reach the steel tow cable overhead.

"What're you doin', man?" Spike shouted.

"I'm going on your recommendation, kiddo. If it looks like that woman's about to fall, it could kill her at this height, especially since we're over rocks here. I've got to try to reach her." I stared at him purposefully. "So you better tell me if you really think she's slipping."

The disappointment and fear in his voice lent him credibility. "She's going. I'm sorry. It's slow, but she's going."

I sighed. I knew the ski patrol would be here soon, once maintenance told them the cause of the shut-down. I also knew that while efficient, such a system took time to get moving, and the first snowmobile hadn't even showed up yet.

I had several things going for me. I'd done rope training similar to this just recently to pass the VBI physical, I was wearing construction boots and coveralls instead of bulky ski clothes, and my work gloves were made of heavy leather. Convincing myself these were weighty advantages, and not thinking too much of my own chances of surviving a forty-foot drop to the boulder field below, I grasped the cable in both hands, swung my feet up so they crossed over the top at the ankles, and began working my way downline.

I was about halfway to Spike's chair, aware of the

aching in my arms but still feeling okay, when I heard the first snowmobile growling in the distance. A few minutes later, a voice rose from the rider who'd had to walk the last distance because of the rough terrain.

He sounded distinctly alarmed. "*Sir. Sir.* You can't do that. It's too dangerous. Professional help is on the way."

I didn't have the energy to deal with that. "Spike," I called out.

Spike was getting into the mood of the thing. "Yo."

"Explain the realities to this guy."

The young man launched into a convoluted diatribe, overriding the voice below that constantly told me to stop, as if that were an option. When I reached Spike's chair, however, I knew not only that my actions had been justified but also that I was possibly too late. The woman, still a hundred feet away, was looking worse than I'd imagined, half out of her seat, her head lolling, one ski free of the footrest, the other one jammed but threatening to join the first and deprive her of any anchor at all.

"I think she's cooked," Spike said softly.

"Not till she hits the ground," I told him, no longer sure that was true.

I looked around for something to help speed my progress, and finally focused on the man below.

"I'm a mountain employee, too. A carpenter. You have any tools on your sled? I left mine behind." I pointed to the distant toolbox next to where I'd been sitting.

He glanced at his machine, parked on the snow some fifteen feet off to the side. "What're you after?"

"A hammer, maybe. Something with a hook. Fast."

He was already moving, no doubt resigned I'd do what I would in any case. "A crowbar."

"Even better. Fast as you can."

He returned in under a minute holding a short crowbar.

"Throw it up. And aim right. I don't want to do this twice."

Unquestioning now, he followed instructions, climbing the tallest rock he could find to reduce the distance between us and then lofting the heavy tool underhanded with all his strength, so it shot straight up at us and then poised in midair. Both Spike and I grabbed it simultaneously.

"What're you going to do?" the teenager asked, letting go.

I hooked the crowbar over the cable above me. "Probably kill myself. Watch your head."

He leaned away as I grabbed the bottom end of the crowbar. The little girl was watching me, her small, pale face tiny in the distance. I considered trying to talk to her but realized the distance made that a waste of more time. I tightened my grip and pushed off.

My intention had been to control my descent by swinging my feet up as I had earlier and using them as a brake, but the angle was so steep and the cable so slick that I shot off as from a catapult, dangling like a streamer on a kite, all notions of swinging my feet anywhere defeated. Instead, I watched with growing panic as the tangled two chairs and the woman squeezing her way between them loomed up with ferocious speed.

The foregone conclusion spoke for itself. Not only would I smack into my target hard enough to be killed or maimed but also the impact would probably jar the woman free, and maybe knock the child off as well.

So much for professional help.

Feeling the strength all but gone in both my arms, I nevertheless gave one convulsive heave on the crowbar, pulled myself up for an instant, and grabbed hold of the whistling cable with one hand, now only some fifteen feet from the chair ahead.

The effect was frightening, extremely painful, and instantaneous. My body, suddenly slowed, swung forward, pulling my arm half out of its socket. The crowbar jumped off the cable, smacked me in the chest, and went sailing into the void. And my right hand, now the only thing keeping me from total free flight, instantly began to burn from the friction.

But it worked. Like some preplanned if graceless circus act, I slid to a stop just to where I could place my feet gently on the intertwined chairs, and I wrapped my free arm around the first hanger arm, subconsciously praying my weight wouldn't bring everything down.

It didn't, and since my face was now inches away from the loose chair's cable grip, I could see that while it had obviously slipped, it was still securely attached. Only then did I look down at the approximately six-year-old face staring up at my feet, her eyes the size of silver dollars.

"Hi, sweetie. What's your name?" I asked, surprised I could even speak.

She didn't answer as I gingerly climbed through the accidental jungle gym toward her, my entire body tingling from exertion and adrenaline.

"Mine's Max. I'm here to help your mommie. She's your mom, right?"

The head nodded. I saw people collecting rapidly far below us, talking on radios, sorting out equipment. I knew they were shouting at me, but I continued to ignore them.

I ended up kneeling on the first chair, which was pressed tightly against the second, squeezing the mother's chest. I stretched out to grab her under the arms when with a slight groan, she slipped again and almost fell free. I snatched the front of her parka and arrested her fall. She groaned with pain and her eyes opened.

"It's okay," I said. "I got you." I tried unsuccessfully to pull her back up.

"My skis are stuck," she murmured.

I looked down. She was right. Both skis were now below the footrest, preventing her from being hauled onto the chair.

I glanced at the young girl. "Sweetie?"

"Mary." Her voice was barely audible.

"Wonderful. Mary it is. Mary, I'm going to ask you to hang on to your mom as tight as you can, okay? I'll help, too, but I've got to use my other hand to undo her skis. Put one arm through the slats in back of the chair, and the other one around her chest, and squeeze as tight as you can. Can you do that?"

Without a word, she followed directions, compressing her lips with serious intent.

Slowly, tentatively, I eased my hold on her mother with one hand and began reaching for her skis, hanging almost upside down in the process. Luckily, the skis were new, the bindings not set too tightly, and the first of them fell away on my first try.

But the second was harder to reach, and as my out-stretched fingers got hold of the binding release, something shifted between the chairs. Mary let out a small cry, and her mother's body began sliding by my head. Fearing I'd lose them both, and my own balance in the bargain, I caught hold of the woman's fanny-pack belt and reared back with all my strength. We shot up, the last ski smacking against the footrest and springing free on its own, and we all ended up staring at each other in a pile on the chair, Mary crying and her mother screaming with pain.

But at least safe from falling.

Which is when I finally took more careful notice of the blood—on me, on the mother, even on Mary. Dark, arterial blood, which accounted for the reduced consciousness.

"Mary," I said. "Get your mom to talk to you. I need her to wake up."

Mary stopped crying and took her mother's face in her small hands, as suddenly calm as any doctor. "Mommy. Mommy. Talk to me."

The woman opened her eyes and asked me feebly, "Who *are* you?"

"Max. What do I call you?"

"Jill." She sounded half asleep.

"Tell me exactly where it hurts so I can try to stop the bleeding."

One of her hands fluttered near her right thigh. "I tried to stop the chair with my pole."

I pulled a folding knife out of my pocket, cut her ski pants at the site, and found a deep puncture wound, steadily pumping blood. I infiltrated my hand through the rip, pressed my thumb hard against where I could feel a faint pulse, and instantly saw the bleeding stop.

My nose was almost touching hers by now. "Jill," I said softly. Her eyes were closed again. "I got it. People are below getting ready to pull us out of here. Mary's fine and she's been a big help. All we need for you to do is to keep on breathing. Keep awake and keep breathing. Will you do that?"

"Sure, she will," Mary said, and I believed her.

Three hours later, Linda Bettina—tall, broad-shouldered, and dressed in stained work clothes—found me at the summit house where I'd finally begun putting up the trim I'd been assigned to that morning. She was accompanied by a young, aggressive-looking woman in expensive, tailored skiwear. It was clear at a glance who between them could decipher the contents of the average toolbox.

"Hey, Linda," I said, looking up from measuring a cut.

"Hey, yourself, Batman. What the hell do you think you're doing?"

I straightened up and parked my pencil behind my ear. "Meaning what?"

She smiled. "Meaning any other dumb bastard would be taking a break after what you pulled. Which maybe you should do anyway if you plan to collect any workman's comp."

I shook my head. "I'm fine. A bit sore. A little rope burn on one hand. The doc checked me out at the base lodge."

That clearly met with her approval, and she dropped the subject.

"How's the patient?" I asked.

"You saved her life. And I think the little girl wants you as a dad."

"Probably not a good idea." I glanced at the young woman, who'd already snuck a look at her watch.

Linda Bettina followed my gaze, her expression hardening slightly. "This is Stephanie Jones from marketing. They'd like to make a little hay out of your trapeze act, if that's okay."

"It's not."

There was an awkward silence as Stephanie froze in midsmile and rethought her opening line. "It's not?" was all she managed.

"Nope." I noticed Linda Bettina smile before pretending to look out a window.

"Why not? You're a hero. The press really wants to see this. It's such good news."

"I'm a private man, Ms. Jones. I did what I did to help out. It's over."

She leaned toward me, all smiles now. "But that's great, don't you see? You're perfect. It's like real Vermont: the reluctant hero. People will love it." She actually winked and added, "You might even be able to make some money out of it."

I shook my head. "Sorry. I'd just as soon forget about it."

The smile faded. "Well, *you* might, but the cat's out of the bag. Like it or not, you saved someone's life, and in this society, you can't do that and pretend nothing happened. People won't let you. I can help you out, smooth the way and make it as painless as possible, or you can go solo and be hounded half to death. Your choice."

I sat on the sawhorse beside me and gazed at her a moment. "Let's be straight here. This is good for Tucker Peak, or it might be if you give it the right spin. And what better spin than some 'yup, nope' woodchuck Vermonter who stared death in the face and told him to buzz off, right? Especially if the resort then makes him employee of the month. Except that if that happens, this particular woodchuck will mention the reason he stuck his neck out was because our ancient, poorly maintained chairlift equipment is just an accident waiting to happen, and that if the press wants something to write about, he'd be delighted to show them all the stuff around here that's threatening to kill the customers."

Stephanie's face tightened. "We'd sue you if you did that."

I laughed. "Now *that* would look good." But I relented. "Ms. Jones, you won't have to sue me, because it won't come to that. I'm an employee. I and other employees helped save this woman from dying. That's your story: Tucker Peak ready for any emergency. You'll have photos of the ski patrol, the snowmaker first on the scene who threw me that crowbar, and everyone'll talk about the team effort instead of me personally because they'll all have been told that I'm a really shy guy who just wants to be left alone. And"—I spoke more slowly for emphasis—"because they know they'll be fired if they give anyone my name."

Jones looked at Bettina, who'd turned back to face us. "Can he do that?"

"He can if we don't play ball with him, and I'll recommend to McNally that we do. He's got a right to privacy, and he shouldn't lose it just because he did something decent. Besides, I like the team effort idea, which happens to be true. Without the rest of 'em, he couldn't have gotten her down from there."

Bettina put an end to it by stepping forward and giving my hand a firm shake. "It's a done deal, Max. Word'll probably leak out anyhow, but it won't be from us." She looked pointedly at Stephanie Jones. "Right?"

Jones made no pretense at hiding her disgust. "Whatever," she said sourly, and left the room.

Linda Bettina looked at me for a moment before extracting a crumpled envelope from an inside pocket and handing it to me. "This just came for you—special delivery."

I took the envelope and studied it. It was simply addressed, "Ski Montin Hero," in a large, childish hand. There was no postage or return address.

"One of the sheriff's people brought it in," Linda explained. "Straight from the hospital."

I tore it open and removed a single sheet of paper. On it was a crude crayon-rendered picture of a broken chairlift, with two stick figures dangling from it, one of them dripping a string of red dots. Above them, sliding down the cable on one hand, complete with cape flapping in the air behind him, was a third figure wearing a broad, carefree smile. A bubble with an arrow pointing at him read, "YOU."

At the bottom of the page were the words, "Thank you for saving Mom. Love, Mary." It was followed by a large heart.

I handed the picture to Linda without comment. She glanced at it and gave it back.

"Tough guy."

After work, and after several conversations with coworkers who were thoroughly enjoying keeping the press in the dark, I wandered into the repair shop on the ground floor of the Mountain Ops building across from my dorm. It was standard fare in some respects, with a greasy floor, scattered tools, and racks upon racks of assorted supplies. Its uniqueness was in the nature of those supplies: a vast array of arcane pulleys, wheels, spring clamps, and other equipment designed to keep the mysterious workings of a ski mountain up and running. In some ways, it resembled what I thought a NASA repair shed might be like, except—I hoped—for the dirt, the machinery, the nature of the business, and the skill level of everyone working there.

One of the latter stepped out from behind a hanger arm mounted in a vise as I let out a "Hello?"

"Who're you after?"

He was tall, skinny, and utterly filthy. On the chest of his uniform shirt, like a mirage in fading light, was the barely discernible name, "Mike."

"You Mike?"

He looked curious. "I know you?"

I stuck out my hand. "New guy. Carpenter. Name's Max."

He was slow to shake. "Pretty dirty." He wiggled his blackened fingers.

I was impressed he'd noticed. "I don't care."

He shook my hand, leaving it oily enough that I did wipe it on my pants.

"Warned ya," he laughed. "What can I do you for?"

"I was wondering about the chair that went for a slider this morning."

Mike shook his head. "Ain't got it. Tramway Board inspectors picked it up hours ago."

"But you looked at it?"

"Sure. I took it down." His face became more serious. "Why you want to know? We're not supposed to talk about junk like that."

"I asked 'em to keep quiet, but I'm the one who saved that woman."

He grew suddenly animated. "No shit? That was some cool move. Dick said you went down that tow line like Spiderman or something. He threw you the crowbar. We think it's great you're telling 'em all to butt out. I heard the PR people were really pissed."

I waved a hand to calm him down. "They'll get over it. They just wanted something to offset the yellow snow."

He laughed again. "Boy, ain't that the truth? I wished I'da thought of that one myself. It woulda been worth getting fired."

I let him recover a bit before asking, "So, I was wondering why that chair let loose, since it almost got me killed."

Mike looked around, crossed to the door leading farther into the building, and checked the hallway beyond to make sure we were alone. Then he came back and said quietly, "It wasn't the chair. It was fine."

"Somebody messed with it?" I asked.

"You got it. Let up on the tension spring so it couldn't hang on when it hit the steep part over the rocks."

"That couldn't have been an accident? Chairs must slide all the time."

"Now and then, yeah, but I know the signs. I been doin' this for years." His voice dropped lower still. "Fits in with the yellow snow you just mentioned."

I didn't bother hiding my incredulity. "You think the TPL bunch did this?"

He raised his eyebrows. "Put it together, Max. First they hang a banner from the chair's tow rope, then they fool with the water supply. All McNally does is offer 'em free passes like they were just kids acting out. Pisses them off, right? Nobody likes that. So they get a little more serious."

"From yellow dye to attempted manslaughter? I guess that's getting serious."

Mike straightened and grinned, spreading his hands wide. "I rest my case."

I waited for Sammie by the back door of the main power house, empty and dark at this time of night, and far from the beaten path. There was no moon. The day's clear sky had succumbed to clouds, and rumor had it we were in for some snow.

"Joe?"

"It's Max," I answered, also in a loud whisper.

"I *know* that," she answered testily, drawing near. "And so will everyone else once your Superman imitation breaks cover."

"You're my first Superman. I can add it to a Spiderman and a Batman so far."

"Are you okay?" she asked, putting a hand on my arm. "You could've been killed, from what I heard."

"The story's improving with age. I wanted to tell you about a little discovery I made. According to Mike, who's been fixing chairlifts for years, this one was sabotaged."

She thought about that for a few moments. "Who gains from that?"

"Good question. I can't answer it either."

She looked off into the night. "Think it has anything to do with Marty Gagnon?"

"I don't see how—not now, at least. We better tell the others we might have a whole different player in motion."

CHAPTER NINE

I SAT IN SNUFFY DAWSON'S UNMARKED SHERIFF'S CAR AT the end of a dirt road some ten miles from Tucker Peak, staring out at a snow-covered field with a frozen pond in its middle, its flat, featureless surface looking like spilled milk at the bottom of a saucer.

"You sure about this mechanic?" Snuffy asked.

"Mike? No reason he'd lie. We could run a check on him, but I doubt we'd find much. I think he was shooting straight."

Dawson stroked his chin with a meaty hand. "You don't think maybe the woman was the target? She have a husband?"

I smiled in response. "No, divorced. And supposedly they get along. Besides," I added, "the eastern lift starts later in the morning, because of how the sun hits the slopes, so what we were on was the first run of the day. Assuming Mike's right about it being sabotage, it must've happened during the night, and there's no way anyone could've known who was going to be in what chair when, or even if any physical injury was intended.

Could've been the sole intention was to show off how dangerous the equipment is."

He didn't react to that. "You said Mike suspected the TPL."

"Only because of their other stunts. They nailed the door shut to an equipment shed this morning. But to do something violent would destroy their cause. Wouldn't make sense."

"Unless they got frustrated, like he said."

I didn't want to make one man's wild guess the only fact in evidence here. "Snuffy, anything's possible, including Mike being wrong and the whole thing being an accident. But if we *assume* he's a good mechanic just for now, then we've got to look at who might've done this, which may or may not have been the TPL. Certainly it was someone with the right tools and some knowledge of machinery. Maybe someone with ready enough access to the equipment so as not to raise any questions."

"Like a maintenance guy."

"Right, an employee with a grudge. The Tramway Board's looking into it, of course, but Linda Bettina's been pretty helpful so far. I'll have Spinney ask her for any insight she might have on any employees past and present with complaints, maybe, or a history of violence and/or vandalism. There's probably someone who fits that category, knows about that kind of equipment, and doesn't give a damn about the environmental movement."

Snuffy finally nodded. "Okay. How're you doing on the burglaries?"

"Still digging. Lester left me a message a couple of

hours ago that he'd like to meet. Could be he found something interesting."

Dawson let out a deep sigh. "I just wish the whole goddamn mountain would go away. All it does is cause problems. I've got my entire payroll working right now because of this protest thing—it's costing me a fortune. I thought bringing you people in would make things easier. Now, I'm up to my neck in alligators. I got towns all over the county bitching breach of contract because of reduced coverage, and the state cops are already saying they won't pick up the slack forever, as if that was a big threat. I just wish I could connect that chair thing with the TPL. Then, whether McNally thinks it's good PR or not, I could bust them all and clear them out of there."

I considered that for a moment. His financial woes didn't interest me much. All cops bitch about money, and the state police's complaints were no less relevant than Snuffy's own. But the question of what the protesters might or might not know brought back Gail's mention of their unofficial leader, Roger Betts. I wondered about the benefits of having a conversation with him.

I opened the passenger door of Dawson's car and swung my legs out, preparing to return to the battered pickup I was using as part of my cover. "It's early yet, Snuffy. Something useful'll surface soon. Don't do anything without telling me, though, okay? I don't want Sammie or me to get caught by surprise."

"Don't worry," he said. "I got enough fires to put out without doing your job for you."

Not a ringing endorsement, but basically what I wanted to hear.

* * *

Getting together with Spinney was less complicated and more comfortable than my clandestine meetings with Sammie and Sheriff Dawson. Spinney merely asked Linda Bettina if he could interview me about yesterday's accident, and she handed us a small conference room on the top floor of the Mountain Ops building.

After closing the door behind us, he smiled and rolled his eyes. "This is too good. There's got to be a way I can convince them that our undercover guy and their hero-for-a-day is not only the saboteur we're after but also a right-winger who hates the TPL, wants to clear-cut the mountain, and works for the Israeli Mossad. It would be a clean sweep. What do you think?"

"I think you need a vacation."

We sat down at the conference table, facing each other in case anyone came in. "Seriously," he asked. "How're you doing after all that derring-do? You ain't getting any younger."

I looked at him wide-eyed. "Up yours. Is that why you wanted to meet?"

He laughed. "Nope. Fun as this is, I think I can make it better." He pulled a sheet of paper from his pocket and slid it across the table. "Rap sheet for Robert Lanier, alias Marc Roberts, Lanny Robertson, and/or Richard Lane."

I looked up at the last name, the sheet still unread in my hands. "Sammie's greaseball ski instructor, the one pawing all his female students?"

"The same. Looks like she nailed him right off." He tilted his chin toward the document. "I gave him the special attention you asked for. First I got nowhere, but cross-referencing aliases led me to that, and Linda Bettina confirmed he was no employee poster boy. He's done a nice job of sampling all the goodies, though—domestic assault, assault and battery, sexual assault, B-and-E, malicious mischief, disturbing the peace, four DUIs, and two counts of burglary, none of which Bettina knows about, by the way. There's other stuff, too, but who cares? He's spent a total of thirteen months in the can for all of it and that was years ago. Since then, he's been cutting deals, pleading out for probation, or snitching for dropped charges. There's probably not a man, woman, or child he's met he didn't eventually beat, rob, or squeal on. And," he added after a theatrical pause, "he was working here—right time, right place—for every one of Marty's phone calls."

I read the rap sheet carefully and returned it to him. "Nice catch. Anything else?"

"Like something we could use for a warrant?" Lester shook his head. "No such luck. Not unless Sammie cuddles up to him and gets him to spill the beans. Still, this gives us someone to look at, someone who might help us flush out Marty Gagnon."

"If nothing else," I muttered.

"Yeah," he said. "I heard about the chair maybe being rigged. Any way you think we could tie Richie or Marty to that?"

"Don't I wish," I said mournfully. I checked my watch and stood up. "No. Not that it necessarily makes more sense, but I think I need to look more closely at the TPL and its leaders to get an answer there. You tell Sammie about Richie Lane yet?"

"Nope."

"Good. I've got something to do right now. Could you find her and tell her we need to talk? With his history,

Richie might've knocked off Jorja Duval looking for Marty, maybe because Marty stiffed him on sharing the loot. That would make for a nice, tight circle, even without the Israeli Mossad. If it's true, though, I don't want Sammie tracking him alone."

Spinney sat back in his chair, looking amused, and indirectly confirmed why he'd shared Lane's history with me only. "Can't imagine why you'd think she would."

I had called Gail Zigman after my conversation with Snuffy Dawson and asked her what my chances were of having a friendly chat with Roger Betts. An hour later, she'd phoned me back to say that Betts was both amenable and eager, but only if she accompanied him and only if we met in private. He was fearful that being found with a cop and the likes of Gail Zigman—from the now bad-guy VermontGreen group—would be viewed by his colleagues as consorting with the devil.

Once again, therefore, I left the isolated world of Tucker Peak after I got off work and traveled to a motel room some ten miles distant, knocking on the door and waiting for Gail to open up.

"Hey, there," she said, kissing me on the cheek. "I like the beard. Tickles my nose."

I laughed. "I know what you mean, it's been itching for days. He here?"

She stepped aside and let me in. Sitting in a chair by the window, staring out a little forlornly at the parking lot, was a thin, white-haired man with stooped shoulders and a much longer beard than mine, tinged with yellow. He looked tired, his skin pale and unhealthy, and he seemed anxious, as if under a lot of pressure.

Gail made the introductions.

Roger Betts rose slowly and gave me a bony hand to shake, smiling wistfully and nodding. "Gail speaks very highly of you, Mr. Gunther. Or is it Agent Gunther? I'm sorry."

I waved him back to his seat and perched on the windowsill nearby. "Joe'll be fine."

"Then you must call me Roger." His voice was a soft, almost musical tenor, very soothing. "I would like to start by thanking you for saving that poor woman and her child. Gail tells me that was typical of you, but I find it quite extraordinary. Risking one's life for a stranger's is something I can only imagine."

His old-world courtliness probably enhanced the man's reputation among his like-minded friends. But I sensed it was natural to him, and that he was no less sincere because of it. I responded in a similar vein.

"I've heard equally good things about you, including that you like a worthwhile fight."

His smile broadened. "I was better at it twenty years ago. I'm not sure how much fire I have left in me."

For some reason, that brought me back to something he'd just said. "Why did you thank me just now? It almost sounded personal."

Roger Betts glanced briefly at Gail, who told me, "Ground rules are this conversation is strictly off the record."

I nodded without comment.

Betts turned his head to look out the window again and seemed to speak more to himself than to us. "I'm not absolutely sure we weren't responsible."

"You suspect someone?" I asked, startled.

"No, not a person," he answered slowly, as if drained of all energy. "More a general mood. I'm not one of those old men who claim the world's going to pot just because my brain's too fossilized to follow current events. I know violence and intemperance have been with us since the cave. But there is a stridency among some of my colleagues that exceeds mere enthusiasm. It's the line dividing righteousness from self-righteousness which allows believers in the latter to turn their backs on common decency."

"As in trying to kill people to throw blame on the resort? Are you saying someone in the TPL did that?"

He paled even further. "I merely think it's a consideration."

"I'm not trying to be contrary," I told him, "but I don't see the logic. People're already whispering about sabotage and pointing the finger at you guys, not Tucker Peak. Surely, if this was done by a TPL member, he knew the risks of injuring someone and putting you in an even worse light was pretty high. So, why do it?"

Betts didn't answer for several seconds, and then finally admitted, "I don't know, and I have no proof. It's just that I can't separate the two in my mind: our actions and such violence. I've seen one lead to the other too often in the past to ignore the possibility."

I looked at him in a whole new light, suddenly filled with a sense of ambiguity. What was his game? Or was he just shouldering the guilt for the whole world's collective ills?

Intrigued by the possibilities, I still wanted to introduce a bit of reality. I held up four fingers. "That lends itself to several scenarios—one of your people went off the deep end; someone did this to make you look bad; someone totally unrelated is indulging in a little terrorism and using your presence as a smoke screen; and, last but not least, nobody did it, because it was an accident. Do any of those sound more likely than the others?"

His response was elliptical at best. "I believe very strongly in the positions I take, and I am convinced that harm will come about as a result of Tucker Peak's plans. But I am a nonviolent man, dedicated to harming no other living creatures. I would be devastated to learn that a cause I was associated with had taken to violence as a means of expression. I merely wanted you to hear that directly from me."

I resisted being too judgmental, although what he'd just said sounded useless as well as self-serving, as if he were here merely to preserve his sainthood by hedging his bets. But Gail respected him, he'd served long and selflessly in his cause, and was obviously feeling both his years and a sense of obligation. I decided to play him straight—for the moment.

"I hear it," I said, "but from you only. Sounds like neither one of us knows what some of your colleagues might be capable of."

His brow furrowed with concern. "I'm not sure what to do."

"Keep me informed through Gail," I suggested, heartened by the chance of forming an alliance within the TPL. "Not about what your plans are," I added carefully. "You have a right to your ideas and to protest if you want. But if you discover that someone inside your group is endangering others, I'd like to know about it."

He was silent for a long while, and finally said, "This

is not the first time I've been made such an offer, Joe. The police have always been canny to the ambiguity of social protest, and they've always been good at driving wedges in among us."

I resisted reminding him that he'd broached the subject first. "I'll put it to you differently, then," I said instead, grateful I didn't have to deal with him on a regular basis. "You and I have now met. You've checked me out and drawn some conclusions. You also know how to contact me if need be. I'll let you look to your own conscience to decide if that need ever comes up." I reached out and shook his hand again. "That okay with you?"

He nodded and smiled, giving me a wink so slight, I wasn't sure I'd seen it. "You're very good at this, Joe Gunther." He then raised an eyebrow at Gail. "Careful around him."

I stood beside Gail at the window, watching Roger Betts drive away in an old Buick, ironically spewing a thin plume of oily smoke.

"Frustrating son of a bitch," I said, slipping my arm around her waist. "He actually winked at me when he left."

"He's no fool," she agreed. "He plays that fuzzy-wuzzy angle like a violin. It forces people to meet him more than half way. He wasn't bullshitting you, though, and he was impressed with you personally."

"Oh, right. I'm sure that's what the wink was all about—a sign of respect."

She looked up at me. "He's eighty-nine. You know that?"

"You mentioned he was pushing ninety. I hope I look as good."

"I hope you're even alive."

I dug a finger into her ribs and she spun away, ending up sitting on the edge of the bed, laughing. I sat down next to her. "Thanks for setting this up, by the way. It was one of the stranger conversations I've had in a while, but at least it makes me feel I have another set of eyes where I need them."

"Who do you think messed with that chair?" she asked, placing her hand on my thigh.

"Don't know. The lack of a clear motive really bugs me. If it was sabotage, I can't see who benefited."

"Maybe it's totally unrelated—a pissed-off employee."

"Yeah, we're looking into that. We'll figure it out soon enough. Whoever did it'll probably get restless and try something else."

A moment of silence fell between us.

"What about the other things you're looking into?" she asked vaguely.

I was struck by something in her voice, having nothing to do with her question. "You okay?" I asked.

She sighed. "To be honest, I'm not sure. I've been staring at a lot of walls lately. How're we doing, Joe?" She sounded suddenly wistful.

I leaned back a little to get a clearer view of her face. "The two of us? I'm okay. What's up?"

She gazed out the window before answering. "I don't know. I'm having a hard time figuring out if I'm doing the right thing."

"Working for VermontGreen?"

"That, and living half my life in Montpelier, away

from you. It's been a crazy few years, you have to admit. I can't tell if I'm making sense anymore."

I could sympathize with her there. Watching her rebuild her life after being raped at the point of a knife several years ago had been an emotional roller coaster at times. But not a directionless one.

"Well, not to sound trite, but are you happy at what you're doing?" I asked.

She looked at me, her expression hopeful. "I think I am. I mean, I know that politicians aren't really normal. They're mostly needy and ego-driven, and some of them aren't bright enough to light the inside of a fridge. But I love the energy of their world—the deal making, the laws that result from it. I hated it all when I was young and looking in from the outside, but I can't get enough of it now. I really do believe it's one way to make a difference. Sort of a logical extension of what brought me up here in the first place, and why I got so active when I was a selectman in Brattleboro."

"I'm not sure I see the problem, then," I admitted.

Gail let out a puff of air and lay back on the bed to speak directly to the ceiling. "Because there's got to be more to life than being politically involved. I don't really have a family anymore, I haven't talked to my parents in so long. I have no husband, no kids, I stopped living with the only man who could put up with me for more than a week. I sometimes feel that in exchange for this new life, I'm about to lose everything else. And then I'll just be somebody wearing a suit and cell phone."

I stretched out next to her, propped up on one elbow. "I've worried about losing you, too."

She stared at me, her eyes wide. "Why?"

"Remember when I was accused of stealing that jewelry and that jerk from the attorney general's office tried to hang me? He described me to the court as an over-the-hill flatfoot trying to compensate for living with an attractive, younger, upwardly mobile woman he was worried would leave him behind."

Gail reached out and squeezed my hand. "Oh, Joe. None of that was true. The man was an idiot. He's not even a lawyer anymore, he was proven so wrong."

"Maybe so, but it hurt. You are all of those things."

"But you aren't compensating for it."

"I joined VBI."

Her mouth half opened in astonishment.

"I love what I'm doing now, too," I explained further. "But part of the reason I took the job was to earn your respect."

She rolled over and hugged me. "My God, Joe. How could you think I didn't respect you? You're the love of a lifetime. Christ, what a screwy idea."

I kissed her. "No, it's not. And it worked out beautifully. You've found something to do that really floats your boat, and I got the kick in the pants I should've given myself years ago. We've never been a conventional couple. Why should that change now?"

"So, you're okay?"

"Absolutely."

"And you don't mind living apart?"

"Sometimes," I answered her honestly, "but it's got its up sides, too."

She smiled at me then. "Oh, yeah? Like what?"

"Being with you now, stretched out on a motel bed."

She chuckled and her hand traveled across my chest.

"What're your plans for the rest of the evening?" she asked softly.

I kissed the corner of her mouth. "I have a meeting with Sammie later. But I've got an hour at least."

She reached up and touched my bearded cheek. "So I can play with this?"

"You rented the room."

A little more than an hour later, I was crossing Tucker Peak's employee parking lot, moving from one halo of light to another, the first fat flakes of a long-anticipated storm barely starting to drift by like albino moths, indecisive and tired.

"Joe?"

It was a man's voice, quiet, vaguely familiar, belonging to a shadow that stepped out from behind a parked car some ten feet ahead of me. The light being directly overhead at this point, his face was shaded in the darkness cast by his baseball cap. His hands, however, were in plain sight and empty.

I stopped and tried to sound innocent first, although I suspected it would be useless. "Who?"

He stepped nearer, still speaking very softly. "It's Win Johnston. You okay to talk?"

I glanced around, both relieved and surprised. It looked like we were alone. "For a minute." Win was a private investigator, an ex-cop, and a friend. But I could only guess that his appearing from behind a car in the dark of night was going to cost me some peace of mind in the midst of an already complicated case.

"I thought I saw you a couple of days ago, but I guessed you were undercover. Your heroics on the chair-lift clinched it, though. Nice beard. How've you been?"

We shook hands and stood closely together, almost whispering. "Okay. You working on something here?" I asked.

"Yup."

"What can you tell me?"

Unlike in the movies, such a question of a good PI played well within the rules. Cops weren't fond of the profession, that much was true, but the antagonisms, at least in a rural place like Vermont, were pretty muted. Win had been a state trooper, had retired in good standing, and was self-employed now because it kept him in the game without forcing him to kowtow to too many bosses. I trusted his integrity and had even worked with him in the past, since PIs could often do things and go places we couldn't.

"Checking up on an employee, seeing if he's above-board."

"Oh, oh," I said. "Sounds like embezzling."

He quickly held up a hand. "No, no. It's much vaguer than that."

"But still interesting to someone with a big problem and a lot of money," I suggested, "like maybe the resort brass?"

His vanity prompted him to admit half an answer. "I'm not cheap."

"So, it's serious."

He wobbled his head from side to side. "Could be. I haven't found anything yet."

"I don't guess you'd tell me the target."

"Sorry."

"Would it have anything to do with that chair breaking loose?"

"Is that why you're here?" he asked.

I considered being as coy as he was but didn't see the point. "No. That came out of the blue. We're here on a string of condo rip-offs."

He looked surprised. "You were just working on that killing in Brattleboro. Is there a connection?"

"You didn't answer my question," I reminded him.

He took my own evasion in stride. "About the chair? I don't know. A contact at the Tramway Board told me it was tampered with. But it's a puzzle piece I haven't been able to place yet."

"No . . . me neither. Win, do me a favor, okay? Keep me in the loop as much as possible. There're a couple of things going on here, and, to answer your question, I don't know if they connect or not, but you already know one woman's dead and another was almost killed. I realize you have confidences to protect, but pay extra attention, all right?"

"Sure, Joe. What's your cover name again? Max something?"

"Lambert. And Sammie Martens is a ski instructor named Greta Novak—bottle blond."

He laughed gently. "Some name. I saw her, I think. Looked like she was having a ball. Didn't recognize her. She's very attractive."

"And very serious, as always."

He shook my hand again. "Keep your head down, Joe . . . Max. I'll let you know if I find anything interesting."

He turned away, passed between two SUVs, and was gone, leaving me to wonder what else might fall into my lap.

* * *

Sammie was waiting for me where we'd met the night before, checking her watch as I walked up.

"I thought we'd have to scrub this," she said.

"Sorry. Ran into Win Johnston in the parking lot. He's working here, too, looking into an employee. I'm guessing one of the management types, given his standard rate, but he wouldn't fess up. The interesting thing is that he's bothered by the chair sabotage, meaning it might play a role in what he's investigating."

"An employee trying to do in the company?"

"He doesn't know, says it doesn't fit, but it makes more sense than the TPL doing it. I asked him to keep an eye open."

"You trust him?" Sammie knew Win only to say hi and shared the common police prejudice against his profession.

"To report anything outright criminal? Absolutely," I told her. "He's proved himself enough times. Plus, he thinks you're very good looking."

"I think he needs to lose weight."

I left it at that. "I also had a private chat with Roger Betts this afternoon."

She gave me a surprised look. "How'd that happen?"

"He's worried some of his folks might be getting a little overenthusiastic."

"As in screwing around with chairlifts?"

"That was the implication, although I told him that, pretty predictably, more people are blaming the TPL for that than the resort, which makes the whole point of the exercise a little weird. Still, after you and I are done, I'm going to call Lester and have him compare notes with

Snuffy's office. They've been building files on the protesters since this started. Could be they have a candidate
we should look at more carefully."

Sammie suddenly shivered, and then checked the time.
"Why did you want to meet? Lester made it sound important."

"We think your Richie Lane might be Marty's contact
man. His real name's Robert Lanier, and he has a king-
size rap sheet."

"Shit," she spat out. "I knew it. Slimy bastard."

"Maybe, but that's all we know. We could pull him in
and sweat him but I'm betting he knows the rules enough
to just sit us out and then vanish. I'd prefer to keep an eye
on him instead, nail him for something crooked if we're
lucky, and then use that to open him up, or maybe follow
him till he leads us to the ever elusive Marty Gagnon."

"Shouldn't be hard to catch him dirty. He aspires to do
something criminal every night. It's in his blood."

"You know where he is?"

"Right now? No idea, but I bet he started out at the
nightclub, 'cruisin' for a lonely lady,' as he puts it. That's
his daily routine—brags about it every morning. Some of
the other instructors told me he might as well be a wall
fixture over there."

"Tomorrow morning, we'll put a twenty-four-hour tail
on him. I'll have Spinney figure out a schedule. If you're
right about his habits, we should have something on him
pretty quick."

"Great," she said, "it won't be too soon."

CHAPTER TEN

I SMELLED HIM BEFORE I RECOGNIZED WHO IT WAS—THAT all-enveloping body odor.

"Max, wake up."

Fred's face was hovering over mine. "Max, wake up. They want everybody on the mountain—fast."

I swung my legs out of bed. "Why?"

"Something about water pumps. We're supposed to meet outside Mountain Ops dressed for weather . . . and it's snowing like crazy."

The scene was out of some Russian movie: a huge, mingling, nighttime crowd of heavily clothed people standing before a tall, dour building, bracketed by bright lights that made the endless swirl of wild falling snow shimmer like a phosphorescent dust storm. Facing them from the deck of a Bombardier, using a bullhorn like a commissar, Linda Bettina was barking out orders.

"People, we've had a power outage in the pump room and a water main break," she announced. "Everyone has to get on the mountain to contain the spill and drain the pipes before they freeze. Report to your department managers and do what they tell you, on the double. Remember, if this mountain goes down, we're all out of work."

She then listed the managers and their locations as they stood in various spots around the equipment yard.

As best I could in my insulated coveralls and heavy boots, I jogged to where I was supposed to be and found my boss directing teams toward a large gathering of grooming machines, four-wheelers with chains, and snowmobiles. I ended up in a group of five men on the open back deck of a groomer, speeding up the mountain in the pitch darkness, our assignment to be dropped off, one by one, at a series of snowmaking hydrants and to open up the drain cocks.

We held on for our lives. The decking was slippery steel diamond plate, the side rails only a foot high and hard to grasp, and the groomer's broad, thrashing caterpillar treads—completely exposed and flashing by with the speed of commercial meat grinders—were as mesmerizing as two cobras, especially whenever the driver hit a mogul or a dip and sent us scrambling to keep our balance.

It was a long night. The storm was unrelenting, the snow cutting off all vision, muffling communications, covering familiar landmarks, and reducing the world in which we worked—mostly soaked in freezing, spraying water—to tiny, frigid capsules of frantic energy. But slowly, pipeline by pipeline, hydrant by hydrant, often using propane torches to thaw what we had to, we all covered the mountain in roaming squads, carried back and forth by screaming, whining, or deep-throated machines driven by people who seemed to know where they were going by feel alone.

By the time the snow-clotted gray veil around us began to take on the dull glow of early dawn, we were told the worst of the crisis had passed and that those of us not specifically assigned to mountain maintenance could leave the line.

We convened in the large room of the base lodge, ironically around the scale model of a perfect, pristine resort of the future, to be fed hot coffee and breakfast by a haggard-looking kitchen crew before the first customers showed up for a day's recreation. It was there I noticed Linda Bettina ducking into a small side office, and I followed her in before she could close the door.

She seemed remarkably chipper for someone who'd just orchestrated a near-military campaign, waving me cheerfully to a seat and slamming the door.

"God," she said, collapsing into a chair, still dressed for the outside and still encrusted with melting ice and snow. "What a night."

She had a large mug of coffee cradled between her hands. "Thanks for your help."

I smiled quizzically. "I'm not complaining, but I didn't know we had a choice."

She laughed. "Yeah, well . . . We try to make that part of the contract a little hard to figure out." She suddenly leaned forward, her eyes bright. "But be straight—didn't you have a ball tonight? Christ, it must be like being in combat."

I thought back to my very real knowledge of that experience and nodded. "It's very close."

She raised her eyebrows. "Oh, no shit. Glad I didn't put my foot in it. Didn't know you were a vet."

"Long time ago."

She slouched back into her chair and rested her head against its cushion. "Jesus. I am glad it's over, though."

"You want to be alone?" I asked, hesitating.

"No, no. Park yourself. I gotta admit, while I wouldn't wish this on my worst enemy, it's times like this that make me think there's hope left for the ski business."

"Ain't what it used to be?"

She turned somber then, closing her eyes briefly and letting her face relax into a mask of exhaustion. "Not even close. It's all about money now, and taking care of number one. The employees just want a job, the managers just want to survive, the corporate heads and stockholders just want a profit, and the guests just want everything now, in perfect order, and for cheap—or else. Nobody remembers that it used to be about skiing." She shook her head and revived somewhat. "And then you get a night like this, when everyone clicks, and it tells me that just maybe I'll stick it out for another year."

"What happened tonight, anyway?"

"Power went out," she said vaguely. "Happens once in a blue moon, but when it does, watch out."

"You don't have backup generators?"

"Yeah . . . well. I guess Murphy was lurking this time. They went out, too. That was a first for me."

"A little unlikely, isn't it? On top of a blown water main? That's a triple whammy."

She took a slow, thoughtful sip of coffee, watching me over the mug's rim. "It's a bad piece of timing. True enough," she cautiously admitted.

"You find out why the pipe broke?"

"Yeah. I did." This time her voice was flat, and her eyes very steady.

"But you're not at liberty to discuss it?"

She put the mug down and studied me for a moment. "I heard someone's been asking a lot of questions around here lately. Would that be you, Max?"

"Linda," I countered, "I'm a mechanically minded man, and a carpenter because I like the freedom, not because I'm an idiot. Something unusual and disastrous happens like it did today, right after a chair lets go for no reason; it seems like a no-brainer to wonder why. I had my nose right up against that chair mechanism, remember? There was nothing wrong with it an accident could explain."

Now I was staring at her, as if she were wrong to hold out on me. She relented, dropping her eyes and muttering, "No. I suppose you're right."

"So, we're talking similar events, then," I suggested. "Someone screwing with the equipment."

She passed a hand across her mouth and pulled at her chin. "Looks that way. But I'll fire you if you repeat it."

"I'm here to help," I said truthfully. "Not add to your problems. Was the water main sabotaged?"

"I'll be going onto the mountain when it gets lighter to find out. It's pretty hard now to tell exactly what happened, but I think so. Lines usually break at junctures: a valve, a Y, a coupling. This one was midline, just where the spillage could take out the top of an entire trail. We'll have to close it till we can recondition the surface. That'll cost us a bundle in expenses and lost revenues both. Insurance only covers so much."

I tried the same line Mike the mechanic had used on me earlier. "Makes sense if the TPL had something to do with it—hits you in your pocketbook while making an issue of water."

She sighed. "Yeah. I thought about that. I'm not sure I buy it, though. Environmentalists are pretty vocal in Vermont, and God knows they have a lot of power. But that also means they've never had to turn violent to get their way. Why do it now? We jumped through all the regulatory hoops, and McNally is still putting up with their crap and holding meetings with them. I know the TPL said we lied to get those permits, but that's a common complaint. We're always accused of being in bed with the politicians . . . Don't I wish."

"You're not going to tell me Tucker Peak volunteered every stat they had available, are you? Including the ones suggesting this water project wasn't such a good idea?"

Her face clouded with anger. "We're not the ones who make this a damn near-impossible process. TPL cooks the numbers and lobbies, too. You better believe it. You work for these people or something? Why're you so goddamn interested?"

I cynically used my current heroic stature. "Maybe because I stopped a woman from bleeding to death. That makes the stakes pretty high."

Linda Bettina stood up, her coffee forgotten in the wake of resurgent frustration. "Look, Max, I don't have the answers you want. I don't know who did what or why. All I know is that a business I used to love is looking more like a used-car lot and I can't do anything about it. That doesn't make us the devil incarnate, and it doesn't mean the TPLs of the world automatically walk on water. It's a screwed up world filled with grubby people gouging out a place for themselves, and sometimes they'll do it at any cost. If that makes me one of the bad guys in your book, then so be it. I'm just trying to do what they pay me to do the best way I know how."

I also stood and laid a hand on her shoulder. "I wasn't blaming you, Linda. You have the best rep of anyone here, better than Phil McNally's. Even Bucky admits you're pretty good—for a girl."

She shook her head with a disgusted but genuine smile and took hold of the doorknob, preparing to return to work. "He's such a woodchuck. I doubt he'd say that about me right now, shooting my mouth off to a total stranger. You never did tell me if you're the one asking all those questions."

I figured I owed her that much. "I'm not. It's a private detective. He asked me a few things, too. I got the feeling he wasn't getting anywhere fast."

She absorbed that for a few seconds and then smiled again, opening the door. "Crazy business, Max, getting worse fast. We're a huge, dysfunctional family, everybody dependent on Big Daddy, only he's bipolar and hiring private eyes to investigate himself. I'd start looking for another job, if I were you. Something safer, maybe— like minesweeping."

Later that day, after a few hours' sleep, I was fitting hardwood panels into the side of the new information booth on the base lodge's main floor—trying not to be stepped on by the lead-booted, canary-colored skiers who were stomping around in a seemingly aimless herd—when Sammie crouched beside me, pretending to adjust her boot buckle. "You got Richie from eight o'-

clock. He'll be fixing himself up at the dorm for his nightly routine at the club. That work for you?"

"Yup."

She moved on and left me amid the chattering, fashion-conscious crowd. The marketing department had worked overtime once more, stressing the triviality of the pipeline "leak," as they were calling it, and the speed with which the closed trail would reopen. Also, the TPL protesters had all but faded from view (since McNally and their leaders were meeting behind closed doors) and the continuing snowfall had made the yellow snow but a recent memory, so Tucker Peak, for all its troubles, was for the moment looking no different from hundreds of other resorts just like it.

Nevertheless, with Bettina's comment about a dysfunctional family fresh in my mind, I watched the resort's guests with new insight. If Tucker Peak's management was Big Daddy, confused and struggling to meet a payroll, cater to the public, and make a profit, then these people with cell phones, fancy clothes, and ever higher expectations were the symbiotic flip side of that equation: a needy, fickle source of revenue as unreliable in its loyalty as management was to its own employees. I was beginning to understand both the nostalgia and the frustration of Bettina, Bucky Arsenault, and the others I'd overheard lamenting the fate of the ski business in Vermont. They were caught between two complex forces, neither one of which they felt they could control any longer, but which, back when they were young and naive, they had helped create. I sympathized with their befuddlement.

Because of my nap, I wrapped up work a little later

than usual, grabbed a sandwich from the kitchen, and went to the dorm to change into clothes more befitting a nightclub.

Shortly before eight, I stood by my second-floor window and waited for Richie Lane to appear crossing the parking lot from the base lodge—discreetly followed by Sammie—before going downstairs to take over the surveillance.

Sammie had been right about Lane's attention to personal hygiene, which, given his plans for the evening, I supposed was a good thing. Better a slicked-hair Romeo smelling excessively of aftershave than my roommate Fred, if you were heading for a bar in search of company.

Nevertheless, it took him an hour and fifteen minutes before he reappeared in the hallway outside his room, shot his cuffs from under the sleeves of his fashionable parka, patted his hair gently and affectionately with both palms, and headed toward the nightclub.

The nightclub, predictably called the Tuckaway, was located across the access road from the base lodge, next to a three-tier garage, and at the foot of the road Willy and I had taken to reach William Manning's condo. It was one story, again faux-Swiss in style, but with no windows, and was one of the resort's newer, and therefore less tattered, additions.

It was also the only clearly designated outlet for after-ski excesses, barring the base lodge's conversation-pit-with-fireplace next to the cafeteria, which closed at ten in any case. The employees had the Butte, and the landed gentry had access to the condo party circuit, but for everyone else, the Tuckaway was it.

It was an enormous, sprawling building. Even on slow

days, after all, the mountain averaged several thousand skiers. Assuming most of them spread out across the countryside after hours to surrounding motels, inns, and village bars, that still left a standard crowd of hundreds to fill the Tuckaway.

In an effort to avoid the low-ceilinged airplane hangar look, the nightclub was divided into different levels and sections for light eating, heavy drinking, dancing, staring into space, and general conversation, which, given the ear-splitting noise, amounted to shouting, pantomime, and lip reading, combined.

It was a scene, almost tribal in nature, that had never appealed to me, more given as I was, even as a child, to solitude, quiet, and reading.

On the other hand, I understood the attraction. As soon as I entered the place, discreetly on Richie's heels, the throbbing, heated, olfactory atmosphere enveloped me like a cloak, stimulating some senses and dulling others, and I easily saw how inhibitions could be temporarily cast aside and new identities assumed. The energy and darkness encouraged boldness and anonymity, and it was clear from the expressions all around me how seductive that could be.

It was certainly familiar ground to Richie Lane. Hanging his parka on a peg by the door, he launched into the crowd like a penguin into the sea, sliding by and around obstacles with ease and pleasure, chatting, laughing, gliding his hands along shoulders, forearms, waists, and occasionally lower. He kissed women on the cheek or more rarely, lightly on the lips, he gave manly hand-shakes to the men, sometimes accompanied by slaps on the back, and through it all, he watched, like a raptor in disguise.

It was a curious thing to witness, and as Sammie had commented earlier, viscerally repellent. In this man's presence, all these happy faces, especially the women's, began to seem vulnerable and frail, like children's at a party being hosted by a covert sexual deviate.

I wasn't sure of his game right off. He appeared to be merely cruising, checking the stock for any changes from the night before. Eventually however, after a couple of hours, I noticed him returning to the same "lonely lady" with increasing frequency, having presumably pumped her for enough information in earlier fly-bys to qualify her for his attentions.

From then on, it became a study in carnivorous stalking. From my vantage point at a small table high and to the back of the room, I looked down on them as from a deer blind, and watched as he slowly turned up the intimacy. Touching shoulders, chair-to-chair, then squeezing a hand now and then to emphasize highlights in his conversation, Richie gradually merged with his quarry, stroking her thigh with his open hand, her breast with the backs of his fingertips, and finally kissing her, long and deep, at around the sixth drink.

Not that similar activity wasn't occurring all around us, probably much of it equally calculated. But my focus was on this man, and I was left with the impression, largely from the deft and practiced way he pretended to drink more than he had, that he was after more than a roll in the hay.

A little after midnight, they rose to their feet, she paid the tab, and they walked outside, she with a marked unsteadiness. Laughing, pawing each other, pausing frequently to kiss, they slowly worked their way to the second level of the garage and ended up next to a dark, late-model Mercedes station wagon. There, as the woman fumbled with her keys, and I memorized the out-of-state registration, Richie gave her a fast kiss, murmured something in her ear, and began walking quickly down to the far end of the garage.

Confused, I quietly followed, keeping cars and concrete support posts between us as visual barriers, noticing over my shoulder that the woman had slipped into the Mercedes' passenger seat.

Richie reached the back of the garage and vanished into the stairwell. As soon as he was out of sight, I jogged to the doorway and listened for which way he'd gone. It was up.

I tried to imagine what he was doing. Fetching something from another car? Meeting up with someone else? Taking the scenic route on the way to dumping his date? As I climbed the stairs after him, I couldn't conjure up anything that made sense.

On the top floor, the double row of cars stretched out with showroom precision under a low ceiling, gleaming in the harsh, monochromatic fluorescent lighting like polished boulders beneath the sea, their rooftop ski racks sparkling like silver.

But there was no Richie Lane. He'd disappeared.

I stopped in my tracks, listening, suddenly tense. There was nothing. Wishing I was carrying a gun, I began to walk quietly down the central corridor, mentally kicking myself both for being lured up here and for not turning back as I knew I should. Caution dictated staying with the woman and awaiting Richie's return. But curiosity, and perhaps arrogance, had gotten the better of me.

As Richie had known it would.

"Don't move a muscle."

I froze in place, except for spreading my arms out to show I had no weapon.

I heard Richie come out from behind the car that had been shielding him and approach me from the rear. A hard, round object jabbed me viciously in the back, making me stagger forward.

"Get on your knees."

I thought back to his rap sheet. A violent man, mostly against women, a sexual predator and an occasional thief. He hadn't killed anyone that we knew of. I tried willing myself to take comfort in that.

I hoped my voice didn't betray my nervousness. "You better think this through, Richie. Or Robert, to use your real name. I'm a cop."

"Cute. Do what I said."

Consciously controlling my breathing, I lowered myself to my knees. The cold concrete bit through the fabric of my pants as my mind began to race. I'd considered this kind of scenario before, as I guessed every cop had. You hope you'll keep cool, stay in control, maybe even talk the other guy into surrendering . . . At the very least, you pray you won't totally fall apart. I had no idea how well I was faring.

"Where's your badge, then?" His free hand began patting me down.

"I'm undercover. I'm not carrying any identification."

"That's convenient. I know who you are anyhow, and

believe me, you're not doin' me like you did Marty. I'm not that stupid, in case you didn't notice."

Gripped by real fear now, I began speaking in a rush. "You got it wrong. My name's Joe Gunther. I'm a special agent with the Vermont Bureau of Investigation. We're looking for Marty. We didn't know he was dead. But that doesn't matter. We're after the same people you're afraid of. If you know who they are, we can nail them for you. You can go back to walking around without looking over your shoulder."

"Right. This where I give you my gun so you can blow my brains out? Maybe make it look like suicide? How dumb do you think I am?"

I couldn't believe the irony of it—to be executed as a hitman. "Not dumb, Richie, but plenty scared. We were thinking you killed Jorja Duval to find out where Marty was, but I guess that's not what happened, right? They knocked her off, looking for you and Marty both. That's what you're telling me, isn't it?"

He didn't say anything.

"They cut her throat, Richie—almost took her head off. Why're they after you? What did you and Marty steal, anyway?"

"We didn't steal anything," he said stubbornly.

I couldn't believe he was still pitching his own innocence, especially given the circumstances. "Maybe you didn't personally," I tried conceding. "But you set it up so Marty could. You were his spotter, finding rich targets like that woman downstairs, checking out their houses and getting some action on the side. He'd call you on the first-floor locker room pay phone a few days before every hit. You did that eight times. Think about it,

Richie. We know all that. That's why we were tailing you. If we were the people you're so afraid of, you'd be dead already."

"Fuck you," he said, his voice revealing his own frustration. "First you say you thought I killed the girl, now you say I'm a sitting duck for the guys that did. You don't even have the number right on the break-ins. You're just jerking me around, and I'm getting sick of it."

I opened my mouth to answer him but was stopped by a blinding flash of searing pain in my head. I didn't even see the floor as I bounced off it with my face.

CHAPTER ELEVEN

I HEARD A FAINT HUMMING AT FIRST, LIKE A DISTANT FURnace, steady and deep throated. It altered as I homed in on it, lightening in tone, but becoming no louder. And it was accompanied by a headache of statuesque proportions that banged off the walls of my skull like a ball with boundless energy. I winced and became aware of a second pain between my eyes, but on the outside. Gingerly, I rolled onto my back and raised my hand, surprised to find it stiff, numb, and difficult to move, and touched my face around the nose and forehead, discovering both to be sore, tender, and crusty with dried blood.

I finally took a deep breath and opened my eyes, instantly closing them against the glare directly above me.

I realized I was cold. Not just chilly, but cold enough to rob my hands and feet of feeling, to make breathing tough and movement a challenge. I opened my eyes again, slowly this time, getting them used to the light, which I realized half a minute later belonged to a fluorescent tube—also the source of the humming noise.

I was still in the garage.

I turned my head awkwardly, looking first one way, then the other, and found that all but a few of the cars had left, including those parked right beside me. People in considerable numbers had walked by me or even stepped over my unconscious and bloody body, and driven themselves home. I checked my watch—four-thirty in the morning.

Perhaps more wearied by that realization than by any of my injuries, I slowly got myself together—going from flat out, to sitting, to standing and leaning against the wall, to finally walking toward the stairwell like an octogenarian—and eventually managed to wend my way back to the employee dorm. There, after getting out of my clothes without waking up Fred, I shuffled into the bathroom to look at myself.

The damage was mostly internal, and I sensed by now it would probably be transient. No concussion, no split skull. I had a hell of a lump on the back of my head, a bloody nose, and a scraped forehead, only the last of which displayed any damage after I washed up, and even that was no more than your average rug rash.

But still I knew, embarrassment notwithstanding, that I better get to a hospital—I'd seen before how convincingly a wounded man can kid himself.

An hour and a half later, sitting on the edge of an ER gurney, rebuttoning my shirt and with my bloodstream full of pain killers, I told Lester and Willy about Richie Lane. Sammie had already heard it driving me to the hospital.

Willy was predictably unsympathetic. "I can't believe you walked into it. You should've called for backup as soon as he went upstairs—sure as shit when you saw he'd pulled a Houdini."

"Thank you, Mr. Kunkle," Sammie said irritably. "Is that how you would've done it?"

He was unrepentant. "People expect me to be a bone-head."

I waved the issue away. "Okay, okay. That may have been a compliment, so let's drop it. The trick now is to find Richie before Jorja's killer does. Lester, you better pull out the stops on every name on Richie's rap sheet— the same drill we did on Marty Gagnon. And let's get search warrants for his room at Tucker Peak, his locker, his residence if he has one, his car unless he took it, and if he did, a New England–wide BOL on it and him both."

"What about his mountain contacts?" Lester asked.

"Who was he closest to among the instructors, Sammie?"

She thought a moment. "Hard to tell, he schmoozed around so much. I guess Kurt Peterson—he actually seemed to like the guy. The rest of us mostly talked behind his back, especially the women."

I touched the nape of my neck with my fingertips. My headache was beginning to descend to normal levels, but the goose egg there was still hot and fragile, as if ready to burst.

"Speaking of women," I continued, "I guess we know how at least some of Marty's targets were selected. We need to go back over each household, find out about any women who might've been involved, like the invisible Mrs. William Manning, and put the squeeze on them as diplomatically as possible. If we're lucky, Richie let a little of himself show through while he was grilling them—

a reference to a hunting camp, a favorite hideout, a relative in some distant town—something that might let us know where he's at."

Sammie had been taking notes, and now looked up from her notepad. "What about the woman you saw him with?"

I nodded, irritated that I'd forgotten about her. "Right. Locate her, find out where they were headed, what Richie's line was." I gave Sammie the Mercedes plate number I'd memorized.

Lester cleared his throat gently and asked, "Are we taking Richie's word for it that Marty's dead?"

After a brief general silence, Willy said, "I'm not. If Richie's really so sweaty about it, why's he still working on the mountain? Doesn't track."

"Might make sense if Marty killed Jorja because of what she knew, and both he and Richie are pretending it was somebody else," Lester ventured.

My headache found a second wind. "That's getting pretty complicated. Let's just keep it open for now. Assume Marty's still alive and working with Richie, and that there's another guy out there gunning for them both. That way, we keep everyone in our sights. We can sort out the realities after we round them all up."

"What about Win Johnston?" Sammie asked.

I considered that for a couple of seconds. "He's a wild card."

"We could tail him."

"Can't justify it. It would cost too much, chances are his client contacts are by phone, and we have no idea what he's doing anyway. Place like Tucker Peak, with its PR sensitivity, my guess would be embezzlement. Anyhow, I think he'll let us know if anything comes up we need to know about."

"Your call," she said mostly to herself, clearly unconvinced.

"That does remind me, though," I added. "Did we get anything from Snuffy's people about the TPL backgrounds he's been running?"

Lester didn't even look up. "Too early yet, he keeps bitching about being swamped. Wonders why in the hell he ever contacted us."

"I'll see if I can't get him moving," I said.

"Oh," Lester added, "I did get a call from the Tramway investigator last night. Definite sabotage on the hanger arm of that chair."

"Okay. Guess that makes it official then."

Willy spoke up from where he was stretched out on an adjoining bed. "On the subject of official business, I take it we've pretty much blown the undercover gig."

I regretfully stroked my beard, which had grown on me in several ways. "Not totally. I doubt Richie'll be hanging around the slopes tomorrow telling people he smacked a cop over the head. Besides, he didn't even believe me."

"And Sammie's still okay," Lester added.

I nodded gingerly in agreement. "I don't doubt Richie'll talk to somebody about me, though, sooner or later, and who knows who might've stepped over me going to their car last night, and who might come squealing later. So, I think I will give it up—Bettina smells a rat anyhow—but let's leave Sammie in a little longer."

Willy sighed heavily and rolled his eyes. "Great. So, Blondie lives on."

* * *

I recognized the car before I even saw the New York plates because it was so flagrantly from out of state: a black, late-model, very shiny Lexus with glittering gold trim. Even upscale Vermonters don't go for a vehicle like that. Too flashy. And too lordly. Might be a good car, but not worth the attitude.

Mrs. William Manning got out hesitantly, adjusting her oversize dark glasses as if to ward off a crowd of clamoring paparazzi. Unfortunately, there were none, and the few passersby took no notice of her.

We were in a convenience store parking lot, halfway between Tucker Peak and Brattleboro, both in separate cars—an arrangement I'd made with her by phone the day before. She was on her way to the condo, where her husband was waiting for her, and had just driven up from the city.

I let her stand there awkwardly for a moment, out of place, out of sorts, and at a loss to explain herself if anyone were to ask. I wanted her own discomfort to melt some of the ice for me before I introduced myself.

Finally, I swung out of the van I was in and motioned her over. She was so relieved she actually stumbled walking my way, looking left and right, presumably still waiting for a shout of recognition—a Jackie-O without foundation or credentials.

I slid open the backdoor and ushered her inside. It was the same van we'd used for our squad meeting a few nights before.

"Glad you could make it," I said, following her in and slamming the door. The light inside was muted and calming, almost like a psychologist's office.

She settled into one of the captain's chairs, tore off her glasses, and glared at me. "I could make it? What choice did I have? I'm being blackmailed here."

I handed her my identification, which she barely glanced at. "Mrs. Manning, you're here of your own accord. The fact that you're worried about your affair with Richie Lane has nothing to do with us."

"As if you wouldn't go straight to my husband with it."

"We wouldn't, in fact, although I do have to warn you, if any of this goes to trial and the prosecution deems it relevant to their case, you could be called to testify."

She covered her forehead with one perfectly manicured hand. "Oh, my God."

"I wouldn't worry yet. It may not come to that."

The hand dropped, she sighed theatrically, blinked several times as if to control tears I saw no sign of, and finally said, "It wasn't an affair. We only met once."

I suspected better, but I couldn't resist. "A one-night stand?"

She stamped her foot. "Christ. It sounds so tacky. You have to understand, I was lonely, my husband and I have been having some problems. I felt my life was falling apart."

I saw her give me the quickest of glances, as if to judge her performance by my reaction.

"Mrs. Manning, I don't care. I just want to know what happened between you and Richie Lane."

She looked faintly scandalized. "You *know* what happened. Isn't that why we're in this . . . thing." She waved a hand around the van.

"I don't mean the sex. I want to know what he said."

She looked at me blankly. I began to think Richie had been underachieving when he put the moves on this one.

"What do you mean?"

I was tempted to tell her he'd not only used her to pay for his drinks and get a roll in the hay, but that he'd scoped out her house to be robbed a few days later, and that she'd been lucky he hadn't threatened to tell her husband for a cash bonus. But I didn't want her to have a fit and storm out the door, not yet.

"We want to get this man," I said instead, "without involving you if possible. He's dangerous, he has a record, and he's involved in things that'll put him in jail for a long time. You were very lucky—unless he chooses to come back, of course—but we don't want some other woman to suffer at his hands."

The veiled threat of his return—of which he'd shown no signs so far—did the trick. She sat forward in her chair, her elbows on her knees, and gave me the instantly sincere look. "What can I do to help?"

"He made small talk when he approached you at the nightclub. Did he tell you anything about himself that might tell us where to find him—some family names, where he was brought up, a favorite summer place, a restaurant he really likes—anything at all?"

She furrowed her brow, which by now only made me doubt her veracity. "It's hard to remember. I wasn't drinking much—I never do—but I was tired and hadn't eaten all day, and I'd been ill the week before. My system hadn't fully recovered, so I'm afraid I was caught unawares."

"You were drunk, in other words."

She frowned and stiffened slightly. I was happy I

wasn't Willy Kunkle right then. "No, I wasn't drunk. I was overtired and my metabolism was off kilter. He took advantage of me."

I tried again. "Do you remember anything he might have said?"

"He talked about Switzerland, how much more fun it was to ski there than here, how the Tyrol was like a magic kingdom. He did make it sound wonderful."

I bit off telling her the Tyrol was not in Switzerland. "How 'bout something closer to home?"

"He told me about a few of the people who work here. That was quite funny. He described some real characters." She hesitated and then shook her head. "He mostly asked me questions. It was very flattering, really. Women don't usually have attractive men ask them about themselves. He couldn't get enough of it. I have to admit, I'm still finding it hard to accept that he's done what you're accusing him of."

"Trust me. Did he say anything about what he does during the off season? Someplace he goes to?"

Her eyes widened. "Oh, yes—that's very good. He did. He said he teaches tennis at Mount Snow."

I nodded. It was probably as accurate as his European geography, but he might have let something slip. I pulled out a card with my name and phone number on it. "Okay, Mrs. Manning. I guess that's it for the moment. If you think of something else, I'd appreciate a phone call."

She held the card between her fingers as if it were covered with glue, which, metaphorically, it might have been. "I don't want my husband to find this."

I took it back, figuring it had been wasted anyhow.

"Vermont Bureau of Investigation. It's in the book. Ask for Joe Gunther or anyone in the Brattleboro office."

She pursed her lips like a child memorizing a poem. "Got it."

I slid open the door. "You're free to go. Thanks."

She crabbed by me clumsily, bent over to spare bumping her head, and stepped onto the parking lot, slipping her dark glasses back on.

"Mrs. Manning?"

She looked over her shoulder at me.

"I'd be careful about being picked up like that. Even in Vermont, these situations can get dangerous."

She scowled at me and opened her mouth to protest. I slammed the door in her face and watched her through the dark glass as she stalked off in rigid outrage.

I then turned to the mobile phone mounted on the van's wall, got directory to locate the Mount Snow employment office, and was routed through to that number. I asked the voice that answered if Donna Repsher was there.

She came on in a couple of minutes. "This is Donna."

"Donna, it's Joe Gunther."

"Joe. I don't believe it. Such a long time. How's the new job?"

"Interesting. Little tough getting other cops to play now and then, but we're working on it."

"And Gail?"

"She's fine. Saw her yesterday. Busier than hell, but that's the way she likes it."

"You watch out. She'll end up governor or a senator someday, and you'll be driving her car. I know you didn't call to chat, Joe, so what's up?"

"Cruel, Donna."

"You going to make a liar out of me?"

"No, you're right. I need to know if you ever had an employee named Richie Lane—said he taught tennis there."

She laughed and told me to hang on. An old friend from where I'd grown up in Thetford, Donna was part of a vast extended family I maintained throughout the state, in part out of friendship, but also because of where they worked or who they knew.

The phone clicked in my ear. "Joe? I'm at the computer and I don't see anybody with that name."

I closed my eyes and struggled to remember what Lester Spinney had told me earlier. "How 'bout Robert Lanier, Marc Roberts, or Lenny . . . no, Lanny Robertson."

I heard her tapping on the computer for a while, before finally chuckling to herself. "Tennis teacher? Cute. Was that his pick-up line?"

"You got it. What was he really?"

"Marc Roberts is on the summer grounds crew payroll—grunt-labor level, basically restricted to picking up trash, cleaning gutters, and other intellectual pursuits. Good place to work on a tan, though."

"You got a home address?"

She did, in West Dover, Vermont, which Mount Snow calls home.

"That current?"

"It's where we sent his last check. I wouldn't know beyond that."

I thanked her, hung up, and called the Dover police department. The chief there, also a friend, said he'd make some discreet inquiries about the address's validity and call me back.

Both Sammie and Lester were conducting interviews similar to the one I'd just had with Mrs. Manning—with married women who'd owned homes ripped off by Marty Gagnon. I wondered if either one of them had picked up anything linking Richie to Mount Snow. If they had, it could mean we were onto something solid. In any case, I could barely believe my luck so far.

While I was waiting to hear back, however, there was a conversation I felt honor bound to have. I started the van up and headed back toward Tucker Peak.

CHAPTER TWELVE

LINDA BETTINA LOOKED UP AS I ENTERED HER OFFICE ON the top floor of the Mountain Ops building. "Where the hell have you been? Your supervisor's been bitching like a jilted girlfriend, which I don't need."

I sat in the chair across from her desk. The office was large, lined with windows overlooking the equipment yard on one side and the ski slopes on the other, and, conceptually at least, could have been outfitted to advertise the high rank of the executive inhabiting it. Instead, it looked like a mad scientist's workshop jammed with piles of computer printouts, strewn-about bits of oil-stained, insulated clothing, and dismembered, arcane pieces of rusting, twisted, broken, or grimy hardware—some quite large—presumably dumped here either to be analyzed, returned to the manufacturer, or maybe because the room's owner wouldn't notice their presence. I'd seen five-car pileups that looked tidier.

"Sorry. I should've called," I told her, reaching into my pocket. I removed my shield and laid it before her. "And I owe you another apology, too."

She picked it up, leaned back in her chair, and studied it carefully. She did not look amused. "I knew you were bullshitting me."

"Not about the private eye, though. He is here and he is asking questions, why I don't know."

She gave the badge one last look and tossed it back to me. "Very fancy. You have fun jerking me around?"

"I did what I had to do. We're running a murder investigation and had reason to believe the man we were after was working here."

"Is he?"

"That's still up in the air. We did discover one of your ski instructors was part of a burglary ring ripping off the condos."

She quickly held up her hand. "Hold that thought." She picked up the phone next to her and ordered, "Get Phil in here—*now.*"

She replaced the receiver and looked at me more carefully. "It'll just take a minute, he's in the building. Where'd you get that bruise?"

"The guy I was talking about. He bushwhacked me in the parking garage."

Her tone hadn't softened any. "You let him get away?"

"I was unconscious at the time."

She laughed despite herself. "Sorry. You okay?"

"I'm all right."

There was a quick knock at the open door and a man in his forties walked in—small, trim, with thick, graying hair. Phil McNally, who'd been spending so much time honing his damage control skills.

"Close the door, will you, Phil?" Linda asked, staying seated.

I rose and stuck out my hand.

Linda spoke for me. "This is Special Agent Joe Gunther of the VBI, whatever the hell that is. He's got a real pretty badge and he's been working undercover here as a carpenter. You know anything about this?"

McNally froze in midhandshake, his mouth half open. "Undercover? No. What's it all about?"

I repeated what I'd told Bettina. McNally felt for the back of the second guest chair and sat down heavily, groping in his pocket for a small pill box. From it, he pinched a tiny tablet which he immediately put in his mouth. "Sorry—bad heart. My God. Who is this ski instructor?"

"You know him as Richie Lane. That's an alias."

"I know him," Linda said disgustedly. "Never liked him. I would've fired his butt if he hadn't been so popular with the ladies."

"His scam was to pick up married female condo owners, get information on their home layouts and schedules, and arrange with another man to burgle them when no one was there. The women, assuming they even realized what had happened, kept their mouths shut to protect themselves."

Phil McNally was beginning to recover, seemingly helped by his pill. "Holy cow. I knew about the robberies. Sheriff Dawson and his men have been working on them."

"He called us in so he could free up more men to deal with the protesters."

"What about the murder you mentioned? Do we still have someone to worry about? I mean, I'm assuming you have Lane under lock and key, right?"

"Wrong," Linda Bettina said bluntly. "They let him get away."

His eyes widened. "So, we have *two* guys out there?"

"I don't think you have anything to worry about," I explained hastily. "Richie Lane isn't likely to come back here, and his partner's laying low. As for who the murderer is, we're still working on that. I should warn you, by the way, that the Tramway Board's getting ready to tell you that chair was rigged to slide back, which, given the nature of the woman's injuries, makes it attempted manslaughter." I looked straight at Linda. "Were your suspicions about the water pipe and generators borne out?"

She looked grim. "Yup."

"What suspicions?" McNally asked.

"They were sabotaged," I explained.

His face reddened, which told me that Linda's veiled resentment about his possibly not having told her about me cut both ways—there were definite issues of turf here. "That goddamned TPL. I bent over backwards to accommodate those bastards. I fed them, for Christ's sake. That son of a bitch Roger Betts, pretending to be some sort of Mahatma Gandhi. What a crock—"

I cut him off, as much for his heart as to staunch his outburst. "We don't have any proof it was the TPL. In fact, this is my first hard-core confirmation that there was any sabotage beyond the chair."

McNally looked from me to his mountain manager, his breathing markedly ragged. "What's that mean? You were keeping this from the police, too?"

Linda glared at him, totally unsympathetic. "Don't

give me that, Phil. He knows and you know we try to keep this kind of shit under the carpet. That's probably why we have a fucking private eye crawling around poking into our business."

McNally's mouth fell open again. "Jesus. We do?"

"Wake up, Phil. You wander around here patting people on the back and playing Dr. Feelgood. This place is a mess. I'm not surprised we're harboring thieves and murderers. We spoil the guests rotten, close our eyes to the underage drinking, the drug use, the sexual highjinks, and hire people who're just short of criminally insane—no questions asked—to take care of them, all to make ourselves more attractive than the next whore up the street and save a few bucks in the bargain. Are you surprised this is where we've ended up?"

I was caught off guard by McNally's reaction. He laughed, raised his eyebrows at me, and jerked a thumb at Bettina while unconsciously massaging his chest with his other hand. "Isn't she great? And right, too."

He pushed himself out of his chair and crossed over to the window overlooking the base area where the lifts angled up the mountain like a fan of black yarn pinned to a map. Throngs of skiers were either standing in line to ascend or simply wandering around, darting to and from the large wooden ski racks like colorful bees around a hive.

"No," he answered her rhetorical question, his back still to us but apparently completely recovered. "I'm not surprised. But unless you have a workable solution, we're stuck—you with your frustrations and me pretending everything's perfect."

At that point he turned and looked at us, his demeanor at last indicating why he was the CEO. " 'Cause that's the problem, Linda. You're not the only recipient of all that shit running downhill, nor are you the only one aware of what this business has become. You and I merely occupy different spots on the same slimy slope." He shook his head and added, "To use a disgusting analogy."

Then he smiled at me. "Welcome to the ski industry, Agent Gunther, where the inmates run the asylum and don't compare notes in the bargain. It does help explain the appeal of moving to Luxembourg." He switched his attention to Bettina. "I'm sorry if you think I'm leaving you out of the loop. You're my right hand and the best mountain manager I know. I trust you enough not to spend much time with you, which I guess makes it seem just the opposite. But I'm not being dodgy, Linda. I'm just preoccupied with an antsy board, a lot of nervous new investors, a shit-load of bills, a penny-pinching CFO, and the definite sense that if this whole reinvention scheme doesn't work out, it'll be my head on the platter."

Linda was already motioning him to be quiet. "I know all that, Phil. I was just blowing off steam at the one person who doesn't need to hear it. You think one of them hired the private eye?"

He nodded. "Oh, hell. I wouldn't doubt it for a second. I might've done the same in their place. Forearm yourself with any dirt you can find, so when the *Titanic* does sink, you've already got the anchor ready to weigh down the captain in case he tries to swim for it."

"I was thinking embezzlement, myself," I suggested.

"Normally, I'd agree with you," he conceded. "And I'll run it by Gorenstein, but since I didn't know about this, I have to assume I'm the target, not some embezzler. Makes more sense, given the current climate around here."

"Well," I said. "If it's any comfort, he told me he hadn't found anything yet."

McNally shrugged that off. "Doesn't matter. If they feel they need it and it's not there, they'll cook it up."

"I know this guy," I disagreed. "He's a straight shooter."

He looked at me with a pitying expression and explained, "Then they'll hire one who isn't."

That didn't leave me with much to say.

Linda had a question for me, though. "Does the Tramway Board finding mean you're going to be wandering around here asking everybody what they were doing on the night of the crime?"

"Something like that."

She looked disgusted. "Great. So, on top of the Phantom of the Opera trying to put us out of business, we've got the sheriff itching to roust the TPL, you guys bugging the condo owners and the employees for both theft and sabotage, and a private dick doing Christ knows what."

"And falling revenues," McNally added. "I got this morning's figures from Conan—ticket sales are nose-diving."

"You think an employee might be behind the sabotage?" I asked her.

"Despite the fact I still work here," she said, "I'm not a total fool. Who else is going to know how to mess with that equipment? A snow bunny?"

"Could be an ex-employee," I suggested, "or someone with eyes in his head, a basic mechanical ability, and the opportunity to get around when no one's watching."

McNally had other priorities. "I suppose asking you to be discreet is a waste of time?" It wasn't really a question.

"It's not my primary concern," I admitted, "but what with the protesters and the deputies going at it these last few days, people have at least gotten used to seeing cops around."

"Sheriff's deputies aren't investigators hassling everyone they meet," Linda said.

I stood up and walked to the door. "We'll try to target who we talk to. You could both help us by giving this some thought—especially you, Linda. You know everyone on this mountain. You've shared their employment records with a couple of my men, which is much appreciated, but it's more about how they interact with each other and with you folks that'll reveal what they're capable of. Like your reaction to Richie Lane—you obviously knew he was warped. If you can think of others like him that we should focus on, it'd be a big help and would get us off the mountain faster."

She wasn't happy with the idea, but I'd used the right bait. "For that, I'll do what I can."

I opened the door and stepped into the hallway. "That's all I ask."

Sammie Martens lived in an enormous studio apartment just down the street from the Municipal Building in Brattleboro. There are quite a number of these places in town—old ballrooms, concert halls, and meeting rooms—high-ceilinged, wood-floored, with huge windows overlooking the Connecticut River and the railroad tracks on one side and the steady activity of Main Street on the other. None of them are used for their original purpose, and some of those purposes have been lost over the years, leaving rooms as tantalizing and inexplicable as catacombs found deep underground.

But they aren't all such wonderful places to live. Often on the top floors of the ancient, red-brick behemoths that make the heart of Brattleboro look like some gritty industrial mill town fringing Boston, many of these apartments are drafty walk-ups. They're poorly wired, hard to heat, and equipped with minimal plumbing. They also suffer from splintery floors, sagging ceilings, and single-pane windows that rattle like rocks in a can on windy wintry days and whenever the trains pass by.

Sammie's occupied a middle range, mostly because she'd put a lot of effort and money into fixing it up, much to her landlord's heightening suspicions. She'd clustered her life in modules throughout its vast space: gym equipment in one spot, sofas and chairs in another, a TV and stereo entertainment area. Her salary precluded anything very fancy—I knew for a fact that she'd furnished it largely from yard sales—and the final result was less Manhattan shabby-chic, and more duct-tape-and-wire livable. But it was her own, had been for years, and, as far as I knew, was the only place she could retreat to when things got tough.

As I guessed they might be now. I'd seen her expression when Willy had made that Blondie crack and figured it might be a good time to continue the conversation we'd begun in the alleyway outside the Butte.

I knew she'd be here—and be alone. Lester had told me she'd gone straight home after our meeting at the hospital, and I'd double-checked on Willy's whereabouts on my own before coming over. I was surprised, however, to find her wearing only a bathrobe when she answered the door, her head swathed in a towel turban. It was barely six P.M.

I also noticed she looked terribly sad, which unfortunately didn't surprise me. "I'm sorry, Sammie. This a bad time?"

She smiled, barely. "Just got out of the shower." She patted her engulfed head. "Had to touch up the Swedish look before I head back to the mountain—didn't want to blow my cover. Come on in."

I followed her into the apartment, once more awed by how it made me feel like a mouse at the bottom of a bucket. My place was the exact opposite of this: a small, low-ceilinged, multiroomed dwelling with its succession of hideaways, all linked by doorways and short, narrow corridors. I felt impermanent here, as if someone might come by, pack me up, and mail me to some unknown address.

"Coffee?" she asked, not bothering to look back, heading across the symphonically creaking floor toward the kitchen lining one wall.

"Sure. Thanks." I followed her and sat on a stool to one side. "How're you doin'?"

She kept busy, collecting mugs from a cabinet, milk from the fridge, not making eye contact. "Fine."

"I'm sorry about Willy."

She paused in midmotion, just for a second, before turning the heat on under the kettle. "What about him?"

I pointedly didn't answer.

The silence stretched until I could almost hear it vibrate. Then she turned to me, her eyes pleading, and said, "Why's he such a bastard?"

I thought about that for a moment, wanting to get it right. "Because he's scared."

"I don't push," she burst out, smacking her hand on the counter. "I don't ask him questions he doesn't want to hear, I don't ask him to do things he doesn't want to do. I bend over backwards not to box him in. What's he got to be scared of?"

I shook my head slightly. "What attracts you to him?" I asked.

She looked at me, startled.

I rephrased the question. "Why do you hang out with him?"

She rubbed her forehead. "I don't know. Why does anyone stay with anyone else?"

"Is it pity?"

She flushed. "No. He would hate that. And he doesn't need it . . . I guess . . . I think it's just the opposite. I mean, I know he's a pain in everybody's butt, but he tells the truth—always. He's the most honest man I ever met. He'll risk everything for that—hurting people's feelings, losing them altogether. It's like a religion."

"Pretty gratuitous sometimes. Not everyone needs to know the truth."

She sighed. "I know. And I know it's mixed in with

other stuff, too. All the sarcasm, the insecurity . . . that goddamn arm."

"The badge of the crippled man?"

She smiled and shook her head. "You should know. You're always pulling his fat from the fire. I should be grilling you. Why do you bother?"

Why indeed? I wondered. "I don't do it to save him."

"Wouldn't he crash and burn without you?" she challenged me.

"Maybe . . . probably," I conceded. "But I think it's more so I can see him save himself someday. I always thought that might be possible."

"Did you know he's an artist?" she asked abruptly.

"I know he'd have a fit if he heard us talking about it. He damn near killed me when I found out. But that's what I meant. He's got that in him, like a gift given to someone nobody thinks deserves it, including the someone himself."

Her eyes widened. "You figure that's it?"

I reiterated what I'd told her earlier. "What do you think he sees when he looks in the mirror, Sam? A recovering alcoholic, a combat vet who worked behind the lines doing things I don't want to know about, a wife beater, a pariah, a physical, social, and emotional cripple. So, he tells the truth whatever the cost, he draws the beauty around him he won't acknowledge in public, and he has you in his life, a stroke of luck he can't believe and won't trust. What do you think set him off about the blond hair and the ski instructor gig?"

She considered that for a few seconds. "I thought it was jealousy at first. The 'beautiful people' thing he's always ranting about. Now I'm not so sure."

"Why not?" I asked, wanting her to hear her own answer.

She fiddled a bit with the cups, spooning in some instant coffee in preparation for the heating water. Finally, she admitted, "I started thinking maybe he was right—I was getting off on it, the glamour of it. He wasn't jealous about me and other men; he was ticked off at the phoniness that I seemed to be liking."

"He told you that?"

She ducked her head and placed both palms flat on the counter's surface before her, as if suddenly exhausted. "No. That's what wears me out. I just *think* that's what he feels. He does that to everyone, puts the burden on us to figure him out. And then, it's like we have to paint the best picture possible of him, or it'll look like we're the creeps. It's not fair."

I reached out and squeezed her hand. She slid over so I could drape my arm across her shoulders. "Sammie, it's only unfair if you make it all your responsibility. He's got to carry some of the weight, too. Feed him some of that honesty back."

"He runs when I try that."

"He runs to think. He always has. Then he comes back. Why do you think he was attracted to you in the first place?"

She sighed so deeply her entire body shuddered. "He likes you a lot."

I laughed. "Christ. Let's hope I don't have enemies." I hugged her once and then turned the heat off under the boiling water. "I like him, too, God knows why. Way down, he's got things to offer, I don't mind carrying some of his load in the meantime."

I looked her straight in the eyes. "But only as long as he shows signs of making an effort, and only as long as you think it's worth your time. Okay?"

She smiled and kissed me on the cheek. "Yeah. Thanks, boss."

CHAPTER THIRTEEN

A VISITOR'S FIRST IMPRESSION OF WEST DOVER, VERMONT, is what its residents struggle with most—it looks like a commercial strip, lining both sides of Route 100, that caters solely to the tourist trade and functions only as an extension of the Mount Snow ski area. It's neither fair nor accurate. West Dover's true identity extends far beyond that narrow corridor and predates all the commerce with a heritage as traditional and sturdy as any other more picturesque Vermont community. But the town's focal point is in fact an unattractive asphalt ribbon jammed with bars, eateries, shops, and gas stations. To make matters worse, on a fun-filled Saturday night, many of the more action-oriented tourist attractions keep the diminutive police department both busy and proficient. If ever I were to recommend a good police cadet training site for processing drunks, the Dover PD would definitely make the list.

Unfortunately, this mirrors a dilemma faced by many towns across the state—what to do when forced to choose between a sense of identity in a marginal economy, and caving in to the lure of the dollar. And it can be a struggle. To choose the former in Vermont is often to be relegated to being a pinprick on a map, a quaint and historical relic groping for some way to keep even marginally alive. The legislature fiddles with controversial methods of spreading the wealth more evenly, but to have a Mount Snow within reach of the local tax assessors can often mean lifeblood.

If at a cost.

Richie Lane had taken advantage of West Dover's contradictory self-image to disappear amid its many low-cost, low-profile, no-questions-asked housing opportunities, to resurface—if just barely—as Marc Roberts. The Dover PD's chief had been good to his word to me on the phone. He'd discovered through discreet inquiry that Mr. Roberts, while not seen of late, was still paying the rent at the address I'd been given by my friend at Mount Snow. So, it was there that I, two local officers, and Sammie Martens all showed up well before dawn one morning, warrant in hand.

It was a ramshackle, two-story apartment house, designed for its present use but built long ago and on the cheap. Its walls were bare, stained wood, the roof threadbare and swaybacked, the windows small, dirty, and made of noninsulated aluminum. It fronted a dirt road and a marginally plowed, frozen-mud parking lot littered with several vehicles of questionable reliability. Lane's was not among them.

Not surprisingly, the senior Dover patrolman, a sergeant, knew the layout well. "Each unit has only one door, facing front. The bathroom windows are along the back and face the hillside, but they're too small to get out of—I've seen people try. Plus, your guy's upstairs, so even if he made it, he'd hit the rocks and make a mess."

We split up, approaching the apartment in armored vests from both ends of the second-floor balcony, two of us armed with shotguns. Then, positioned to either side of the door, we used the manager's key to quietly turn the lock, and poured into the place like marines taking a beach.

It was done by the book, even though we were virtually positive that we wouldn't find anyone home. And we didn't.

Turning on the lights after making sure we were alone, Sammie looked around, her distaste of Richie Lane enhanced by what she saw. "Jesus, what a shit hole."

It wasn't destined for any hygiene awards. Dark, smelling of mildew, dirty clothes, and rotting organic matter of vague and possibly threatening origins, the apartment reminded me of a human-size hamster cage. The donning of latex gloves was as much to keep our hands from touching anything disgusting as it was to spare the scene our own latent prints.

Not that fingerprints were an issue on most of what we found. An acknowledged clotheshorse, Richie had festooned the place with piles of shirts, slacks, jackets, quasi-pornographic underwear, and an inordinate number of socks. He was also big on prepackaged food, the apparent advantage being less the ease of preparation and more the fact that once eaten, it could be dropped, container and all, wherever he happened to be at the moment.

There was also an ample supply of hard-core videos, many of them stolen rentals, presumably withdrawn under one of his pseudonyms, and a correspondingly wide collection of triple-X-rated magazines. I hoped this wasn't where Richie brought his dates.

It was clear, however, that he'd been here within the month. Thirty minutes into our archeological dig, Sammie found a newspaper dated two weeks earlier.

She pointed at a phone near the rumpled bed. "You think he conducted business from here?"

"We can only hope. Get the number and we'll run it by the phone company."

"If he did," she suggested. "Maybe we'll find some records or files or something."

We both instinctively paused to study the room from a different perspective. The sergeant, having sent the other officer away, looked from Sammie to me and back again. I could tell he'd stayed behind in large part to keep her within sight. "What's up?"

Sammie tilted her head, her eyes going from wall to wall, as if reading a map. "We've been here long enough to have found a desk or a filing cabinet or a briefcase. If he did do business here, given his past criminal history, he probably figured this place would get tossed sooner or later."

"Meaning he hid it," he concluded for her.

"If we're lucky."

She began walking the floor perimeter, where the kickboard met the wall, moving clothing, trash, and debris as she went. I took her cue and studied the framing over each door. I got lucky first, noticing how a board over the bathroom entrance was slightly soiled at both ends, as if from repeated handling.

I reached overhead and tugged at it gently. "He's a tall

guy," I reasoned out loud. "Be more natural for him to work high than to get on his knees."

The board came straight out along two long wooden dowels fitting a pair of holes in the header behind. The narrow gap between the top of the header and where the sheetrock ended served as a perfect clandestine shelf.

I reached into the gap and withdrew a thin, curled up accordion folder made of lightweight cardboard. This I handed to Sammie, to mollify her obvious disappointment at not having made the discovery.

She placed the folder on the kitchenette counter and slipped the rubber band from around it with a snap.

"What've you got?" the sergeant asked, his expression overly keen, as he stood close enough to her to be almost touching.

She poured the contents out, ignoring him, too used to law enforcement's gender imbalance to take much notice of its occasional juvenile excesses. "Looks like some notes, letters, a list of names and schedules." She opened a small envelope. "And—damn, this is handy—photographs of houses looking suspiciously like Tucker Peak." She held one up by its corners. "Including the William Manning residence."

I forced the sergeant to step back so I could examine the list. "All the burglaries are here, plus a few."

She glanced over from studying the photographs. "They had more planned?"

I read more carefully. "They were either going to knock off more than they did, or they've already hit a few no one told us about. Look at the dates in the schedule."

Sam compared them to the electronic dates stamped on the front of each photograph. "Richie quizzed his girlfriends about their calendars while they were rolling in the hay and then gave Marty the heads up. Wonder who took these pictures?"

I was now staring at the wall before me, thinking back. "What's up?"

"Something Richie said about the break-ins before he creamed me—'You don't even have the number right'—this must be what he meant."

She riffled her thumb through the notes in her hand. "I guess we better figure out who we're missing."

I pointed to the small pile of letters. "And check out his pen pals."

For the next three days, the four of us did a collective autopsy on Richie Lane's private archives, interviewing the owners of those houses listed but not known to have been robbed, and chasing down the names of those people, mostly women, who'd written him.

It was not easy going. Most of the condo owners were only occasional residents and some only owned their property in order to rent it for a fortune through the resort's booking service, leaving us to interview baffled renters who had no idea what we were talking about. We did meet an owner who had noticed a few items missing—and a broken window—but who still hadn't thought that he'd been robbed. Our visit turned on a light bulb over his head, and caused Willy to restate that most people are morons.

We also met two residents who admitted that around the time we knew their homes had been targeted, they'd had sudden changes of schedule, which we assumed was why Gagnon and Lane had passed on the opportunity. On a tangential sociological point, I also discovered that not every house had been scrutinized through Richie's bedroom antics alone. In many of the houses we studied, there was either no woman inhabitant, or she was too old or incapacitated to frequent the Tuckaway or take ski lessons, or hadn't been at the resort at the right times, meaning Richie had probably gained his knowledge from a male. With each and every mark, however, the common denominators of either regular attendance at the nightclub, or slopeside lessons from Richie, reinforced our hypothesis that he'd been Marty's spotter.

Tracing the writers of Richie's letters also turned out to be tricky. Several of them were married, prompting the same discretion I'd used with Mrs. Manning. Others were located far away, usually back in their urban homes near or in New York, Boston, Hartford, and elsewhere, which forced us to conduct the interviews by phone. Others were simply impossible to locate. Richie hadn't kept all the envelopes, and some of them didn't have return addresses anyway. Usually, by cross-referencing the signatory with our list of homeowners, we could figure it out, but in one case, specifically, we hit a dead end. Unfortunately, she also looked very promising.

She'd signed her name Shayla, and made mention of Steepway Road, a road which—according to the 911 database we consulted—was located in Newfane, about twelve miles northwest of Brattleboro. There were others, too, Steepway being about as unique a designation as River Road, but this one was the most proximate to Tucker Peak, in next-door Windham County, and seemed as good a place to start as any.

Also, the tone of Shayla's letter implied that she and

Richie, whom she called Bobby—his real name—were friends of long-standing acquaintance. Unlike most of the other correspondents, which ran the gamut from the pleading to the pornographic, she maintained a familiar, joking tone, almost like that of an intimate sister.

After checking all available databases and finding nothing on Shayla, I picked up the phone and called the Windham County sheriff and asked if his department could shed any light. He was no help there, but recommended I speak with the town constable, Eric Blaushild.

Constables are a curious Vermont institution, dating back to before the state joined the Union. The root of local law enforcement, and once listed along with the sheriff as the primary police agents in the state's constitution, they had not weathered the march of time well. Dropped from the constitution during a rewrite in the seventies, they'd assumed a second-class status in a world increasingly interested in better police training, uniform standards for all departments, and more legally defensible policies and procedures.

Constables—at best part-time certified by the state in a one-week training course, and often elected by a public who had no idea what or who they were—frequently were seen as dinosaurs, useless appendages, or even dangerous, gung-ho, gun-wielding wannabes who hadn't cut the grade to make it into "legitimate" police work. There was some truth to all this, of course, and examples could be trotted out on demand. But by and large, the town constable remained, while a bastard child of the law enforcement establishment, a good tool for local ordinance enforcement, especially involving dogs and occasionally quarrelsome residents. They could also be good sources of neighborhood information.

It was for this last resource that I'd been steered toward Eric Blaushild. A lifelong Newfane resident, a jack-of-all-trades who plowed driveways and serviced cars in the winter, and did anything he could think of to make a living the rest of the year, he was a man I'd known about but had never met, and was reputed to be a walking who's who.

I found him in a makeshift garage, behind a battered 1940s tract house, similar to what had made Levittown synonymous with suburbia. It didn't look out of place in Vermont, however, despite the calendar shots of Greek Revival farmhouses that the Department of Tourism cranked out in great volume. In fact, although I doubted anyone had actually done a count, I guessed that Blaushild's kind of home—inexpensive, nonpicturesque, a little threadbare, and eminently practical—outnumbered the other by a considerable margin.

The garage was wood-floored, dark, and none too warm, despite the fiery glow leaking through the gaps of an ancient makeshift wood furnace in one corner. Following the instructions of the woman who'd come out to meet me when I drove up, I shut the rickety door behind me, and called out, "Eric Blaushild?"

A voice answered from under the pickup beside me. "That's me."

"Joe Gunther. Vermont Bureau of Investigation. I was wondering if I could ask you about someone."

With a chorus of squeals, a man slowly rolled out from under the truck on a creeper, his hands resting on his stomach and his head supported by a small, very dirty pillow. He didn't bother getting up. "I heard about you—and the VBI. Never thought I'd meet both at the same time. Who do you want to know about?"

I liked his no-nonsense manner—no jokes about VBI, no kowtowing either—just the facts. I perched gingerly on a dubiously constructed sawhorse. "All I've got is a first name: Shayla."

"Rossi. Lives on Steepway. Owns a rottweiler named Ben," he said without hesitation.

That caught me by surprise, which he obviously enjoyed. But it also made me wonder what else I should know.

"You friends with her?"

He shook his head. "Barely know her, and didn't like what I met. Had to give her a warning a few months back—dog was on the loose. That's why she's fresh in my mind. What's she done?"

"Nothing I know of," I answered truthfully. "Her name came up in a case, and I just want to talk to her."

Blaushild finally rolled off the creeper, got onto his knees, and stood up, pulling a rag from his pocket and wiping his hands. "Good luck there. Attractive woman, till she opens her mouth."

"Violent?"

He shook his head. "She just sounds off, is all—got an opinion about everything and everybody and isn't shy about sharing it. I got an earful about the dog ordinances, the selectmen, the road crew, the sheriff, her neighbors, the governor, and the president of the United States, all in the time it took me to fill out that warning."

"She live with anyone?"

"Nope, and I can see why."

"What about the dog?"

"He's fine. Potentially lethal but trained to a gnat's eyelash. When I rounded him up, all he did was try to lick my face off."

I asked him for directions and for any other information he might have on Shayla Rossi. He escorted me outside to his vehicle, where he retrieved a metal clipboard from the front seat. Sitting on the car's fender, he leafed through its contents until he reached a copy of the warning he'd written her months ago. It had her birth date, social security number, and mailing address.

I copied it all down, commenting that this was a lot more information than I'd ever put on a warning back when I was in uniform.

Blaushild smiled ruefully. "Saves time later, when I give 'em a ticket, which usually happens pretty soon after. Always has to cost money before they pay attention."

I thanked him for his time and drove back to Newfane village and the parking lot in front of the Newfane market and called my office on the cell phone.

Judy, the secretary, put me through to Lester Spinney.

"Goofing off?" I asked him.

"Going nuts is more like it. Chasing all these people down is gettin' to be a royal pain in the butt."

"Good. I got another one for you." I gave him Shayla's name and statistics and waited while he entered her into the computer.

"Nothing," he finally reported. "She's got an old Toyota wagon she's driven too fast a few times, including once under the influence, but that's it. She one of the letter writers?"

"Yeah. Got her name from the constable up here. I'm in Newfane."

"You going to see her? Want some company?"

I mulled that over. It was good procedure to team up, and Newfane was only fifteen minutes north of Brattleboro, but we'd been conducting interviews nonstop for days, and had gotten nowhere fast. There was no indication this encounter would be any different.

But there was the dog, and Lester was sounding stir-crazy.

"What the hell," I told him. "I'm at the market."

It turned out the aptly named Steepway was closed during the winter. Being a challenge to climb in summer and an impossibility with snow on the ground, it was ignored by the town's snowplows. For all intents and purposes, it was a dead-end street unless traveled with a snowmobile. Lester and I approached it from the bottom, following Blaushild's instructions, and discovered, just shy of where the plows gave up, a brown house so modest, it looked plucked from a toy box. It was tucked under the trees and clung to the edge of a truly abrupt, overgrown incline—dark and claustrophobic even in the middle of the day. A thin plume of smoke drifted out of the metal chimney.

"That the one she drives?" I asked Lester, pointing to a rusty Toyota wagon parked in the yard.

He read the license plate. "One and only."

Typically, no great effort had been made at snow removal, resulting once more in our stumbling across a series of frozen ruts until entering a slit trench aimed at a small porch sagging with cordwood and trash cans. Evidence of the rottweiler was abundant—a zip line with a leash attached, a dog house, several metal dishes, and countless paw prints—but no dog.

I was first in line and heard Lester slip and almost fall behind me. I looked over my shoulder in time to see his acrobatic recovery.

"Legislature should pass a shovel law," he said, catching his breath. "It snows, you gotta shovel it, or a year in prison."

I was about to tell him how the constable's description of Shayla Rossi made her the perfect candidate for such a conversation, when both his startled expression and the small, almost indiscernible click of a door opening made me violently face forward.

I was too late. My entire field of vision was filled with the huge, open-mouthed head of a rottweiler coming at me in midair, as silent and lethal as a cannonball.

I only had time to throw up my left arm before we collided with tremendous force, the impact throwing me back onto Lester and forcing the air out of the dog's lungs into my face.

The pain in my forearm was electric in intensity: crushing, radiating, mind-numbingly sharp. I opened my mouth to yell but could only gasp for air, noticing all the while the total silence around me, filled solely with the labored grunting of the dog as he tried to adjust his grip, his hind legs scrabbling against my thighs.

"Get off me, Joe. I can't reach my gun."

I was on top of Lester, and we were locked inside the icy trench—an idiotic spectacle if it hadn't been for the dispassionate brown eyes, mere inches from my own, of the hundred-pound animal trying to eat through my arm to my throat.

But Lester's words had some effect nevertheless, cutting through the shock of the initial assault and forcing me to think of what to do next.

Wrestling with the dog, whose front claws were now swatting at my head, I rolled enough to one side to reach my belt for my own gun. But I didn't have enough room to clear the holster.

The pain was beginning to make my head swim. "Push, Lester. Get me out of here."

We did it in one clumsy, spasmodic heave—I pushing against the dog, Lester against me—spilling us out over the confines of the trench. In the process, the rottweiler broke loose, rolled away, and coiled up to spring again as I finally wrenched my gun free.

We both aimed at each other simultaneously, he with those enormous jaws, I with an instinctive shot from the hip, noticing as I pulled the trigger a man pointing a rifle from the porch.

"Gun," I yelled, firing as fast as I could into the chest of the airborne dog.

At the same moment the lifeless dog hit me again and sent me sprawling, a large-caliber explosion filled the air and a heavy thud slapped into the ground near my head, immediately followed by three fast, high-pitched shots from Lester.

Then, finally, as if following a battle-filled nightmare, the silence returned—utter, complete, absolute—leaving me only with a ringing in my ears, and the smell of gunpowder in my nostrils.

"You okay?" Lester asked, sounding far away.

The dead dog's head was nestled in the crook of my neck, his blood and saliva coursing down inside my collar. Wincing with a lightning bolt of pain from my mangled arm, I half rolled, half heaved him off of me, and propped myself up on my good elbow, gun still in hand.

"Yeah."

Lester and I were staring at the porch, where the body of Richie Lane lay sprawled across the steps, his rifle useless to one side, his motionless chest mottled with dark red blood.

From beginning to end, this whole mess had lasted thirty seconds, if that.

Lester was halfway to his feet when he froze again, both our attentions caught by something moving inside the open doorway.

"*Don't move*," we both yelled.

"We're the police," Spinney added. "Come out with your hands in plain view."

Slowly, tentatively, like a ghost taking shape, the figure of a woman emerged into the dim light, her expression frozen, her face pale, walking as if in a dream. Stepping out onto the porch as Lester moved toward her, she glanced down at Richie's corpse and let out a small whimper.

Lester was not sympathetic. He grabbed her roughly, spun her around, planted her facedown in the snow and put a knee in the small of her back, one hand holding her wrist in an armlock, the other still pointing his gun at the house.

"Anyone else in there?" he asked her.

"No," was the muffled response.

"What's your name?"

"Shayla."

Having unsteadily regained my feet, I stumbled past him, dripping blood as I went, and positioned myself just outside the door. Lester quickly frisked and cuffed Shayla Rossi and joined me.

It took us under two minutes to check the interior of the tiny house.

Back on the porch, I sat heavily onto some cordwood, feeling faint, cradling my left arm in my lap, while Spinney stood beside me surveying the carnage.

He gently tapped the toe of his boot against Richie's inanimate leg. "I've never had that happen before."

I looked up at his sad, reflective face. "Shot someone?"

He didn't answer at first, and then said, "Damnedest thing. Civilians think we do this all the time." He sat on the top step beside the body, quietly, almost as if it were only sleeping, and added, "I wonder how one of them would feel right now."

CHAPTER FOURTEEN

WILLY KUNKLE APPEARED IN THE DOORWAY BETWEEN MY woodworking shop and the rest of the house, having let himself in, as did everyone who knew me. I lived on Green Street, across from an elementary school, in what had once been the carriage house tucked behind a truly exotic Victorian showpiece, now my landlord's residence. It was quiet, affordable, with lots of light, and it had a postage stamp–size yard beside a small, attached barn I'd converted into the wood shop.

"Hey," I said. "Come on in. There's coffee on in the kitchen, if you want."

He waved his one good hand in the air dismissively. "I've had a gallon of that shit already today. Heard you tried to replace me as token gimp."

I turned away from the workbench where I'd been ineffectually but meditatively sharpening a chisel on a water stone and showed him my slinged left arm. "No cigar, though. Doc said I should be in good shape in a week or two—no broken bones, not too much muscle damage. Just an interesting scar. What brings you by?"

He reached inside his jacket pocket and withdrew an envelope, which he placed on the bench beside me. "Snuffy Dawson's report on all TPL members with any kind of record. I took a look. It's mostly predictable, protest-related stuff, but a couple of 'em got a harder edge. Guess not even the tree-huggers can deny human nature."

It was a throwaway line, typical of the man, but perhaps because of the late hour, or my encounter with Ben the rottweiler, or even my recent conversation with Sammie Martens, I challenged him on it.

"And what is that nature, Willy?"

He pointed at my injured arm. "You should know—dog eat dog."

"Dog eats man, at least," I conceded. "I'm serious, though. What's your take on the human race?"

His expression soured. "This the shit I gotta put up with for seein' how you're doin'?"

I didn't see any value arguing the point. "Yeah."

His eyebrows arched. "You must be pretty dense if you don't already know what I think."

"I don't believe it."

He slapped his forehead. "Oh, I get it. You know me better than I know myself. 'Cause deep down inside me, there's a goddamned saint struggling to be free."

"If there were, he'd have committed suicide long ago," I told him. "I'm just saying that if you really believed all the crap you hand out, you wouldn't be doing this job. Nor would you care about Sammie."

He scowled at me darkly, didn't answer immediately, and finally admitted, "She said you'd been by."

I picked up the envelope and dropped it again. "Which

is why you're here now—this could've waited till tomorrow."

He didn't answer.

"Right?" I pushed him.

His mouth twitched angrily, and he turned away. He walked over to a table saw and brushed its cool, smooth surface with his hand. "I don't . . . Damn."

"You didn't break up, did you?" I asked, suddenly alarmed.

"No," he said heavily. "I just can't . . . We probably should, for her sake."

"Isn't that her decision, too?"

He glared at me. "What's this? Amateur shrink time?"

"All right," I agreed, getting a little angry myself. "Then straight talk. She loves you, you love her, but you've fucked up before and you're scared you'll fuck up again. You think she doesn't know that?"

"I'm not sure."

"Find out, then. Tell her. Ask her questions. Open up a little. You're wrapped so tight, your eyeballs're bulging. And if you don't know she hasn't called you a total asshole a few dozen times over the years, you're living in a dream. Except," and I held up a finger for emphasis, "that she chose to be with you anyway, at least for the moment. Give her some credit for that. Honor her taking a risk by taking one of your own. If it falls apart then, it falls apart. At least you won't have to blame yourself for not trying. Is that nonpsychobabble enough for you?"

He took a long time to say, "Yeah," in a quiet voice.

More advice boiled inside me, more ways of saying roughly the same thing, but despite my eagerness to unload years of pent-up frustration, I realized it wasn't my time.

"Go talk to her, Willy . . . Now," I said instead, and turned back toward my sharpening stone.

I was in bed when Gail came in, both the day's trauma and the painkillers having finally taken hold. I sensed her standing there before I opened my eyes, and wasn't startled when I saw her outlined against the dim light from the window.

"Hi. I didn't expect you."

She sat on the edge of the bed and kissed me. She smelled of fresh, cold night air. "I didn't, either. I've been thinking about us ever since the motel room, feeling happier than I have in a long time. I finally decided, the hell with it, and came down. I'm sorry I woke you, though. I thought you'd still be up. I guess surprises like this aren't ever a really good idea."

I extracted my hand from beneath the blanket and laid it on her thigh. "I'm not complaining—and your timing couldn't be better."

She leaned over me again and accidentally brushed my left arm with her elbow. I shut my eyes and winced. She straightened abruptly and stared at me, her face barely visible in the gloom.

"What's wrong?"

I pulled out the bandaged arm.

"Joe. What happened?"

I shook my head and touched her cheek. "Nothing. I got fanged by a dog today—nothing bent, folded, or mutilated. It's more embarrassing than anything." I flexed my left hand to show her it worked fine. "Right up there with a firefighter falling off a ladder—occupational hazard."

The toll on me hadn't been purely physical, of course, nor was my pleasure in seeing her as lighthearted as I was pretending. Being shot at by another human being and seeing him die as a result was not something I could shrug off casually, no matter how many times I'd been exposed to it in the past. But I decided to spare her the details until later.

"You're sure?" she asked, visibly relieved.

"Yes, and really happy you're here." I sat up and returned the kiss. "Try and deny we're kindred spirits now."

She smiled then and stood back up. "Stay there."

She undressed slowly, playing to the half-light, letting me see her in carefully measured degrees. Finally, totally naked, she leaned forward and gently pulled the covers off me, trailing her fingers down my body as she went.

"What a great way to end the day," she said softly, climbing into bed.

Little did she know.

The next morning, over an early breakfast, I told Gail the rest of the story, grateful she'd chosen to listen to music instead of the news in the car on the drive down. In a state with Vermont's low crime rate, where simple vehicular manslaughter routinely made the front page, my OK Corral imitation with Lester was at the top of every hour.

"And this happened in the afternoon?" she asked. "I still don't understand why I didn't hear about it."

"They didn't release it till after the post-shoot. The

AG's office sent two guys down to make sure we hadn't assassinated Richie and had the dog attack me to cover it up. After that, I met with Snuffy to quiet the politician in him, and then drove to Waterbury to offer my head to the boss and the commissioner."

"With that?" she asked incredulously, pointing at my arm, now back in its sling.

"I could've done it later," I admitted. "But I knew they were feeling the heat. Spinney was happy to do the driving. It let him blow off some steam. He went code three all the way—probably took us forty minutes, if that, so it wasn't as bad as it sounds."

She pursed her lips, bit into her toast, and said as she chewed, "Always the team player."

"Most of the time," I agreed. "When do you have to be back in Montpelier?"

She instinctively checked her watch. "I have a meeting at ten. Why? What's up?"

I retrieved the envelope Willy had delivered the night before and opened it. "I asked Snuffy to give me a list on all the TPL people with rap sheets. I was wondering if you'd give it a look, see if any of them rang a bell—unofficially, of course."

I placed the sheaf of documents I'd extracted before her on the breakfast table. She looked at it dubiously for a moment, not touching it. "I'm not sure I'm comfortable with that."

I shrugged. "That's fine. It was a straight question. I'll go over it with the folks at the office." But I left it where it was as I crossed over to the stove for more coffee.

Not subtle, but effective. "You are such a twerp," she said. But I heard the fondness in her voice and was all the happier we'd had a chance to talk in that motel room. Over the years, we'd had our rough spots, some of our own making, others inflicted by outside events, and certainly her move to Montpelier had contributed to a vague sense of estrangement. But for the first time in quite a while, I felt I was totally back in sync with her—and knew she was feeling the same.

She picked the papers up.

We didn't speak for a while, as I let her do her homework, but eventually she put the last sheet down and looked at me. "That's a lot of people. Most of them are friends."

"I thought they might be. Actually, I was hoping that would make it easier."

"How's that?"

I pointed my chin at the documents. "Because you could give me a gut reaction on eighty percent of them and tell me not to waste my time. Save us the effort and maybe stop somebody from getting killed."

"That supposed to be a delicate guilt trip to help me along?" she asked, smiling.

I shook my head. "Just the truth. Only thing that saved that woman on the chairlift was dumb luck."

"You think one of these people did that?"

"It's a possibility, even Betts seems to agree."

"Maybe management did it to put the finger on TPL—get the sympathy vote."

I couldn't argue with her. "True."

I sensed that a combination of curiosity, friendship, and a feeling of responsibility made Gail pick up the top sheet again. But her tone of voice betrayed her discomfort. "Roger you already know. If you think he'd put someone's life at risk to make a point, this conversation just ended."

"Gail," I said soothingly, knowing I was pushing her, "that list was generated by hitting a few computer keys. That's why there're so many names."

Her mouth made a rueful twist as she relented. "I know. I'm being thin-skinned and close-minded—two things I hate about most of the people I work with. It's catching. I'm sorry." She took up the entire batch and weeded out three sheets that had obviously caught her eye early on. "If I were you, I'd start with these. One I don't know, one I don't like, and the third has the reputation of being as cold-hearted as anyone he's ever opposed."

I studied the three. "Toussaint, McPherson, and Davis," I read.

"Toussaint's the wild card," she told me. "Looks like he's been around: Seattle, Philly, San Francisco, Boston. All the right places for all the right causes. 'Resisting arrest' could mean anything, but he does have one assault on a police officer.

"McPherson is a flamer, if you ask me—superopinionated, supershort fuse. He's a self-righteous, pompous, stuck-up little creep. He's also British and an ex-Greenpeacer—claims to have been where it counted when it counted, like hassling those French ships that were trying to set off the atomic test in the Pacific. But anyone can say that—there're loads of liars in this business. It's just that no one wants to be so un-PC as to check them out and call their bluff."

"Let me guess," I suggested, "he's the one you don't like."

She saluted me with her cup, "Two points. Davis has a reputation that does stand up. Tough as nails, very persuasive, a committed fighter for the cause. I've never seen any proof of it, but I wouldn't be surprised to find out he'd broken a few rules to get what he wanted."

I put the three on the top of the pile and returned them all to the envelope. "Why just them?"

She swallowed some coffee before answering. "You asked for a gut reaction. It could be one of the others, but from what I either know of them or have heard about them, they'd be unlikely violent types. I'm not sure what made me pick Toussaint—maybe because all the places he was busted were where things turned ugly and people were hurt. Left a bad taste in my mouth. When you meet him, he'll probably turn out to be a Don Knotts look-alike, scared of his own shadow."

"You also picked people who either have been or claim to have been all over the place geographically. Most of the rest of them seem to be pretty home-grown."

"Maybe, but from my brief career as a prosecutor, I found rap sheets can be misleading. If you don't get busted out of state, it looks like you never left home. Still, there aren't as many hard-core radicals here—typical of Vermont, they tend to be more pragmatic."

That sounded about right and made me think back to when that attitude had led to a private meeting in a motel room recently. "You think Betts might be willing to talk to me after I do a little homework with all this?"

"He did the first time, for reasons I don't pretend to know. My bet is he's expecting a call, and I'd be happy to be the go-between again."

Gail checked her watch one last time, stood up, washed

her cup and plate in the sink, and set them in the drying rack. "I better take off. Hope that helps."

I escorted her to the door and gave her a kiss. "Thanks for coming down."

She looked at me and touched my cheek, her eyes soft. "That was pretty weird, almost like I knew you'd been hurt. One doozie of a relationship, huh?"

I kissed her again. "Yup. One in a million."

CHAPTER FIFTEEN

I SHOWED UP LATE AT THE OFFICE, MILKING MY BUM ARM FOR all it was worth. In fact, I'd taken a small nap after Gail left to catch up on the sleep she'd so pleasantly interrupted. Once I arrived and had awkwardly shucked my coat, though, I wished I'd heeded the commissioner's advice the day before and taken a few days off. The ringing phones and pink message slips emphasized how popular Lester's and my little escapade had become. As our director Bill Allard had mournfully commented, it was just the kind of high-profile event VBI had been hoping to avoid, especially during its honeymoon phase. In fact, leafing through the slips, I noticed that many of the callers hadn't been reporters and politicians, but fellow cops, no doubt seeking some indication of what this might tell of the future. Despite the mistaken perception of what makes law-enforcement appealing to those who join it—chases, shoot-outs, and undercover pyrotechnics—it is just those kinds of uncontrolled events that make officers nervous. Cops, more than most, hate surprises.

Which didn't mean I saw myself as the one to calm their nerves. I dropped the entire pile on Judy's desk and told her to forward them to Allard. Better he than I, I rationalized, in these times of delicate image molding. I'd let him give me hell later.

Still, Richie's spectacular death did change how I wanted to approach the several problems facing us, which is why I'd called for a squad meeting from home.

And they were all there: Sammie at her desk, studying the contents of a computer screen; Willy, reading a back issue of *Guns & Ammo*; and Lester, tilted back in his chair with his feet up on his desk, wearing his customary bemused expression.

"How're you feeling?" he asked me.

"I liked it better when they had me doped up. How 'bout you? The adrenaline settle down yet?"

His demeanor changed to something closer to melancholy. "The adrenaline's okay. Having killed somebody still needs work. Last night wasn't great for sleeping."

Willy looked up briefly from his reading. "It's like losing your cherry, Les. No big deal."

Spinney glanced from me to him and back, and then silently raised his eyebrows, the half-smile returning, if tinged with incredulity.

I leaned toward him so the other two couldn't hear and murmured, "You're being stress debriefed for this, right? Or do I have to quote the rule book?"

"No, no," he reassured me. "I've seen the shrink once already, last night, and we've got a repeat in a couple of days. I'm okay—promise."

I nodded, sat on the corner of my desk, and addressed

them all, "Okay, now that we're really under the microscope, I thought it might be a good idea to see where we're standing and decide on a possibly revised course of action. Snuffy Dawson is sweating bullets over the Richie thing, since that's the investigation he asked us to conduct, so in fairness to him and in light of the fact we may be looking at multiple homicides now, putting that one first seems pretty reasonable. Where's Shayla Rossi right now?"

"Downstairs," Sammie said, "but not for long. 'Course we can talk to her in Woodstock after they arraign her and ship her north."

"Any of you had a crack at her yet?"

"A once-over-lightly," Sammie admitted. "You might have better luck, but she didn't sound like a great source to me. Could be why he chose her to hide out with—clueless barely covers it."

"If you think it'll do any good. Otherwise, I won't waste my time."

"No, no. Have at it."

I was almost disappointed to hear her say that. Not because her caution wasn't reasonable, but because there was an added element of self-doubt I was forever hopeful she'd lose. On the other hand, Shayla was the only one we had available from the whole Marty-Richie-Jorja Duval mess.

"Maybe I will, if only to ask her why Richie was so desperate."

"Gee, there's a tough one," Willy said sourly. "He was shitting bricks about whoever iced Jorja."

"He was shitting bricks when he had Joe in the

garage," Sammie commented. "Why didn't he kill him then?"

Willy shook his head dismissively. " 'Cause he wasn't sure. When Richie saw Joe the second time, at Shayla's, that convinced him Joe was a bad guy, especially since he had Lester riding shotgun. It pushed him over the edge."

"And reintroduces an interesting point," Lester added. "Richie didn't know who was after him, not even by name, or he would've confronted Joe with it in the garage."

After a long, reflective pause, I suggested, "Which still doesn't mean it couldn't have been Marty."

Not surprisingly, Willy then countered his earlier, dismissive comment with an interesting suggestion. "What we should be asking is, why this level of violence against a B-and-E lowbrow? The other thing Richie would've spilled in the garage—if he'd had the slightest idea—was why he was being targeted and why he thought Marty'd already been killed."

"Damn," Sammie muttered. "Maybe they both stole something they didn't know they had."

"Maybe," Lester said doubtfully. "But when whoever they stole it from pounded on the guy who fenced the watch—"

"Walter Skottick," I interjected quietly.

"—he wasn't asked what else he might have, just where the guy was who sold it to him."

Willy seemed to come to Sammie's aid by saying, "Then it was something they saw, or somebody."

Sammie's enthusiasm was still obvious in her voice.

"Or maybe the killer was after Richie all along. He's the one who spent all the time with those women, milking them for personal info. Could be one of them said something important he didn't realize."

"And her husband, boyfriend, or whatever decided to be careful and plug the leak," Lester filled in, tilting his head to one side. "That would play to the theory that Marty's dead, too. You'd think we would've picked up on that kind of family dynamic during all the interviews, though."

"We haven't talked to everyone, yet," Willy reminded him.

That jarred loose an idea. "Speaking of people talking," I said, "Jorja Duval's the only one we know for sure who met Richie's bogeyman face-to-face, whether it was Marty or not."

Willy jumped straight to where I was headed. "Meaning you're hoping he left something behind the crime lab missed."

"It was a frustrating scene," Lester commented. "A ton to process, most of it useless . . . But they did process it. Still, sounds like a long shot, and you'd expect signs of Marty to be there, anyhow."

"I'm going to call David Hawke at the crime lab," I persisted, "see what he says. In the meantime, we need to put all our energies on building clear and complete backgrounds for Richie, Marty, and everyone else: spouses, caretakers, anyone with even a remote connection to the houses listed in Richie's hidden documents. I know we're partway there already, but the heat's on now, and it's only going to get worse until we solve this. Along those lines,

Allard has assigned us three extra people from the Bennington office. Sam, you can coordinate with them as to how many, if any, come over here, or if you want them to just stay put and work the phone lines and computers from there."

"What about the TPL investigation?" she asked.

"Back burner again," I answered her, immediately thinking of the three names that Gail had indicated might have potential. "If anything comes up accidentally, great—spread the word. Otherwise, we're going to have to divide and conquer here. TPL will have to wait."

David Hawke had started out at the state crime lab as a civilian scientist back when it was run by the Vermont state police. That it was now an independent branch of the Department of Public Safety—just as we were—and directed by Hawke instead of a state police captain, spoke volumes about recent efforts the DPS had been making to distribute its resources more efficiently, much to the distress of state police old-timers nostalgic for the days when they'd controlled almost every law enforcement function beyond the municipal level. The VSP was still king of the mountain in terms of size and political muscle, but that mountain was visibly, if slowly, changing shape.

The metamorphosis of the crime lab had been gradual, smooth, and driven by increasingly stringent and sophisticated scientific necessities, antiquating the erstwhile practice of having uniformed troopers do forensics rotations and then leaving just as they became competent. But Hawke still understood the pain of organizational change, and thus knew how loaded his opening question was when he asked me on the phone, "How're things in your neck of the woods? Cold and lonely?"

I could only laugh and admit, "Yeah, pretty much. At least I'm not being taken for a state food inspector quite as often."

"But you're still not Vermont's FBI?"

"Not even close. How're you settling in?"

"Great," he said cheerily. "We're now nationally accredited, and I just had to break the news to the powers that be that in order to stay that way, we'll have to get out of this building and into something that doesn't date back to the eighteen-hundreds. So, I'm a happy camper, but I have a lot of depressed bosses. Speaking of which, you call to cry on my shoulder, or are you scrounging for a favor?"

"Ouch," I said. "I sound that desperate?"

"I read the papers, Joe. How's the arm?"

"It hurts."

"I am sorry about that." Then he admitted, "But it may be just the beginning. The buzz downstairs is that none of them would've ever fallen into something like that with their pants down, and that they sure hope you boys get your shit sorted out before one of you gets killed—all quote-unquote, of course."

I sighed. "Them" in Hawke's parlance meant the state police, and in particular their Bureau of Criminal Investigation.

I ducked that debate altogether. "You're right, David, I am scrounging for a favor. You still have access to Jorja Duval's body?"

"So long as it's an unsolved case—you bet."

"Then can you get anything more out of her? We're heading straight up the creek with this one."

There was a long pause at the other end as David Hawke considered the request. "We pretty much gave her the full battery, more than just the standard checklist. We could run her blood for specifics, if you have any suggestions. What're you looking for? Drugs? Environmental chemicals?"

"That's the problem," I had to tell him. "I don't know. We have no idea who killed her, or who spooked the guy we just killed. Basically, she's the only one left we can interrogate, even if it's after the fact."

I could almost see him nodding at the phone in comprehension. This was, as I'd hoped it would be, just the kind of problem he and his colleagues liked to tackle most.

"There is something I could try," he finally said slowly. "There's a retired guy in Florida who's been trying to sell people on how to lift prints from human skin. Has something to do with temperature differences between the skin surface and the material you want to transpose the print to. Anyhow, he's been fiddling with it since the late seventies, and just recently started getting some consistent results."

"That sounds perfect," I said, almost cutting him off.

"Yeah, well, 'sounds' may be the operative word. This is still considered iffy stuff, and it has a pile of variables that'll render it null and void: the body's temperature, exposure, cleanliness, extent of decay, and a bunch of other things. They all have to work together, more or less, as do factors like was the assailant wearing gloves, were his fingers oily enough, was it the right type of oil, did he press too hard or not hard enough, and so on. You get the idea."

"Unfortunately," I admitted.

He sounded apologetic for overdoing the caveat. "Hey, don't get depressed until I give you good reason. I will try this out, right on the bruises we think his hands left on her arms. In fact, I've been looking forward to giving this technique a shot."

"Okay," I said. "I appreciate it. And I promise not to hold my breath."

He laughed. "You can if you want to. This won't take long. I'll call you tomorrow or the next day and let you know what I've found."

Shayla Rossi was being housed in the basement, courtesy of the Brattleboro police, sitting in a narrow cell with the traditional metal toilet and a bunk. There were no other short-term residents at the moment, so instead of moving her to the interrogation room upstairs, I left her behind bars. I merely dragged a folding chair to the other side of her door and made myself comfortable.

"Who the hell *are* you people?" she demanded.

I remembered what the constable had said about her cranky personality. "Vermont Bureau of Investigation. My name's Joe Gunther."

"Never heard of it." She was sitting on the bunk, her back against the wall, her knees drawn up before her. My mind flashed back to what I'd just told David Hawke about our persistent low visibility, a problem I sensed I'd soon be yearning for.

"We work on major felonies, Ms. Rossi—the really bad stuff."

"That has nothing to do with me. That's Bobby's rap."

I flapped my injured arm slightly, remembering that she'd known Richie Lane by his real name of Bobby Lanier. "Your dog gave me this."

"I didn't set him on you."

"You trained him," I said.

Shayla Rossi merely pressed her lips into a thin, straight line.

I glanced down at the file I'd brought with me. "I see the gun Bobby fired was yours, too."

"I didn't know he was going to use it."

"You knew he was on the run."

"So?"

"That's harboring a fugitive, Ms. Rossi, and aiding and abetting. And say what you want about Vermont being soft on crime, we still take assaulting a police officer pretty seriously. Unless you help me out, you could spend a long time in a cell." I thought back to her isolated home and what it said about her choices in life, and added, "Except that you'd be living with dozens of other women, some pretty nasty, all piled on top of one another. We have a real overcrowding problem in our jails."

Her arms slipped around her knees to hug them closer to her. "You're so full of shit you can't see straight. I didn't do a damn thing. My lawyer'll have me out of here like that." She tried to snap her fingers, but either her technique or her sweaty hands betrayed her—there was no sound beyond a pathetic plop.

I referred back to the file. "Right—your lawyer. Public

defender. Seems like he had a little trouble spelling your name, kept writing down 'Sheila'."

I actually had no idea if that were true. There was no mention of it in my paperwork. But it had the desired effect.

"That fucking idiot," she said, her hot, narrowed eyes watching me as if I might suddenly strike out.

I shook my head sympathetically. "Shayla. I know you don't think much of us, or the system in general. But you're between a rock and a hard place here." I paused before suggesting, "It's not where you have to be."

"What do you mean?" she asked slowly.

"Let's face it, you're dealing with a bunch of very embarrassed people. Here we were, running all over looking for Bobby, and you had him tucked away, nice and safe, right under our noses, not twenty minutes from this building. That makes us look pretty bad. My bosses, the prosecutors, everybody's scrambling for cover, you know how it works. And guess who they're planning to hang most of this on?" I pointed to her.

She opened her mouth to say something, but I leaned forward suddenly and gestured to her to stay quiet. Her mouth snapped shut with surprise.

"Shayla, you know that's bullshit, right? *I* know it's bullshit. I also know it doesn't need to be. I can get you out of this. A little slap on the wrist, a little kowtowing to the judge and the others, and you go back home, free as all-get-out."

She looked at me suspiciously. "How?"

"You tell me what you know—here and now." I pulled a tape recorder out of my pocket, turned it on, and placed it through the bars onto the end of her bunk.

She tucked her heels up even closer. "I don't know anything."

"I'm not saying you do, not consciously. I just want to hear your perspective: how Bobby contacted you, what he said, how he got you to take him in. You and I know you're just the innocent bystander here, the one who gave an old friend a place to stay, but until I can tell my bosses exactly what happened, item by item, they're going to try to pin it on you."

She looked both confused and disgusted. "This is such a crock."

"Talk to me."

She scratched her head. "I don't know . . . Bobby and me go back. We were hot once, but then he went one way, I went another. No big deal. We talked now and then . . ."

"About what?"

She stopped, surprised. "Normal shit. What he was doin', what I was doin'."

"And what was he doing?"

"Working at Mount Snow and Tucker Peak the last two, three years—longest time he ever stuck with anything. It wasn't much, but he said he liked the people. He was big on that, always liked being around people. Just the opposite of me."

"He had a scam going at Tucker Peak," I said. "He ever talk about that?"

She hesitated.

"Shayla," I tried putting her at ease. "If you didn't have anything to do with it, you can't get into trouble."

"He was pretty proud of it," she finally said. "Like he was a spy or something—James Bond the rip-off artist."

"He ever mention Marty Gagnon?"

"Not till he came to hide out at my place. Before then, I just knew he had a partner, that was it."

"How did he describe the operation?"

"He called himself the inside man. He'd sweet talk the ladies or con the guys, whatever it took to get into their homes. Then he'd take pictures or draw a map, figure out which windows were alarmed, if any, find out when the owners would be away. That's what he thought was like being a spy, 'cause he had to be real slick about it, not show his hand. It did sound pretty cool."

She'd stretched one leg out during this, which I hoped was a sign she was becoming more comfortable with me.

"But then it went wrong," I suggested.

She stared at her foot for a while, apparently thinking back, maybe wondering how things had turned out as they had. "Yeah. He called me up, said they'd killed Marty and were closing in on him. That was the first time I heard of Marty. He also told me he'd hit one of them over the head who claimed he was a cop, 'cept the name of the police department he mentioned didn't exist. Bobby was really scared."

"Who did he say was after him?"

"He wasn't sure. He thought it was the druggies."

I glanced at the tape recorder to make sure it was still running. "Who were they?"

But her answer was a disappointment. "I don't know, probably one of the people he ripped off. That's what scared him—not knowing. And that it all fell apart super-fast."

"Do you think Bobby stole drugs from someone?"

She shook her head. "He didn't do drugs himself and he didn't have the connections to move it. Maybe he tried—I'm not saying he didn't—but if he did, it's news to me."

"Let's talk about Marty a little."

"I told you, I didn't—"

I interrupted her. "I know, I know—you'd never heard of him. But you were told he'd been murdered. Did Bobby know that for a fact?"

She stared at me, looking confused. "He's not dead?"

"He might be. We haven't found a body."

She became thoughtful. "Bobby just said he'd been killed, not that he'd seen it happen."

"How do you think the two had been getting along?"

There, she seemed clearer. "Not so good. He bitched about how Marty wouldn't move the stuff fast enough, how he had to keep at him all the time."

"Did it sound like Marty would get angry?" I asked, my interest growing.

"I guess. It wasn't like they were ever buddy-buddy. Bobby thought he was low-class, not a people person, which was a real putdown from him."

Which made me wonder what he'd seen in Shayla, aside from her being the perfect person to hide out with.

"Did Bobby ever say Marty had threatened him?" I asked.

She shook her head. "Nah."

I considered continuing, going over the same ground again in the hopes of learning more—that was certainly standard practice. But chances were good that Sammie had pegged this woman's usefulness from the start.

Still, the drug angle was new, if not well defined, and

offered the slim possibility of a new line of inquiry. It also helped explain, if true, why the costs in human lives had been so high. From a simple case of unsolved burglaries, we were now facing the possibility of something far bigger—and more lethal.

All that was left now was to hope that our interviews, phone calls, background checks, and general data crunching would yield just enough light to let us see what was going on.

And maybe lead us to Marty Gagnon, a man I was now very much hoping I'd meet alive.

CHAPTER SIXTEEN

I STEPPED INSIDE THE WARMTH AND DARKNESS OF MY HOUSE late that night and leaned back against the closed door, feeling all the muscles in my body suddenly begin to relax.

The medicine I'd been given to both control the pain and fight off any infections had fogged my brain and made me groggy. All day, I'd been struggling to maintain concentration, which ironically had probably helped make me more efficient than usual. But now I was wiped out. I worked my way out of my coat, dropped it on the floor, wandered over to the sofa, and collapsed, falling asleep before I could remember to remove my shoes.

The respite didn't last long. Like an approaching train whistle in a dream I wasn't sure I was having, the phone's ringing crept into my head as from far in the distance, only finally waking me up when I couldn't explain its source.

I opened my eyes and stared up at the dark ceiling, feeling like a huge weight was pinning me in place. My hand groped over my shoulder, fumbling for the side table next to the sofa, until it finally located the incessant phone.

"What?"

"This Joe Gunther?" The woman's voice sounded doubtful.

"Yeah."

"Must be a bad connection. This is Linda Bettina at Tucker Peak. We've had another incident you probably want to look at."

"What is it?" I asked, slowly sitting up.

"The new pumphouse we've been building just went up in smoke." She hesitated and added, "You told me to call you if anything else happened."

"I know, I know. Sorry. I'm a little under the weather. You sure it wasn't a short or something?"

Her voice regained its usual slightly acerbic edge. "The pumps hadn't been installed yet."

"I'll be right over."

The air was so cold, it felt brittle, and was bathed in a full moon turned up to full wattage. As I drove between the dark mountains leading up to Tucker Peak, I kept twisting in my seat to look around, overwhelmed by the deep stillness of the snow-shrouded trees, which were tinted a faint, lunar blue by the shimmering radiance overhead. At times like these, I felt irrelevant in the world's grand scheme, and totally powerless. I knew that we humans were wholly capable of burning, polluting, stripping, and altering the landscape to a lethal extent. But on special occasions, under just the right lighting, I trusted that the winner in this struggle would be the same force that had preceded us in history, and which would, in the long run, treat us as a minor blip in time. The car I was in, the road I was traveling, and the few house lights I could see in the distance seemed as impermanent as snowflakes on a hot stove.

I drove to the equipment yard as Linda had instructed on the phone and was met by the same crooked-toothed, bearded snowmaker named Dick who'd tossed me the crowbar when I was stranded in the chairlift.

He gave me a big smile as I got out of my car. "Boy, you sure had us goin', pretending you were a carpenter. Good thing you never got one of us pissed off. We mighta pounded you good and never known you were a cop."

I looked at his eyes, watching for some double meaning there, but he seemed to have merely uttered a bizarre statement of fact.

He did, however, suddenly step back and give me a more careful appraisal. "Where's your arm?"

I'd put my coat on with the left sleeve empty. "I still got it. It's in a sling."

"Cool," was all he said, before taking my good elbow and steering me toward an idling Yamaha snowmobile. "Linda said to get you up there pronto. Hope you're dressed warm."

He got on first and gave the throttle a couple of hormonal revs. I tucked in behind him and had just looped my hand through the thick strap binding the seat when he took off with a jolt that should have sent me ass over backward. So much for not pounding on a cop.

The trip was the exact opposite of my drive over: windy, freezing, lurching, and noisy. I held on for dear life, seeing little beyond the hairy nape of Dick's neck, feeling my face and hand going numb and the muscles in my back and legs beginning to spasm as I unsuccessfully tried to anticipate which way to lean and when to brace for a bump. By the time we came to a sudden, sliding stop, I felt like simply falling into the snow and asking someone to cover me up.

Instead, I was grabbed under the right armpit and hauled to my feet, where I found myself staring into Linda Bettina's face. "It's over here," was her greeting.

I followed her as best I could, regaining my land legs and trying not to stumble in the thick snow. Ahead of us, surrounded by tall, somber trees as if cupped in a pair of hands, was a pile of red embers, against which human shadows moved back and forth like black specters. In the distance was a wide, featureless opening, flat and opal pale in the moonlight, which I took to be the frozen pond.

Linda stopped as we entered the warm air bubble engulfing the glowing remnants of the pumphouse. She pointed at a large, round man in a white fire coat who was giving orders to a group of others.

"That's the fire chief, if you want to talk to him."

"He know what started it?"

"He just showed up with his crew and put it out."

I looked around as someone started a generator and ignited a ring of bright lights on tripods.

"And destroyed any chance of finding tracks," I said half to myself.

"Wouldn't have been any anyhow," Linda said. "It's a construction site—*was* a construction site. A dozen guys have been stomping around here for weeks. Too bad, too—I've really been cracking the whip on this project.

We were about to get this done two months ahead of schedule."

"Who reported it?" I asked.

"Snowmakers saw the glow. We hit it right off with water from some portable snow guns and called the fire department to back us up. Didn't make any difference. It was going full blast from the start." She turned to face me. "You smell anything?"

I took my time before responding, sniffing carefully. "Gas?"

"That's what I think—this was torched."

"Did the snowmakers notice anyone or anything unusual when they first arrived?"

She shook her head. "Nope. Same as the dye job on the other pond, the generator sabotage, the water main break, and the chairlift accident, not to mention all the other shit that's been going on. Whoever's doing this is luckier than hell."

I didn't voice the other obvious possibility of it being an employee.

"Linda?"

We both turned as Phil McNally loomed into the light, squinting slightly, stopping in his tracks as he recognized me. "Oh. Are you all right?"

Linda looked at me more closely. "What's wrong with you? Break an arm?"

"Dog bit it," I explained, realizing just how isolated this bunch could be in their closed-off world. As far as I knew, no paper or radio or TV station in the state had failed to run the story, and yet nobody here seemed to know about it.

Nor were they particularly interested, since both Linda

and Phil went back to staring at the remains of the pump-house.

"TPL?" McNally asked.

"We don't know," Linda told him, jerking a gloved thumb at me. "That's why I called him."

He passed a hand across his neck. "Great, one damn thing after another. This morning, somebody chained about eight snowmobiles together—took an hour to untangle them. I guess I messed up big time playing footsie with those guys."

"They may not have done this," I suggested.

They looked at me.

"You kidding?" McNally asked. "It's perfect for them—nobody hurt, and the whole pump project delayed for months, not to mention the money we already spent on pumps that have nowhere to live now. I'll have to tell the manufacturer to hang on to them and probably end up paying a storage fee to boot. Christ. What next?"

It was an interesting question, and one I wanted answered before it caught me by surprise.

My next meeting with Roger Betts didn't have to take place in a clandestine motel. Phone calls by Phil McNally to my boss had forced the TPL case off the back burner, if only briefly, and the fire the night before now made it reasonable for me to invite him to my office in Brattleboro.

I did, however, want Gail in attendance, as before, hoping her presence would show how I wanted us all to work together against a common foe.

They arrived as a couple, Gail having picked Betts up

at Tucker Peak on her way in, and entered the office chatting amiably.

The others were out, so the office was ours. I dragged two chairs across the room, and we all sat in a circle, like three card players in search of a table.

"Roger," I began, "I really appreciate your coming down. I know it's a hassle with everything you've got going."

"Not at all," he countered, his voice once again reminiscent of some old-world gentleman. "I understand entirely. You must have questions concerning the fire."

I nodded. "True enough. But you should know that the ground rules are a little different this time. We're no longer off the record, and I am less inclined to settle for a pledge of cooperation from you. Things are getting out of hand."

"I agree entirely," he said, to my surprise. "These events are not reflecting well on us, either. I am scheduled to meet with Mr. McNally in two hours and I suspect that will not go well."

"I saw him last night," I admitted. "He ain't happy."

I reached for a file on my desk and opened it in my lap. "Which leads me to the point of this meeting. Last time, you said you feared one or more people within your ranks might be doing these things, but you had no names to suggest. This time, I have some names, and I'd like you to react to them."

He studied me passively for several seconds before saying, "That may not be ground I wish to tread."

"Maybe so," I agreed, pulling out a single sheet of paper and handing it to him. "Nevertheless. Look at them first. Then we can debate."

The names included the three Gail had chosen earlier from Snuffy's list, along with others we'd added as a result of our own research. There were eleven overall.

Roger Betts took his time, presumably pausing at one name or another and running it through his mind. Several times, he gazed out the window before continuing.

Finally, he put the sheet down and looked at me. "What are you asking of me?"

"You know the dates and approximate times of each event that took place at the mountain. They're listed at the bottom of that sheet if you don't. What I'm asking is two questions: Do any of those names stick out as people we should check out? And do certain activities of any of them correspond to when the events occurred? I'm looking for unexplained absences, generally odd behavior, reactions or the lack thereof when news of these things broke out—you name it."

He thought for a while and finally shook his head regretfully. "I am sorry. I don't feel I can do that. To have told you of my misgivings was a moral duty, to put my finger on an actual individual with no proof beyond a hunch would be inappropriate and careless."

"If you're being truthful," I told him, "which I choose to believe, that tells me *a*, that you do have a hunch, and *b*, that you didn't see any of these people fitting the profile I outlined, at least not consistently."

He smiled thinly. "Correct on both counts, although I have to admit that *b* is only true because I don't watch my colleagues like a den mother. We work shifts and we handle various assignments. Several days may go by without my seeing any of them." He waved his hand toward the empty office around us. "This is most likely true for you, too."

I leaned forward in my chair to emphasize my seriousness, hoping he wouldn't see my irritation. "If you have any knowledge that might help us solve these crimes, and you don't share it with us, it could put you and your organization in legal hot water, cost you a bundle, distract you from your purpose, and open the door to a real public relations black eye."

He pursed his lips and glanced down at the list. "Perhaps you could give me the opportunity to investigate a little on my own?"

I sat back. "Fair enough, but we're going to keep pushing from our end, too."

I escorted them to the door, catching Gail's elbow so she'd stay back a moment. She nodded to Betts. "You go ahead. I'll be right there."

We watched him walk down the hallway, his white hair haloed by the light from the window beyond him, and enter the stairwell.

"Be careful what you say right now," Gail warned me before I opened my mouth. "I have loyalties running both ways here."

"I understand that," I conceded. "But he raised the red flag first on this. I'm just hoping he'll see it through to the end. Whatever he says won't be enough to bring charges against anyone, that much is pretty clear. I'm only looking for a little guidance. We can waste a lot of time and money and put everybody in TPL under the microscope, or he can help us, give that same attention to a select few, and maybe save a life—don't forget that woman in the chairlift almost died. Either way, the same guy will end up in the limelight eventually. I don't see this as the moral dilemma he does."

She kissed me on the cheek. "I'll see what I can do."

Spinney had set up two long tables in the middle of the room and covered them with dozens of differently colored file folders, each folder labeled with someone's last name. He and I were alone in the office.

"Okay. Red names are primaries, like Marty Gagnon, Richie, Jorja, the TPL crowd, and all the homeowners that were either known to have been robbed, or who appeared on that list we found in Richie's apartment in Dover. Blue names are secondaries, mostly people only associated with the first group but with interesting wrinkles to their makeup, like an old rap sheet." He pointed to one. "Shayla Rossi, for example, and a bunch of other folks who used to run with either Richie, Jorja, or Marty. Finally, we have the yellows, made up of cleaning people, caretakers, co-workers, etcetera, none of whom appear to be involved in all this, but who might have something to offer anyhow, such as being witnesses to events they maybe didn't understand at the time."

"Okay." I nodded, waiting for more, standing beside him and considering what amounted to hundreds of hours of research.

"In the red category," he continued, "we still have a few gaps among the homeowners. Turns out a lot of condos belong to people who've never set foot in Vermont and just keep them as investments and as sources of revenue through time-sharing leases arranged through the resort."

"Tucker Peak handles all that?" I asked.

"Yeah, that's apparently pretty typical. The places are rented out on a forty-sixty basis, with the resort getting forty percent for management and maintenance—things like arranging leases, handling custodial care, and seeing to any necessary repairs, as well as supplying electrical, plumbing, and cable services. Also, snow removal in winter and lawn care the rest of the time."

"Pretty big operation. They have a separate division handling that?" I asked.

"No. It comes under Conan Gorenstein's responsibilities—the CFO. I guess once you've got it all computerized, it's not that bad. At least that's what I was told. They have whole staffs handling it at the larger mountains, but I guess, so far, they haven't seen the need here."

"You dug up anything interesting among the owners or renters?"

He smiled and raised his eyebrows. "You bet—no great surprise, I guess, but they turned out to be the best part of the whole deal. The more we dug, the more I thought of inviting any one of a half-dozen federal agencies to join in, starting with the IRS. We came across multilayered corporations, wives and kids owning things I doubt they even know about, PO box addresses by the handful in places like Delaware and abroad, and Christ knows how many lists of officers that may or may not be alive and kicking. It was almost weird to come across a Mr. and Mrs. Jones or Smith who just had a condo and a home in the flatlands and nothing else. Our old pal William Manning, for example, looks as crooked as a dog's hind leg, he's got so many irons in the fire."

Unfortunately, I could see the bad news coming. "But nothing connecting to Marty's B-and-E operation."

He surprised me then. "I'm not so sure. Nothing that slaps you in the face, that's true. But there are a couple of things we could go after." He leaned across the table and plucked a folder from its midst. "Smallest nibbles first—remember when we did the preliminary go-around after finding Richie's secret paperwork, when we talked to everyone on the target list? At least one of them said he'd noticed something missing, along with a broken window, but hadn't thought he might've been robbed till we suggested it."

I remembered what Willy had thought of the man. "Yeah."

"Well, one reason he was so dense was that he was used to finding stuff damaged or missing, even when the place hadn't been leased out during his absence."

I looked at him carefully. "What?"

"People were in his place when it wasn't being rented, more than once. He thought it was the caretaker or maybe some of the resort staff taking advantage of an empty house to screw around a little, have a party or something. He said it hadn't bothered him because he'd come from a blue collar background himself and could sympathize with a few folks wanting a piece of the rich life. He told me it had never been too bad and that he'd chosen not to report it."

Lester replaced the folder onto the table. "There was something about this that caught my eye—I mean, it is kind of weird. So once I got a list of dates from the homeowner, I went to his neighbors, to find out if they'd seen or heard any activity next door when the place was supposed to be empty. They had, but nothing like the guy had thought. It hadn't been rowdy employees having a good time on the sly, it had been what looked like regular renters: people with cars and skis and kids and what-have-you spending a few days on vacation."

"It was being rented without his knowledge?" I interpreted.

Spinney smiled. "Sounds like it. Only he wasn't making any money off it."

I mulled that over for a moment, for the first time in quite a while thinking back to Win Johnston, the private investigator, and wondering if this had anything to do with his being on the mountain. "It is odd. You look into it more?"

"Nope. I just thought I'd mention it. I figured I had bigger fish to fry." He picked up another folder. "Like this one. Andy Goddard. Aged forty-five, retired stockbroker, year-round resident. He was one of the ones on Richie's list, complete with exterior photographs of the house, but no sheriff's report and no complaint from the homeowner of any break-ins when we asked during that first canvass. The man is squeaky clean—no hits anywhere. Pays his bills, minds his manners, been up here about three years. Unmarried, no kids, no steady girlfriend that we could find, and no complaints from the neighbors."

I knew I was being set up. "All right, all right—a saint."

"Except we found that the resorts maintenance department had replaced a shattered bathroom window right after the date that was electronically burned into the corner of Richie's pictures of the house. Using bathroom windows is the same MO we've seen with most of the other burglaries."

"Suggesting Goddard was robbed but didn't report it."

Spinney's enthusiasm grew. "Right, which made us dig a little deeper. The guy's a local, right? At least a permanent resident, which is rare with this bunch. We started asking around, found out not only was he a regular at the Tuckaway, like all the other marks, but also that he had the rep of being a coke tipper."

"A user?"

"No, no. I meant literally. He tips people with little samples of cocaine. He's known as the local high flyer— flashes his cash, makes with the ladies, and hands out little samples to the ones he favors."

"We have someone on record saying he did this?"

"No such luck," but his expression didn't dim. "This falls under what you might call credible hearsay. This morning, though, we found out that one of his best buddies is an acquaintance of ours: Kurt Peterson."

I thought back a moment, my brain temporarily drawing a blank. "Richie's best friend among the ski instructors," I finally recalled.

Spinney laughed. "Damn, good memory—didn't know you had it in you. But you're right, which is why we think he'd be worth squeezing a little. Sammie loved hearing that, so she's busy right now trying to get enough dirt on Peterson to make him talkative."

I remembered Sammie's distaste of Richie's manner with every woman he encountered. "Is Kurt Peterson the same level of operator? We never bothered checking him out after we discovered Richie's apartment. He fell by the wayside."

"A poor man's version, maybe. From his rap sheet, we think he could be Goddard's supplier, or at least one of them, but we're hoping that what Shayla told you about quote-unquote druggies coming after Richie might have something to do with Andy Goddard. You gotta admit, the dominoes line up nicely."

"Except that aside from recreational coke, Goddard looks like a bored premature retiree, not a killer. Any reason we're not trying to squeeze him instead of Peterson? Sounds like the long way around."

"No argument, 'cept that Goddard's more careful than he seems. All we heard were rumors of this coke tipping thing. One guy told us that no one would ever fess up to it, either, 'cause Goddard makes sure the people he favors pass his scrutiny first. That's where we figured Kurt would come in handy—from his record, he's obviously not as discriminating."

"Okay," I agreed. "I'll go along with that." I waved my hand over the spread of files before us. "Anyone else look promising?"

Lester tilted his head to one side. "Not *as* promising, but if Goddard peters out, I got other options."

"What about our favorite missing person?" I asked. "Does Marty Gagnon have any ties to Kurt, maybe through Richie?"

"If he does, we haven't found them," Spinney admitted. "Whatever role Gagnon might have in all this, he's keeping it well under wraps."

I recalled what Lester had said about Sammie's present activities, and a quasi-parental concern crept into my head. "You said Sammie's getting dirt on Peterson. What's she doing, exactly?"

He looked at me like an ambivalent confidant, unsure of how much he should divulge. "Exactly? I'm not sure. She did say something about knowing just how to get to him, though."

"And you were happy to let her do that?"

The true source of his discomfort surfaced. "Willy's with her."

"Swell," I muttered. "You better take me there."

CHAPTER SEVENTEEN

WE FOUND SAMMIE AND WILLY IN THE BASEMENT OF THE Mountain Ops building in a back room of the Tucker Peak security office. He was taping a mike wire from just under her brassiere, around to the back, and down her spine to a transmitter below her waist. It was now early evening, and already dark outside.

I leaned up against the doorjamb, knowing Sammie's lack of modesty on the job, and pointed at the mike. "At what point in this operation were you going to clue me in? Tomorrow morning?"

Willy laughed, his eyes on his work, his one hand moving expertly. "Only if we hit the jackpot." He tore some tape in his teeth and pressed it against her skin.

"Assuming you hadn't gotten her killed by then."

He glared at me as Sammie cut in, "It was my idea."

"I don't care whose it was," I told her. "It's half-baked and rushed. That's a lethal combination."

"You don't even know what it is," Willy said.

I looked at her instead. "Gee, let me guess. You're

going to pretend to be a talent scout for a recording studio and ask Kurt Peterson to sing into your cleavage?"

Willy glanced at Lester for support. Lester merely
spread his hands to both sides, palms up, and raised his
eyebrows.

"It'll work," Sammie said, pulling her sweater down
and smoothing it into place. "I'll tell Kurt I'm hard up for
some drugs, make a buy, and bust him. I know he's using
the Tuckaway as a drugstore."

"Sam," I tried explaining, "you haven't been on the
mountain for a couple of days, you've been helping
Lester. How're you going to explain your absence?"

"That's what makes it perfect. I need a fix—I'm strung
out, on the prowl. That's where I've been—lookin' to
score."

"You don't think word's gotten out that there were
cops undercover here?" I asked. "I was on the mountain
last night and got ribbed for it."

"Did my name come up?"

"There was no reason for it to, Sam, but what would
you think? Two new employees appear out of nowhere
and then vanish almost as fast. One turns out to be a police officer and suddenly the other, looking like an
Olympic athlete, starts bar crawling, claiming she's a
hophead. What would that smell like if you were a bad
guy?"

"It's worth a shot," she persisted.

"I'm not saying Peterson's not worth a shot," I said.
"I'm saying you're too high profile to deliver it. Why not
switch with Willy? Have him go in after we take the time
to set it up properly."

She gave me a scornful expression. "He's the wrong sex, Joe. Kurt has the hots for me. He spent so much time ogling my ass when I was Greta Novak, he barely took time to do his job. And I played with it, too, figuring it couldn't hurt to fake being friendly, just in case. The man thinks with his pecker. I know it. He won't make me, and he'd make Willy in a heartbeat. Besides, Willy's been around here as a cop, he's more exposed than I am."

"I don't like it," I said, adding, "I don't guess you got a wire warrant."

Now they were standing side by side. Willy tapped his breast pocket. "Signed and sealed by the judge."

"It'll go down in the Tuckaway," Sammie explained. "He asks me to step outside and we pull the plug. I'll be watched all the way."

"That's where you think he'll do the deal?" I asked incredulously, "right at the bar where everyone can see him? *Of course* he's going to ask you outside."

But she was shaking her head. "No, no, he doesn't. We know that. We're not going in blind here. We *have* done our homework, Joe. I promise. Peterson does do all his business in the Tuckaway, probably for his own safety— and it is in front of everyone, literally under the table, money for dope, tit for tat."

"She's just going to fan his cock a while," Willy chimed in, "do the deal, and we'll bust him, right there. No muss, no fuss."

I passed my hand across my face, every instinct fighting this scenario. I finally glanced at Spinney. "What do *you* think?"

He shrugged. "Sounds okay to me. We don't do it now,

we will lose Sammie's cover story and any inside track to this guy."

Spinney and I sat in the car, the engine on to run the heater, a radio receiver plugged into a tape recorder between us. We were positioned out of the lights on the edge of the parking lot behind the Tuckaway. The only sound came from the recorder's small speaker—the monotonous ruckus of voices common to all bars, and the steady back-and-forth between Greta Novak and her date—made scratchy and hard to hear by the typically poor reception of all undercover wires. In addition to the two of us outside, Willy Kunkle sat at a table inside, silent and alone and watching from a distance, a minuscule earphone in his ear through which I could reach him on a radio. He was pretending to tie one on with a string of ginger ales, which, as a recovering alcoholic, was an act he had down pat—I'd seen him do it.

We'd been there an hour already, listening to Sammie and Kurt Peterson play mental tag—he trying to get her out of the bar and into the nearest bed, she trying to get him to supply her with the coke she claimed would make the experience all the more memorable.

They were beginning to get on each other's nerves.

"Come on, Kurt," she pleaded. "Give me something. I'm hurtin'. I'll pay you, if that's your problem."

He laughed. "Oh, I want payment, all right, but not with money."

Spinney and I heard a sudden scraping on the microphone that made us both jump in our seats.

"Hey," she said. "Hands off. You want to turn this into a business deal, that cuts both ways."

He didn't seem fazed. "Ooh, the brass cupcake surfaces. And I thought you liked me for my potential. Maybe we could swap a sample first. I get a feel, you get a teeny, weeny sniff."

"You got some on you?" she asked.

I winced slightly in the dark, worried she'd push him too hard. Deals like this took patience, sometimes several repeat encounters, and this had been moving at breakneck speed from the start.

"Wouldn't you like to know," he answered her. There was the familiar rattling of ice in a glass, followed by, "Boy, who knew? Greta Novak, a cokehead. First time we met, I pegged you as a total jock. Figured you were probably a vegetarian, too—body a temple and all that shit. Not that I'm complaining about the body. I'd just like to see more of it."

"I am a vegetarian," she lied. "Coke comes from a plant, right?"

He laughed. "Good point. All right, you win, but you better be as good in the sack as you are on skis. I'm talking major leagues here. You do that and I'll not only not charge you, I'll make this a standard arrangement."

"You kidding me?" She made her voice soft and seductive, "It'll be the best deal you ever made. You won't be sorry."

"You got it, babe. Let's get outta here."

I looked sharply at Spinney.

"Give it to me here," Sammie said. "I'll do it in the bathroom."

Peterson laughed unpleasantly. "Oh, right. And then tell me to fuck myself. I don't think so, Ice Queen. I got 'stupid' written on my face somewhere? No, no. We do this at my place or you can get somebody else to powder your nose."

"Come on, Kurt. You won, okay? I do it now, I'll be in the right mood when you'll really appreciate it, instead of waiting around. I mean, where'm I going to go? We work together. You'll see me tomorrow morning on the mountain. I won't stiff you. I just gotta have it now." She tried softening her voice again. "I won't let you down."

But it wasn't working. We could hear his voice grow distant as he stood up. "Sorry Greta—my ball, my game."

Now was the time to either call his bluff or break off the engagement, either way guaranteeing that Sammie stayed inside the safety of the nightclub. Predictably, she did neither.

"All right, but don't bitch to me later that I wasn't in the mood."

His voice was closer now, and we could hear the background noise varying as they worked their way through the crowd. "Don't you worry about the mood, sweet meat. I got enough for both of us."

I picked up the radio I had cradled in my lap. "Willy, you on them?"

There was a pause during which I could visualize him digging his own radio out of his pocket and finding a discreet place to use it. "What do you think?"

Just before he keyed off, Spinney and I both heard a loud crash. Then Willy's radio went dead.

"What the hell was that?" Lester asked.

"Sounded like a tray of glasses. Maybe a waitress dropped it."

I waited for thirty seconds before calling him again. "Willy. We heard a loud noise. You still on them?"

Nothing came back.

A cold dread swept over me. I told Spinney, "I knew this was a bad idea. Drive around to the front door. We'll see if we can pick them up there."

Suddenly, Willy's voice filled the car, almost drowned out by what sounded like a riot behind him. "I lost 'em. We got a bar brawl in here. I got cut off."

Spinney slammed on the brakes as a car pulled out of a parking place ahead of us. "Shit." He rolled the window down and blew his horn. "Move it, goddamn it."

I laid my hand on his arm. "Quiet. Listen. Roll up the window."

Between us, Sammie's voice was saying, "What's happening back there?"

"Beats me. Sounds like we got out just in time. Here, this way. I'm parked over here."

"I thought we were going to your place?"

He laughed. "The dorm? No way, baby. First time I fuck you, I want it done in style. We're borrowing a condo for the night."

The car ahead apparently stalled, since it stopped moving at a diagonal, blocking the exit entirely. Swearing, Lester threw the gearshift into reverse and began backing his way around the parking lot. "We know what he's driving?"

"Of course not," I muttered angrily. "We didn't take enough time to find out. Nor do we know where this condo is, assuming it exists."

Sammie was obviously aware of the same things.

"That's really cool. I used to have a Camry. And the same color, too—dark blue. I loved that car. I thought it had class."

There was a slight pause before he said, "It runs. That's all I care about. Get in."

We heard the thud of two doors closing. Lester finally found an opening in which to turn around and began driving recklessly fast toward the front of the building.

"But if you want class, baby," Kurt told her, his voice muffled by the coat Sammie had been forced to put on "you won't be disappointed. This is some place we're goin' to."

"Sounds beautiful. Where is it?"

"You'll find out soon enough."

Spinney squealed around the corner and almost collided with one of the mountain's security cars, its bar lights flashing off the nearby trees and snowbanks. Just as we were about to speed by it, the driver's door opened and an officer stepped out in front of us, shining his flashlight directly into Lester's face.

"Shit," Lester yelled and hit the brakes again. He threw open the door and screamed. "We're cops, you stupid son of a bitch. Get the fuck out of the way."

I used the radio. "Willy, you out yet?"

I could hear him panting. "Almost."

"They got into a dark blue Toyota Camry. We're blocked in around the corner."

"Gottcha."

Spinney was out of the car by that point, still yelling and showing his badge. I stayed put to listen to whatever else Sammie might tell us.

"Wow," she said. "Something's happening back there. Lean back a little. I can't see past you."

"What do you care? Just a bunch of drunks."

Spinney returned to the car. The security officer, looking grim, slammed his own door and stepped out of the way as we roared by.

"She just said we're on the driver's side of Peterson's car," I told him. "Which means she's headed up that road." I paused and added, "I hope."

The radio blurted, "I'm out. I don't see them."

"They've already left, Willy. Take the other car and head up . . ." I stopped and looked around.

"Summit Road," Lester said.

"Summit Road," I repeated.

It was dark and twisty and empty of traffic, including any taillights ahead.

"We can't've lost them already." Spinney muttered angrily.

"Doesn't seems likely." I said. "He implied it was nearby, though." I leaned forward and narrowed my eyes, as if that might improve visibility. "Maybe they're already there."

Spinney was twisting his head back and forth, talking to himself. "We're passing side roads here . . . Come on, Sammie, talk to us."

As if she'd been eavesdropping, Sammie suddenly said, sounding distant and scratchy almost beyond comprehension, "Snowflake Circle? Where do they come up with these names?"

Suddenly, there was that sound of the microphone getting mangled.

"Hey," she said loudly, "Hands off. What do you think you're doing?"

Kurt Peterson burst out laughing. "You need a blueprint? Jesus, Greta, loosen the hell up. I'm getting in the mood. If you weren't selling, you shouldn't have advertised, wearing that sweater."

"You'll get what I want to give you when I want to give it. You're the one who turned this into a business deal, Kurt. Keep your pants on."

Careful, I thought.

"What the fuck is it with you, girl? You can't make up your mind? I'm not sure this is worth the hassle."

From the way Lester was driving, I could tell his frustration was building to a boil.

A small element of panic crept into Sammie's voice, "What was that sign? I missed it." Her transmission was now breaking up so badly, I had to guess at half her words.

"I don't know. I don't pay attention to the stupid signs. Why do you care, anyhow? This isn't a tourist ride."

She tried to laugh casually. "I just like the names—they're so corny."

"So call it Corny Row." Peterson's tone indicated some of his previous passion was dulling.

"We must've missed it somehow," Lester growled. "Shit. Can you understand a goddamned thing they're saying?"

I held up a hand to quiet him. Sammie had picked up on the same mood change I had. Her voice soft and caressing again, she said, "I'm sorry, Kurt. One toot and I'll be okay. I'm just a little strung out. I *am* looking forward to this . . . Ooh, what a beautiful house—a log cabin. I love those. Is that where we're going?"

Peterson sounded slightly mollified. "Nah. That one's nothing in comparison."

Spinney slapped the steering wheel with his hand. "Damn. We blew it. I knew it. We haven't passed any log cabins. We're on the wrong road."

I picked up the radio. "Willy. She's off Summit Road, somewhere below . . ." I flashed a light out the window at a sign, "Pine Ridge. She said she saw a large log cabin. It must be on one of the three roads we just passed."

His answer was tightly controlled, almost deadpan. "Roger that. I'll take Powder Lane."

I could only imagine what he was going through.

"Okay, Lester," I said calmly, "Let's take the next one down and see what we find."

"Must be nice to live in one of these houses," Sammie told us, as best as I could piece it together. "Look at that—I can see right down to the base lodge. Who owns the condo, by the way?"

Peterson laughed. "He doesn't. He's the caretaker. He gave me the key. It's like a frigging palace, though. You're really gonna love it: huge windows, master bedroom like a football stadium. It's even got a marble bathtub with water jets in it, right next to a picture window. I thought maybe we could put that to use, too—light a few candles? That sound good?"

She poured the honey on once more. "Oh, yeah. You really know how to treat a girl."

Spinney shook his head. "Christ, what movies does she rent? That stuff's terrible."

"Maybe," I murmured, "but at least it's coming in clearer. We must be closing in."

"This it?" Sammie finally asked.

There was more rustling of clothes and the sound of doors opening and closing. From a slight distance, he said, "Yeah. What d'ya think?"

"It's amazing. Cedar shingles, slate roof . . . and look at the porch. Number sixty-eight—it's like *Lifestyles of the Rich and Famous*. I could get into that."

"Yeah, right. Don't kid yourself, Greta. You and me, this is as close as we get to this life—stealing their keys at night and putting up with their shit the rest of the time." He paused and added, "Maybe that's what makes this so sweet. Ladies first."

"Willy?" I said into the radio, "Wherever she is, it's Number sixty-eight: huge place with slate, cedar shingles, and a porch. You seen the log cabin yet?"

"Negative."

I looked over at Lester. We'd been driving along our road long enough to have seen the same landmark twice. "Double back," I told him. "We must be parallel to them."

"Willy? We're heading for the middle road. So far, she seems fine. They just got there."

There was no response.

"Holy cow," Sammie's voice said. "This is incredible."

Peterson's voice was husky. "You're what's incredible."

"Hold it, Kurt," she warned him, forcing a laugh. "First things first. Where's my nose candy?"

"Give me a squeeze first."

"I'll give you a squeeze you won't forget—later."

"God, I like your tits."

"Very romantic. You come up with that?"

Ouch, I thought. Ever since we'd turned around, reception had worsened, heightening the feeling we might lose her altogether.

His voice hardened. "Fuck you, too, bitch. What makes you so goddamn special?"

I heard Spinney murmuring, "Come on, come on, come on," as we slithered along the snowy road, moving dangerously fast.

Of the options available to her, Sammie took what I thought was the boldest. She screamed at him. "You are such an asshole, Kurt. We have the whole fucking night ahead of us. I'm going to do things to you you've never even dreamed of, and you're about to screw it all up because you won't hold up your end of the bargain. *Give me my goddamned coke.*"

It worked. "All right, already. Save some of that for later, for Christ's sake. I got it right over here."

"There it is," Lester suddenly said.

"We got the log cabin," I told Willy, and gave him directions.

I heard Peterson and Sammie moving around, at last quite clearly, presumably positioning themselves so the coke could be lined up and then snorted. She made a cooing sound as Peterson tore something open.

"It's supergood shit," he said, "hardly cut at all."

After a slight pause, Sammie said, "Yup, tastes like the real deal."

"Go ahead," Kurt urged. "Let's get this party going."

"There's the view of the base lodge," Spinney announced. "Gettin' close."

Sammie's voice had dropped to a familiar, stronger, more authoritative range. "The party's not going anywhere, Kurt. You're under arrest—"

His response cut her off. "*What?* You bitch. I knew it. I fucking knew it. You goddamn bitch. I knew you weren't going to put out."

In the background, we could hear her monotone, ". . . You have the right to an attorney. Should you . . ." But there was something about his outrage she wasn't hearing. He wasn't angry that she was a cop, he was upset about not getting the night he'd been hoping for. That his fantasy was still holding sway had me worried.

There was a sudden loud report.

"Put it down, Kurt," she said warily. "I'm a cop. You mess with me now, you'll never get out of jail."

"Mess with you? That's exactly what I'm going to do. You promised me that much, and that's what I'm going to get."

Headlights appeared behind us. Kunkle driving at breakneck speed, threatening to put us in the ditch.

And then Sammie's mike went dead.

"That's it," Spinney said, shouting now, the adrenaline making us all crazy. "Number sixty-eight."

He cut into the driveway, fishtailing. Behind us, Willy didn't bother braking—he just smashed into the rear of the Toyota. He was halfway to the front door before Lester and I had gotten out of our car.

"Willy," I shouted, "*think.*"

He wasn't in the mood. He wrestled with the locked door for all of two seconds, pulled his gun out and shot it five times, finally kicking it open. He, Lester, and I all ran into the house like we were storming a beach and found Sammie, her skirt hiked up and her sweater torn, resting with one knee in the small of Peterson's back, holding his wrist at an excruciating angle. He was facedown on the floor, semiconscious.

She blew a strand of blond hair out of her face, "Where the hell've you been?"

Suddenly calm, Willy holstered his gun, extracted a pair of handcuffs, and walked over to her. As he bent over and slapped the cuffs on behind Peterson's back, he gave Sammie a quick kiss on the cheek. "Nice job, kiddo."

CHAPTER EIGHTEEN

OLD STOMPING GROUNDS—I WAS IN THE BRATTLEBORO PO-lice department's closet-size interrogation room off the detective squad area, sitting at a small table against the wall, catty-corner from Kurt Peterson. He was looking a little the worse for wear, Sammie having given him a sizable black eye, a mild concussion, and a kick between the legs that still made him limp.

Introductions, Miranda rights, and other amenities had already been dealt with.

"Kurt," I began, sounding sorrowful, "you've made a real mess of things. You're looking at some serious time behind bars."

He'd been staring at his feet, but looked up at me. "I know it looks bad, sir. I don't know what got into me." His tone of voice reminded me of an insincere bully toadying up to the principal.

"You tried to rape a police officer, among a raft of other things, so you can stuff the choirboy imitation. And while you've never done time, you have been in trouble before, which makes me think our prosecutor'll throw the book at you. She's a woman, by the way, very sensitive to how other women get treated by guys like you, and she's not overworked like a state's attorney. She only gets our cases. You understand?"

"Yes, sir."

I sat back and crossed my legs. "Which is not to say I can't be useful to you."

A silence filled the air before he asked timidly, "How?"

"I'm the guy who advises this prosecutor, who testifies in front of the judge, and who's the boss of the officer you tried to rape."

"I didn't really try to rape—"

I smacked a hand flat on the table and made him jump, but when I spoke, I did so softly, "I smell any more bull-shit coming from you, I walk straight out that door and we never meet again. Do you understand?"

"Sorry."

"I can influence how people see things."

Again, I let silence prompt him to ask, "What's that mean?"

"You tell me something you know and I don't—and which I find useful—and I'll ask our prosecutor to maybe knock off one of the offenses we have against you. Small offense for small news; bigger offense for bigger news."

He looked at me pleadingly. "I don't know anything."

"Don't sell yourself short, Kurt. You've got half a dozen things up your sleeve I'd like a look at. Try this: Where'd you get the key to that condo?"

His eyes widened slightly. "The key?"

"Yeah. Who gave you the key to get in?"

"Rusty Warner," he blurted out. "He's the caretaker."

I nodded. I already knew about Warner. We'd dealt with him just an hour earlier. "Very good. Rusty Warner. See? I can use that—very helpful. How'd you two meet?"

"I don't know. You work on the mountain long enough, you get to know almost everybody, sooner or later."

"Especially if you're a social butterfly, right? And the instructors tend to get around. You had a good guide there, didn't you?"

Reinforcing my schoolyard image earlier, he even squirmed a little. "I . . . guess."

"Richie," I prompted him.

He broke into a smile. "Oh, right. Yeah. Richie. He cruised all night. You're right there."

"And he tucked you under his wing, from what I heard."

His pride stirred slightly. "We hung out. I don't know about tucking under any wings."

I feigned surprise. "You were the ringleader?"

"No, no. Ringleader . . . Jeez. No. I guess if I think about it, I suppose he sort of took charge . . . sometimes."

I scratched my head. "Huh, this may be tougher than I thought. If I'm going to put you in a good light, I got to know in my gut how you fit into all this. There're a lot of people involved, after all—we need to know who does hard time and who gets a slap on the wrist."

His forehead began to glisten. "What do you mean, 'all this?' You make it sound like I'm part of some mob or something."

I downplayed his panic with a wave of the hand. "Oh, a simple foot soldier, you and I know that. Small fry. Still, we had to kill Richie—he's history. You, you're a bird in hand."

He began speaking rapidly. "I don't know what you're talking about. I really don't. I mean, I know I did a bad thing, being drunk and all, and she did kind of lead me on, if that's okay to say. But you're putting me somewhere I don't belong."

I got up and walked around the tiny room a couple of times, as if totally befuddled. "Kurt, you had the drugs, you had access to the house, you kept company with a known bad guy, you attacked a police officer after she'd identified herself, and I've got a small army of witnesses willing and ready to tell the judge that this wasn't just some isolated night-gone-bad. You were a dealer, Kurt—plain and simple. Maybe not a top player, maybe just selling what fell between the cracks, but still a dealer. If you're going to tell me you did this all on your own, how am I going to tell our prosecutor to go easy? She'll bury you alive."

I stopped and leaned on the table, so my face was inches from his. "You need to tell me where the bigger fish are swimming, Kurt."

His face was now covered with sweat. "I can't."

I stayed put. "Before, it was, 'I don't know.' Now, it's, 'I can't.' I translate that as, 'I won't.' Is that what I'm hearing?"

"No. I want to help."

"You better want to help, Kurt, or we'll throw away the key on you."

He swallowed. "I'm scared."

I sat down again. "Can't blame you there. It's a scary business . . . especially if you're alone. A man like you needs a man like me in times like this."

He showed a little petulance. "Being in jail is better than being dead."

I laughed softly. "That's only because you think it's an either/or choice. It's not. It's a little more complicated than that. See, what you did last night? That was all against us—cops. No innocent bystanders were involved. You broke the law and we can put you in jail, but we can also cut you loose. Merely spread the word that we had a long and fruitful conversation with you, and are throwing you back like the little, helpful minnow that you are."

I paused and added, " 'Course, there's no guarantee the next guy who picks you up will be as friendly, knowing how chatty you'd been."

"That wouldn't be legal," he said tentatively.

"Sure, it would. Just because it sounds like something from a TV show doesn't mean it doesn't happen all the time." I leaned toward him again, "Especially when the stakes are high enough, like my wanting to know who your supplier is."

He wiped his face with his hand. "This isn't fair."

I didn't respond.

"I think I better talk to a lawyer, after all."

"Be my guest. We won't overwork him. Like I said, we'll just say, 'Thanks for all the info,' and let you walk. There's a phone right outside this room."

He didn't move. "What happens if I tell you?"

"Depending on how much you say, a lot can happen. You could even start life over with a clean slate, if the planets line up right. Of course, for that, you'd have to be *really* helpful."

"No jail time? A new identity?"

"Whoa, remember who you're talking to. I'm just a

cop. None of that's up to me. You talk, I listen, then we let the people upstairs decide."

"But you'd tell 'em how I been. You'd tell 'em I was a big help."

"Everything that's been said in this room is on the record."

He placed his elbows on his knees and his face in his hands and let out a heavy sigh. After half a minute, he straightened up. "Okay. The guy you want is Andy Goddard."

Kathy Bartlett still worked for the state attorney general in Montpelier, even though she'd been permanently assigned as VBI's special prosecutor. Her office was a standard box, one of many lining a large central room filled with desks and head-high, sound-absorbent paneling. But it had a door for privacy and a window overlooking the gold-domed state capitol, one of the smallest, most toylike, and curiously modest such baubles in the nation. On the grand scale of Vermont's diminished bureaucracy, often shoved into some pretty eccentric nooks and crannies, Kathy's quarters were pretty plush.

"I'm not saying I don't like Kurt Peterson's sworn statement," she was telling me. "I am saying that in order to get a search warrant that'll stand up later, it'd be nice to have another leg to the stool. We're not just running up against some public defender and a judge here. As the new boys on the block, we're also coming under the scrutiny of every legal entity in the state, many of whom would love to see us fall on our faces."

I kept to the subject at hand, choosing not to discuss something I could do nothing about. "We don't have much more to use against Goddard. Whoever he is, he's been very careful up to now. We have Peterson's testimony and general scuttlebutt that he's peddling dope, but no one else'll go on record."

"How 'bout wiring Peterson and getting him to make a buy off Goddard?"

"I suggested that. Peterson wasn't interested, said he'd take hard time over being dead."

"Goddard's that scary?"

I waggled my hand in midair. "Peterson thinks so. We discovered Goddard via some roundabout backtracking from the Duval homicide, but I'm not making him into a killer till I know more."

"Any ties to Marty Gagnon? Maybe that's our key to opening this up."

I shook my head. "I tried Gagnon's name out on Peterson and drew a blank. Richie apparently never introduced them. And Lester Spinney couldn't find a connection anywhere between Gagnon and Goddard."

Kathy looked at me helplessly. "Surveillance?"

"I'll do it if I have to, but it takes time and money, and ever since Richie's death, patience hasn't been the boss's long suit. That's the flip side to the moving-too-fast scenario—if we don't move fast enough, the same people'll pound us."

"Maybe you can bluff," she suggested. "Let Goddard know you're breathing down his neck. Force his hand."

But I didn't like that idea. The hand I might force could simply become a disappearing act.

I did, however, have another idea. "It occurs to me," I said, "that there may be more than one way to conduct a surveillance. What if I were to get hold of something incriminating from inside Goddard's house, without entering it and without using a knowing proxy to enter for me?"

She smiled encouragingly. "Okay, I'll bite. What've you got in mind?"

I didn't drive all the way to Montpelier to have a conversation with Kathy Bartlett I could have conducted by phone. I'd timed my arrival to coincide with the end of the workday, and so now crossed the street and walked down the block to meet with Gail at a local pub.

She'd beaten me to it and was sitting at a small table by the window, waving to me as I drew abreast.

"I hope you don't mind," she said as I kissed her and sat down, "but I asked Roger Betts to join us."

"What's he in town for?" I asked, caught between curiosity and mild disappointment.

"He's around here almost as much as I am when the legislature's active. What're you having?" She signaled to a waitress.

"Coke," I called out from halfway across the room. The woman gave me the high sign and turned on her heel. The place was full of people whose purpose in town was made obvious by their very nonrural clothes.

"How's Kathy?" Gail asked, waving to someone she knew over my shoulder.

"Her usual, hard-nosed self. She said to say hi."

Gail sipped from her drink, which looked like a Scotch and water. "And the arm?"

I was no longer wearing the sling. "Better. Still sore, but not throbbing like it was. What's on Betts's mind? He got something useful to tell me?"

"I think he will have," she admitted. "I've been leaning on him like you asked, mostly because of what you said last time we were together—that someone had almost been killed already, and that all you wanted was a little time-saving guidance."

"I also think he's wanted to clear his conscience from the start." I added. "He's just had a hard time using a cop to do it."

She poked at the ice in her drink with her fingernail and smiled. "Good thing he chose you, other cops might not have been so tolerant."

I shrugged, my mind flashing back to my conversation with Kathy Bartlett, and the internecine squabbling we'd discussed. What an opinionated, stubborn, suspicious, and only occasionally innovative bunch we were in law enforcement, all disguised under the generalized, bland austerity of the uniform and the badge. "Maybe. Maybe not. People put us all in the same box, whether we deserve it or not."

Gail pursed her lips, obviously weighing that in her mind. "True," she said slowly, "although you have to admit, most of your colleagues have more of a siege mentality than you do."

I looked at the flow of pedestrians passing along the sidewalk beside me—close enough that if it hadn't been for the glass, I could have reached out and touched them—and pondered this philosophical tangent. The paradox of proximity combined with isolation seemed pertinent to Gail's comment. Police officers were expected to be enmeshed in society, were even urged to get out of their squad cars and become interactive—joining neighborhood associations and school groups and being seen as regular citizens, lending a hand to the public good. But they were received differently from firefighters or EMTs or anyone else, for that matter, having to deal with inane jokes about speeding, tickets, jaywalking, and with suspicion bordering on hostility about their motives for intermingling at all.

And unfortunately, it cut both ways. Younger cops especially saw themselves as latter-day knights, chosen to walk the battle line between society and a hostile wasteland, little understanding that there was no such easy divide, that crime and society were as symbiotic as a human body and the ailments attacking it every day. These civilian-soldier hybrids tended to wear militaristic haircuts, affect cynical, swaggering attitudes, and keep one another's company as much as possible, citing the general population's lack of understanding as their own explanation for standing aloof. Thankfully, the older they got, the more blunted became this self-protective, unimaginative, almost paranoid edge, although the after-effects remained. But since most of those veterans were off the street anyway, flying desks instead of cruisers, whatever benefits of maturity they might have gained became lost to the troubled kids on street corners who were most in need of them. And so the cycle continued, with small, hard-won improvements, and those generally achieved with the speed of growing grass.

There were times I found the whole debate both insoluble and overwhelming, and certainly nothing to chat about idly at the end of a long day. Ironically, Roger Betts's arrival at that point rendered the point moot and now struck me as fortunate.

Settling in gingerly, so his knees didn't smack against

ours under the tiny table, Betts apologized for being late.
Gail put him at ease and tried to catch the increasingly
busy waitress's attention. As she did, he told me how dis-
tressed he'd been at hearing of my encounter with Richie
Lane—or more properly, Rossi's dog—and asked how I
was feeling.

"I'm fine," I told him. "Gail tells me you've come to
some sort of decision."

He ducked his head slightly and smiled. "Yes, well.
Why don't we get down to business?"

I didn't react, although Gail cut me a hard look.

"The reason I took this long to tell you what was trou-
bling me," Betts began to explain, "was because the nature of what caught my eye was so obviously embroiled
in a human drama, I didn't want to add to the agonies this
man was already suffering, at least not without being
more sure of myself."

"And now you are more sure?"

He looked crestfallen. "Sadly, no. But I can no longer
take the responsibility of possibly risking another life by
staying silent. There was a time my idealism would have
lent me comfort and resolve in such a dilemma, but age
has a way of eroding such self-serving certainties."

It was like hearing a confession on *Masterpiece The-
atre*, his diction was so precise and his choice of words so
antique. However, I clearly sensed beyond it the pain of
his decision, so while I'd been irritated by his earlier wa-
vering, I couldn't fault the thoughtfulness that had put
him here at last, and I stayed silent to allow him to continue.

"Eight years ago, a dear colleague and friend of mine
married a younger woman with whom he'd fallen terribly

in love. He'd believed himself beyond such happiness after losing his wife to cancer fifteen years before and had thus given himself totally to the environmental cause. There are many different types of people in our ranks—as I'm sure is true everywhere—but we may have a disproportionate number of true believers, even romantics. Norman Toussaint is such a person. But he is also dedicated, idealistic, passionate, and vigorous in standing up for what he thinks is true."

The waitress had come within hailing distance by now, but none of us cared. Betts was staring at some focal point near the middle of the table, and Gail and I were hanging on his words like kids hearing a bedtime story. I remembered Gail's mentioning Toussaint and thinking at the time that he seemed the least defined of the three we'd discussed: a well-traveled man with a minor record of resisting arrest, who always seemed to be where the action was hottest among the environmentalist battlefields.

"Norman and I met over two decades ago, when he and his first wife were young and recently married. They were absolutely devoted to the cause, to the point of choosing not to have children until the world was made a healthier place to live. An extremist position, of course, and a naive one, especially in retrospect, but not uncommon at the time. In any case, you can imagine how that made Norman feel when his wife was then taken by cancer."

I could, in fact, since my own wife had met a similar fate even longer ago than that, a distance in time that had in no way dulled my memories of her and the happiness we'd shared. It wasn't something Gail and I often discussed, but she knew about Ellen, and now cast me a sympathetic look.

"Norman took the loss the same way Joan of Arc seems to have taken to those famous voices she heard." Betts continued, "He became absolutely driven, even obsessed. All his energies were given to environmental protection. When I'd known him first, I'd wondered about his apparent inability to break off from a task and relax a little. Lord knows, the rest of us knew the value of a vacation. But there were others enough like him that what might have been identified as a form of mental imbalance was merely dismissed as zealotry."

He paused and sighed gently. "And then he met Abigail—a wonderful girl, light-hearted, broad-minded, and generous. She was like a magical elixir, cleansing his soul of the dark clouds within it. It wasn't quite like a Hollywood movie, of course. In fact, it was quite rough going to begin with. He was very resistant to a much younger woman trying to reintroduce him to life. It was almost comical at times to see her, loosening him up, making him laugh despite himself. But the transformation began working; he began to melt like an iceberg in the sun, and finally, after much hemming and hawing, they announced they were to be married."

He smiled sadly. "Looking back, I wouldn't doubt a part of Norman now hates that day, when he sacrificed his own twisted logic and committed himself to another human being. He probably feels that had he stayed the course, his and Abigail's world wouldn't now be so haunted and crippled by misery and debt. He's just the type to take responsibility for the simple vagaries of fate."

"I'm losing you here," I told him quietly. "What happened?"

He laid his hand on mine. "I'm sorry. I ramble, given half a chance. Going against all his earlier instincts, Norman agreed to have a child with Abigail. That child, in the cruelest of ironies, has developed leukemia. It has driven Norman and Abigail apart, and perhaps pushed Norman over the edge."

Roger Betts turned and fixed his tired, pale blue eyes on mine, and added, "I have no idea if he is the man you are after. I do know that suddenly, he's been able to pay for medical treatments that were previously beyond his means. I only know this because Abigail told me about it in confidence. I have never asked him outright to what he owes this good fortune, but the rumor is a rich relative left it to him in a will."

"And you don't believe that."

He sighed again. "I'm ashamed to say, no."

"Implying there's something you're leaving out."

He nodded without speaking, seemingly at odds again about being here.

"Is it something he's done?" I tried.

That got him going again. Again, he patted my hand. "No. I mean, not actually. I'm not accusing Norman of anything. But he's been erratic lately—moody, forgetful, quick to judge—but most of all, inconsistent, which he's never been in the past. He's as driven as ever, but not by our mutual interest. It's as if his concentration is elsewhere . . ."

"With his sick child, perhaps," Gail suggested.

But Betts disagreed. "It's different. Now you can understand why I was so loath to bring this to you. Something is eating this man up from within, beyond the guilt of his family situation. And given his almost maniacal sense of purpose, it frightens me. I truly no longer know of what he may be capable."

The wash of noisy, clashing conversations swelled around us in the silence following Roger Betts's last words. I looked up and around in mild surprise and saw that the after-work, predinner crowd was at its max, laughing, drinking, making deals, and eyeing one another with a variety of intentions.

"Roger," I finally asked, "given the timing of the various accidents and Norman's schedule, do you think he might have been involved in any of them—specifically?"

Betts looked at me haplessly. "I wish I knew. It's not the kind of organization where we use a time clock. People show up at odd hours, work for however long they can. It's terribly fluid, and to be honest, I haven't pried into it."

"Not to worry," I tried easing his discomfort. "We'll do that, and we'll try to be subtle about it, although we will act on what we find."

"I understand," he said simply.

"I will do my best," I added, "to keep you out of it, though."

A small look of distaste crossed his worn face. "I deserve that because of the surreptitious way I approached you. But don't worry about it. I am not an informant—I acted on my conscience. If it comes out, it comes out—it might even be for the better."

I noticed how Gail was looking at her old friend and figured the best way for me to end this conversation was by leaving the two of them together to commiserate. I'd catch up with her later.

I did, however, have one last question. "Would you say Norman was mechanically inclined?"

Betts's face momentarily cleared. "Oh, good lord, I should say so. He trained as an engineer in college and was always the one we called on to fix things. He built his own house—he's very handy. Why?"

I rose to my feet and squeezed Gail's shoulder in farewell. "Just curious."

Outside, after sunset, the wind had kicked up and was blowing down the street in ferocious, snow-dusted gusts. The headlights of passing cars glittered off the airborne ice crystals, making me feel all the more like I was walking inside a huge freezer.

The chirping of my cell phone, deep inside my coat, introduced an incongruous and ineffective springlike note.

I groped around, my glove in my teeth, until I successfully tore the phone from its inner recesses and flipped it open, shoving my head into a doorway to hear better.

"Joe, it's David Hawke. Are you okay?"

"Yeah, I'm freezing my ass off on a cell phone. What's up?"

"I'm sorry it took me longer than I thought to get back to you on those prints. I did get a set off of Jorja Duval's body—textbook lift. Worked just like the guy said it would. I might have to write him a note of appreciation."

Why is it, I thought, that when you tell people something like, you're about to die of hypothermia, they immediately prolong what they have to say?

"That's great, David. Did you get a hit on the prints? Were they Marty Gagnon's?"

"That's the cherry on top. I sure did. The FBI coughed it up pretty fast. But they weren't Gagnon's. They belong to someone named Antony Busco, nicknamed Tony Bugs."

All sensation of cold and discomfort vanished. "Does that mean what I think it does?"

Hawke laughed, not often being the bearer of such heady news. "You bet. Very connected man, as they say. I sent the rap sheet to your office." He hesitated before asking, "Was that okay? I didn't know you were on the road. You going back there?"

"I am now."

CHAPTER NINETEEN

THE HEATER MADE THE CAR BALMY AND COMFORTABLE, AND completely at odds with the weather outside, which had turned gray, cold, and blustery. The blasts of wind I'd experienced the night before in Montpelier had developed into a sustained northern blow, and weather reports were calling for more snow later in the day.

I was happy it hadn't started falling yet, though. Using the windshield wipers during a covert surveillance was poor form, and right now, I was very interested in keeping a low profile.

Willy Kunkle was sitting next to me, one foot propped up on the dash before him. In the distance, behind a thin screen of denuded hardwoods, was Andy Goddard's generously sized house, which, like most of its upscale brethren, was blessed with a view of the snowbowl beyond. We were parked on the service road, near some Dumpsters and a few other vehicles: pickups and sedans belonging either to guests or maintenance crews. Aside from actually being in the car, we didn't stand out from our surroundings.

"What the hell're we doing here, anyway?" Willy asked. He'd left his own vehicle at the bottom of the hill and had joined me just a few minutes earlier.

"Waiting for Mameve Knutsen," I said, knowing the lack of further explanation would irritate him. Every once in a while, I found it irresistible to turn his crank slightly. He did it so routinely with all of us.

He sneered at me. "Cute. Where'd you come up with that?"

I smiled. "Didn't, that's her name. She's one of the cleaning ladies around here." I pointed at Goddard's house, "She's working in there right now."

Willy didn't need a more detailed explanation. "Isn't that a little risky, using her to search for us?"

"We're not. She doesn't know we're interested yet, which means she's not acting as our agent. If we pick her brains after she comes out—and she cooperates—that puts us in the clear."

"Which, combined with Kurt Peterson's affidavit about Goddard being a user, maybe gives us enough for a search warrant," he concluded.

"Right."

"Except there's no reason she should tell us anything."

I checked my watch. "That's why Linda Bettina's meeting us here in about ten minutes."

Willy nodded without comment, apparently satisfied.

"How's Sammie doing?" I asked after a pause.

"Good. She's tough."

"Maybe. The guy did try to rape her."

He pressed his lips together, his eyes fixed straight ahead. I didn't say anything, hoping the silence would work for me.

"She did smack him down," he finally said. "That counts."

I couldn't disagree. Had Gail been able to do what Sammie had, years earlier, I didn't doubt that the trauma of her own rape would have been easier to handle. Still, the threat alone was bad enough, and nothing to dismiss.

I thought I might approach the subject from a different angle. "How did you feel about it?"

He snorted. "You guys hadn't been there, I would've killed him."

"I thought what you did was great."

He mulled that over awhile, and eventually said quietly, "I was proud of her."

"It showed."

He didn't respond. I was wondering what to say next, a little curious why I was even pursuing this with him instead of with Sammie, when he suddenly said, "Spinney told me we're dealing with the Mob, all of a sudden."

I hesitated, disappointed at the abrupt change of subject, and then conceded defeat. Sammie was right, he was a tough nut to crack. "Looks like it. We put out an inquiry on the whereabouts of Tony Bugs Busco." I reached into my pocket and handed him a copy of Busco's mug shot that I'd received as e-mail just before leaving the office. "Got this from the FBI. There's a long rap sheet back at the office, too, but no current information. If it turns out he's dead or in the joint or we get proof he's in the South Sea islands, we'll go from there, but if not, I'd like him to explain how his prints ended up on a corpse in Vermont."

Willy grunted, staring at the picture. "In the meantime, we wait for Mameve Knutsen. What the hell's with that name?" he said irritably.

A pickup truck with the Tucker Peak logo on its side pulled into the lot not far from us. "You can ask her yourself. Bettina just arrived."

We got out of the car, buttoning our coats and turning up our collars against the cold, as Linda Bettina—tall, broad-shouldered, and seemingly immune to the weather—strode toward us wearing her usual uniform of heavy boots and insulated coveralls.

"She out yet?" she asked. She didn't offer to shake hands or trade amenities. We were a necessary evil, as she'd explained again on the phone this morning, and cooperating with us was just a means of getting us gone faster.

I glanced over to Goddard's house and saw some movement by the small car parked in his driveway. "Looks like it."

Bettina walked by us, heading that way, "Then let's get this over with."

"Remember," I warned her, catching up.

"I know, I know. I'm just here to support her, not twist her arm. I got it the first time."

Mameve Knutsen was a small, slightly built woman with a lively face and an engaging smile, which she turned on us as we all drew near. Given Bettina's mood and Willy's routinely grim expression, I gave her high marks for not running to her car and locking the doors.

Instead, she put down her vacuum cleaner and bucket in the driveway and greeted us amicably. "Hi, Linda. How're you doin'?"

"Okay," Bettina said, sounding surprisingly pleasant all of a sudden. "You all done in there?"

"Yup. Just heading off to my next stop."

"Great. Well, this won't take long, but these two men would like to ask you a few things. They're police officers, from the Vermont Bureau of Investigation."

To my relief, Mameve's smile broadened. "I've heard of you. You're part of that new outfit, supposed to be like the Untouchables or something."

"Or something," Willy muttered under his breath.

I shook her hand and introduced myself and Willy, explaining, "We don't want to take too much of your time, but we're here on kind of a sensitive mission. I understand from Linda that you have a habit of starting each job with a fresh vacuum cleaner bag."

Mameve looked mystified. "Yeah. I know it sounds dumb, but I like to start fresh, the vacuum works better that way, and I don't have to stop in the middle to change bags."

"So, you started on this house with an empty one?"

She stooped down and pulled a rectangular wrapper from the bucket by her feet. "First one out of a bag of three—got two left."

"And the other one's still in the machine?"

She glanced at Linda, as if hoping she'd explain the joke. "Sure is. I put them in my trunk and throw them out at the end of the day."

"Okay," I said. "Well, here's probably the weirdest question I have for you: Could we have that bag?"

The smile faded. "The vacuum cleaner bag? Why?"

Linda Bettina spoke up from behind me. "Mameve, they're suspicious about Mr. Goddard for some reason and think you might have picked something up that'll help them out. The bag's your property, though, and you can tell them to get lost if you want. That's why I'm here, to make sure that point's made crystal clear."

Again, I was relieved by her reaction. The smile returned with a crafty look. "Wow, that's great—like the crime lab on the Discovery Channel. I love that show. Is that what you're talking about?"

"Yeah," I admitted, "exactly right."

"What're you looking for? I may have seen something."

I felt more than heard Bettina let out a sigh, assuming there was either a policy or at least encouragement not to talk about the guests in such a fashion.

Not that I was going to mention it. "Are you thinking of something specific, Mameve? I don't want to be accused of planting ideas in your mind."

She turned thoughtful. "Gee, I don't know. I know they party a lot in there. They're pretty messy. But I can't say I've seen anything I haven't seen in other places."

"Nothing that would strike you as illegal?"

She shook her head. "Nope. Sorry."

"Do you know Andy Goddard?" Willy asked for the first time.

"We met a couple of times, by accident. They try to have us come by when the people aren't here. We get a schedule every week." She patted her pocket. "But that's harder with year-round residents like Mr. Goddard, since they're on-mountain all the time. Even so, I bump into guests pretty regularly, year-rounders or not, which I guess means the system isn't working too good."

Linda spoke up. "What do you mean, 'pretty regularly'? You should've said something."

"It didn't bother me and it doesn't seem to bother the guests, so there wasn't much to say. I've always thought it was pretty silly pretending all us custodial people were invisible, anyway. Besides, I did report the schedule wasn't working. That other man told me he'd look into it."

We all three looked at her with renewed intensity, causing her cheeks to flush.

"Did I do something wrong?" she asked in a small voice.

"What man?" Linda asked first.

"I don't remember. It was days ago and I forget his name. Come to think of it, I'm not sure he told me."

"What did he look like?" Willy asked.

Mameve pointed at me. "About his height, rounder, light brown hair, and a mole right here." She touched her cheek. "And he had a funny way of pulling his ear when he asked questions. I usually report to Barry—he's my supervisor—but he was out of the office. This new man said he'd take care of it."

I feigned ignorance—something Willy and Linda didn't have to do, the description meaning nothing to them. I merely shrugged and instead asked a tangential question that touched on something Lester Spinney had discovered earlier. "But you're being told people aren't supposed to be in these homes when they actually are, right?"

Mameve was obviously embarrassed by now. "It's not a big deal. I shouldn't have mentioned it."

Linda Bettina didn't hide her irritation. "Of course

you should have. This is just some screwup where one hand doesn't know what the other one's doing. I'll probably get a memo in six months like it was late-breaking news." She turned to me and explained, "Mameve's right, it's a PR scam. The guests are supposed to get this feeling their places are always miraculously pristine. It's fantasy bullshit and adds to the complications, but if they want a schedule, I give 'em a schedule. I don't know who this guy is she's talking about—the way they hire consultants and advisors and God knows what, I'm not surprised."

"Who's they?" I asked.

"McNally, Gorenstein, the Board, the brass. I'll have to get back to Gorenstein and sort it out. It costs us money to do it this way, so if it's not working, we ought to can it."

"You don't do both the housing and maintenance schedules?"

"Just maintenance," she answered. "Gorenstein does housing 'cause it's a revenue maker. As they see it, I just spend the stuff. Anyhow, none of that's why you're here. Let's get this over with."

"Right," I agreed, happy to get past the subject. I faced Mameve again. "Would you be willing to give us the bag and sign an affidavit later that it was empty and factory-fresh before you entered the building today?"

"Oh, sure," she said. "This is really exciting."

"We'll also ask you to sign a consent-to-search form allowing us to open the bag and examine its contents."

I was pulling the form from my inner pocket as I spoke.

Mameve nodded eagerly. "Sure, sure."

Linda Bettina turned and walked away a few steps. "All right. If you don't need me anymore, I got stuff to do."

I waved to her. "No, that's great. Appreciate the help."

We completed the consent form, secured the bag from the vacuum cleaner, and I shook Mameve's hand again. "It's been a real pleasure. One last question: When you work on that house, what do you do exactly?"

"Pretty much just vacuum, mop, do the bathrooms, clean the kitchen sink and stove. We're told to do a thorough job, but not get into the guests' belongings, so I don't go poking around." She smiled again and winked at me.

"That's going to be harder to do from now on. What is it you think Mr. Goddard's up to?"

I patted her shoulder. "This is where it gets really unfair, and I'm sorry, but we can't tell you that. It's just an investigation, and if it turns out we're all wet, talking about it could cause problems. In fact, you might want to think about that yourself, in case you were planning on telling anyone about this."

Her disappointment was palpable. "Oh."

"Yeah," I reinforced the message, "and if word does get out, since Linda was right here, she might come looking for you for an explanation, not to mention Mr. Goddard himself. He could think you've really done him a number. It's your choice, of course, but I'd be careful."

Something in my own words suddenly made me hesitate, struck by a long shot. I touched her arm as she turned to leave.

"Mameve? I'm sorry to keep bugging you, but I guess I lied—I have one other question."

She looked at me expectantly. "Sure."

I reached into my pocket and showed her Tony Busco's mug shot. "You ever seen this man?"

She glanced at it and looked at me quizzically. "You kidding?"

I exchanged looks with Willy. "No. Why?"

"That's Mr. Goddard. I thought you knew him."

I bit down on my surprise and answered her poker-faced. "We never met. I just needed confirmation. Thanks again for your time and remember, mum's the word, right?"

Slightly crestfallen, given her earlier enthusiasm and helpfulness, Mameve Knutsen loaded her equipment into her car and drove away without further conversation.

We watched her leave, Willy still holding the bag in his hand.

"Depending on what's in here," he said, "let's hope she does keep her mouth shut. Those guys wouldn't think twice about making her disappear."

"Let's not get too carried away too fast," I cautioned. "And as for whatever we find in there," I pointed at the bag, "I'll make sure she's kept under wraps."

We turned and walked back to where the car was parked. "What was all that crap about the guy asking questions about the schedule?" Willy asked. "You acted kind of funny."

"It was Win Johnston, the private eye. I didn't want Bettina to know it, but I'm guessing he was loitering around the office and took advantage of Mameve's confusion to collect a little information. I sure would like to find out what he's up to."

CHAPTER TWENTY

WILLY AND I DIDN'T GET BACK TO THE OFFICE UNTIL LATER that afternoon, after hand-delivering the vacuum cleaner bag to David Hawke at the crime lab in Waterbury and asking him to give it his highest priority, a request that only generated a tired smile of acknowledgment.

We found Lester as expected, surrounded by his folders plus a few more piles of paper from his research into Tony Bugs Busco, a man I now wanted to know a whole lot more about. Surprisingly, however, Lester wasn't alone and was about to grant me my wish—and then some—from an unexpected source.

He stood with his guest as we entered and made the introductions, "Joe, Willy, this is Al Freeman from the U.S. Marshals Service."

My arm halfway out of my coat sleeve, I stared at Freeman for a split second of stunned silence. "*Damn,*" I then said. "Of course. What an idiot." I freed myself of the coat and shook hands with a nonplussed young man with a broad chest and watchful eyes. "Andy Goddard and

Tony Bugs, right?" I challenged him. "The Witness Protection Program—he's one of yours."

Freeman smiled carefully and took a half-step backward. "Oh, hold on. That's a big leap. I'm just here because we heard you were interested in Busco. Nobody's saying we have him under wraps."

Willy let out a short, unpleasant laugh. "Give me a break." He walked over to his desk, dropped into his chair and slapped both feet noisily onto its hopelessly cluttered surface.

I couldn't fault him. Freeman hadn't done his own credibility much good with that. "You heard we were interested?" I asked. "How'd you do that?"

Freeman ignored the question, resuming his seat beside Spinney's desk. "Why're you looking at Busco?" he asked.

I studied him quietly, considering which way to go. As trite as it sounds, relationships between agencies are pretty much what you make them, and a lot of local and state cops had stopped cutting the feds much slack as a result. The prejudices between and about both sides were common and familiar, and pervaded all ranks. I had to wonder if young Mr. Freeman was under orders, and had bought the party line, or whether his own personal dealings had led him to his present attitude, in which latter case, my telling him he was being a jerk would merely confirm his opinion.

On the other hand, did I really care? I wasn't sure the Marshals were going to be of much use to me right now. I had Busco's prints on a murder victim and Mameve's statement that Goddard and Busco were one and the same. If the vacuum bag's analysis came back with evidence of illegal drugs, I had more than enough for search and arrest warrants both. In fact, if Kathy hadn't recommended waiting for the analysis, just for the extra credibility it would give us, I would've been knocking on Goddard's door right now.

"It was Al, right?" I finally asked.

"Yeah, that's right."

"You mind taking a little walk with me, Al? Just out in the hallway, no need for a coat."

He hesitated a moment, both Willy and Lester staring at him—Willy with his smirk still in place—before slowly getting to his feet. "Sure."

I opened the door for him, muttered to Judy that I'd be back in a few minutes, and escorted him out into the hallway.

"Where're we going?" Freeman asked.

I strolled over to the window at the end of the corridor, which overlooked a snow-blanketed parking lot between the Municipal and State Office buildings.

He joined me hesitantly, his arms crossed before his chest.

I spoke as if addressing the small cars below. "I asked you out here so we could stand on neutral ground. I know what it's like being in the other guy's office, surrounded by his people. It can make you dig in your heels a little."

"I—"

I interrupted him with an upheld hand. "Let me finish. I also know the Marshals are professional, hard working, good at their jobs, and give 'tight-lipped' a whole new meaning. So, don't think I'm about to start laying into you, okay?"

His reflection in the window nodded without comment.

"That having been said," I continued, "you did come to see us, not the other way around, and I seriously doubt you did that without having something to trade."

I now turned and handed him the picture I had of Tony Busco, looking him directly in the eyes. "Start trading. Is this the man we're calling Andy Goddard?"

He smiled very slightly and nodded. "He's one of ours."

"Thank you. That confirms what his cleaning lady just told us. Given Busco's nickname, I can guess his background, and I could tell from Lester's face in there that he was dying to give me what he's dug up so far—you want to beat him to the punch?"

"You going to tell me why you're interested?" Freeman countered.

"Yup." But I offered no more.

A slight pause swelled up between us. "Okay," he conceded, "Tony Bugs was West Coast, deep into medical waste dumping and the theft and redistribution of controlled pharmaceuticals—part and parcel of the same thing, since it all involved hospitals. Anyhow, DEA and EPA hooked up, nailed him, and got him to turn against the Mob. They collected a bunch of convictions, and we got to tuck him away as Andy Goddard."

"What did they use to squeeze him initially?" I asked. "They just catch him red-handed?"

"No. It was unrelated. He was peddling drugs. They were about to arrest him on that when one of his customers OD'd on a bad batch, so they tacked a manslaugh-

ter charge on him, too. They leaned on him pretty hard.
He's a two-time loser."

"And probably told him what a great life he could have
afterward under your wing," I suggested.

Freeman bristled a little. "If you have him doing something crooked, that's a contract violation. He's on his
own. We don't screw around with that. Ninety-five percent of the people in the program have criminal backgrounds. Only twenty percent of them relapse into old
habits. And none of them end up with us unless they've
sent a ton of people to jail. It's a good program."

I patted his shoulder. "Relax. I don't give a damn, anyway—it's out of my hands. I've just got a good suspect I
want to build a case against. That's all."

"What kind of case?"

"Well, with your appearance, a pretty serious one now.
We thought Goddard was just distributing coke, but now
that you've confirmed he and Busco are the same guy, it
looks like he's graduated to murder. We lifted a print of
his off the corpse of a girl named Jorja Duval."

Freeman's eyes widened slightly. "I read about that.
Jesus Christ. How many people know about this?"

I knew what had him concerned. "That Busco's involved and that he's in the program?" I pointed down the
hall. "Those two and me. There'll be a few others: the
sheriff, my boss, our special prosecutor, another of my
field agents. We're not much chattier with the press than
you are, but if you want to stay discreet and help us both
out, we can keep it that way by working together."

He looked at me without comment for several seconds,
clearly hearing the implied threat behind my offer. "You
got it," he finally said.

I bowed slightly and swept one arm toward the VBI office like a welcoming maître d'. "Then let's get back to the party and work out a plan."

That plan, however, was dependent on factors beyond our control for the moment, such as David Hawke's finding something incriminating in the vacuum bag, and Kathy Bartlett putting together a tightly bundled package with her federal counterparts with which to sway a judge. Not that we were guaranteed success even then, of course—it was within the purview of the U.S. Marshals to take this case over. However, given the implied warning I'd made to Freeman, I was hoping they'd feel it was also not in their best interests.

In the meantime, therefore, I decided to tackle Roger Betts's concerns once more by looking into Norman Toussaint, the under-the-gun, mechanically inclined environmentalist.

Norman and Abigail Toussaint lived in the hills several miles outside the small Vermont town of Jamaica. There were no landmarks of note indicating the entrance to their property, just a dirt track butting into the paved road. The deputy sheriff who'd given us directions had stressed that point: "No mail box, no road sign, no power lines, not a goddamned thing—they wouldn't even put a 911 number up, in case they get in a jam. Granola-heads with an attitude."

It was pretty remote. Sammie looked out the side window as I slowly negotiated the ice-filled ruts, and commented, "I like the countryside okay, but this gives me the creeps. It's like living in the middle of nowhere. Wonder what they do for entertainment?"

"From what Betts told me," I answered, "that's not high on their list right now."

"Still," she said softly, "it's like going to Transylvania or something."

I empathized with her there. The farther I drove into the woods, the more encased I began to feel. No effort had been made to trim or thin out the trees. In fact, it was more like the forest was being encouraged to take back the road, with limbs sticking out to rake against the car, and the overhead canopy low and dense enough to imperil the passage of a regular-size delivery van. Despite the relative brightness of an admittedly overcast day, the tunnel we were traveling was dark enough that I eventually turned on the headlights.

Conceptually, I could see a logic to keeping the approach to a house this overgrown—it would heighten the delight of coming into a clearing fully equipped with a hundred-mile view. I was therefore doubly disappointed when we rounded one last curve some two miles into this journey, and almost smacked into a dented, rusty old Jeep Wagoneer parked outside a completely hemmed-in, low-profile, almost windowless log cabin so covered with snow, it looked like a bear den. It reminded me of the marginal shelters thrown up against the elements during the Alaskan gold rush a hundred years earlier. Like the driveway leading up to it, the house was shrouded in gloomy darkness. I pulled alongside the Jeep and killed the engine.

Sammie frowned, imagining the flip side to this

frozen, glum setting. "Must be a joy when the bugs're in full force."

We got out and tentatively approached the heavy wooden front door, sensitive as always out in the country to the sounds of any dogs readying themselves to attack. I was especially prepared to use my right arm as a defense this time so I could balance out my scar tissue. But all was still, both inside and out.

The term "log cabin" nowadays usually evokes images of a pampered conspiracy between a hormonal Lincoln Logs set and someone with buckets of cash. This was another thing entirely: small, crude, emphatically home-built, and almost purposefully oppressive.

Sammie pounded on the door with the heel of her hand, creating a series of dull thuds as if she just whaled on a tree stump.

We waited for half a minute, fully expecting a no-show, and thus both gave startled jumps when the door suddenly and soundlessly swung open.

"Yes?"

The woman facing us was small, thin, dressed in heavy layers, wearing a pair of granny glasses and a wool watch cap. She looked dressed for a hike outdoors, although her appearance belied the physical ability to do that.

"Mrs. Toussaint?" I asked.

"I'm Abigail Evans," she answered tiredly, seemingly without curiosity about who we might be.

I showed her my badge. "We're from the Vermont Bureau of Investigation—Agents Martens and Gunther. We were wondering if we could speak with your husband."

She was hollow-eyed and gaunt, and merely blinked in response.

"Is he here?" Sam asked.

"He's on the platform," she replied finally, gesturing feebly beyond where the cars were parked. "Just follow the trail."

We both glanced in the direction she'd indicated and discovered in the meantime that she'd quietly closed the door on us.

Sammie raised her eyebrows at me. "And I thought my relationship was under stress."

The hike up the trail gave new meaning to a walk in the woods. Emulating the drive to the house, it was narrow, overgrown, rutted and uneven, and as dark as a tunnel leading far underground. Sammie and I stumbled and caught our balance repeatedly against the nearby trees before settling down to a slow, steady pace that saw us through the better part of a one-hour trip.

Along the way, I couldn't resist following up on her one-liner at the cabin. "Things going any better between you and Willy?" I asked, watching the heels of her boots as she marched ahead of me.

She didn't bother looking back at me. "Yeah, actually. I think they are."

I didn't say anything, making the subsequent long pause do my prodding for me.

Her hands flapped out to either side of her in a frustrated gesture—faintly comical when seen from behind. "What the hell do I know, Joe? Out of the blue, he said we ought to get away for a few days after this case wraps up. This from a man who wouldn't know a vacation if it bit him in the butt."

"You know where you'll be going?"

At that, she quickly glanced back at me, laughing and rolling her eyes. "You think I'm picky? I don't care if it's Guilford."

Guilford was the next town south of Brattleboro, and not much more than a crossroads.

"Besides," she added, "We're only talking a long weekend, if that."

"Still," I said after a couple of minutes of reflective silence. "Must be nice to be back on track."

I wasn't sure how that comment would go over. As their recent falling out had established, Willy and Sammie were hardly a match made in heaven. And for all my maternal meddling in their business, which of course I pretended was for the good of the squad, I wasn't sure if the best thing might not be a permanent breakup.

But the tone in her voice as she spoke straight ahead, leaving her words to drift back and surround me, was soft and hopeful and filled with optimism, and let me think that perhaps my efforts weren't quite so misguided.

"It is nice," she said. "Feels really great. And I know in my heart we can make this work."

Finally, mercifully, on the verge of thinking Abigail Evans had just conned us into trekking halfway to New York City, we came upon a wooden ladder heading straight up into the canopy overhead.

Sammie leaned against a nearby trunk and peered into the crisscross of pine and denuded hardwood branches. "There's a platform, all right—way the hell up." She kept her voice to a near whisper.

I tested the ladder, obviously homebuilt and covered

with the green skin of some slippery fungus. "Feels solid enough."

"You want to knock, or make like a lizard?"

I thought how I might respond if I were camped out on top. "Knock," I said, stepping back and cupping my hands around my mouth.

"Hello on the platform. Is there anyone there?"

A long silence elapsed during which we heard only the slight creak of the trees in the breeze high above.

"Who wants to know?" The voice was clear, neutral, belonging to a man.

"It's the police, Mr. Toussaint. We'd like to talk to you. Could you come down, please?"

"You come up. There's no danger."

Sammie made a face. "Wish he hadn't said that."

"No history of violence," I tried soothing us both.

She wasn't interested. "That we know of."

I grasped one of the ladder rungs. "I'll go first. You cover. Just make sure you don't shoot my ass off from below."

We headed up slowly, discovering the platform to be much higher than it appeared. The ladder was actually made in multiple parts, ingeniously connected across several large trees, and hinged here and there to compensate for any movement caused by the wind. The more we climbed, the brighter it got, and the more prevalent the snow that the lower branches had stopped from reaching the gloomy forest floor. I was reminded of an article I'd read in *National Geographic* in which researchers had lived for months in the top of the jungle canopy, studying Christ knows what. Only here, the ladder was cold and increasingly slippery, and was beginning to sway much more than I found comfortable.

We paused some distance below the closed trapdoor of a solid wood platform that blacked out about a fifteen-foot square of sky.

Sammie's voice was barely audible below me. "Okay—all set."

She linked one leg through the rungs and braced both her hands around her gun, taking a bead on the door just over my shoulder.

Unhappy with the William Tell positioning and unable to come up with a better suggestion, I finished my climb, leaned out to one side, and rapped on the wood overhead.

The trapdoor opened almost instantly to reveal a clean-shaven, thin man with a wrinkle-free face and what looked to be prematurely white hair.

"Come up," he said simply, and vanished from view.

I motioned to Sammie to follow and climbed into a small, warm, glassed-in tree house the size of a very large, square closet. It was flooded with the blinding light we'd been missing for over an hour by now and over-looked the view I'd been hoping for from the log cabin—miles and miles of tree-choked hills and valleys, with a horizon of snow-covered mountains in the distance. It was exactly like one of the fire warden towers of old, including a narrow cot, a small wood-fired stove, and a pair of binoculars balanced on a window sill.

I could appreciate all this because our host was standing at one of the windows, his back to us, his hands in clear sight, spread out and leaning against an overhead beam—as if he was consciously trying to appear non-threatening.

It worked. Sammie holstered her weapon.

"Mr. Toussaint?" I asked.

He turned then and nodded wordlessly.

I made our introductions as I had to his wife earlier, repeating, "We'd like to ask you some questions."

"I'm sure you do."

"You don't sound surprised."

He crossed over to the one chair in the small room—a rocker—and sat carefully, leaving us to stand over him. I noticed the whole cabin was swaying slightly from side to side, which made me wonder what it was like to be up here during a storm.

"I'm not," he said. "I've been expecting you."

"Why's that?"

"Because of what I've been doing at Tucker Peak."

"What've you done, exactly, Mr. Toussaint?" Sammie asked, sitting on the cot beside him.

He smiled sadly. "This where I confess my sins and ask for mercy?"

I pulled a small recorder from my pocket and turned it on. "You're not under arrest here, but if you want to confess to something, we're willing to listen." Given what little we had against this man, I was silently praying all this meant what it seemed to.

"I did it for my son," he admitted after a pause.

"We heard about that," I said. "How's he doing?"

"Not well. He's alive, but too damaged to appreciate it. It's one of the great ironies of my life that after decades of fighting for a cleaner, healthier environment, I've fathered a doomed and crippled son."

"He still might make it," Sammie commented. "Especially nowadays."

He looked at her with scorn. "You sound like his mother. You people are fools. You don't get the joke."

I decided to return to something more tangible. "What did you do on the mountain, Norman?"

"I rigged the chairlift—almost killed that woman and her child. Christ, what a piece of work that would've been."

I wondered how long he'd been up here, herding his thoughts into ever tightening circles, perhaps hoping that eventually he'd turn into himself entirely and drift out among the treetops like a ghostly black hole.

"What else?" I asked.

"I blew the water main to flood the ski slope."

"And the pumphouse fire?"

He'd been staring at his hands resting in his lap, but now looked up at me quizzically, "No. I don't know who did that. After the water main, I came here. I couldn't handle the guilt."

"What about putting the dye into the storage pond?" Sammie asked.

He let out a small, mirthless laugh. "That was classic—environmental guerrilla tactics, one-oh-one, just like nailing that shed door shut and chaining the snowmobiles together." He then shook his head. "No, I left that stuff to the firebrands. I had more serious work to do. Private work. Feats of redemption." He returned to studying his hands.

I crouched down before him to better look into his eyes. "Norman, you were making money doing these things, right? To pay for your son's treatments."

"To do that; to buy back a lost love; to betray the beliefs of a lifetime. I can't believe I almost killed another human being."

His tone was that of a man in a near suicidal depression. I was glad we'd located him when we did.

"When you blew the water main, the power went out, too—a two-man job. Who paid you? Was he also the other man?"

Toussaint finally locked onto my gaze and shook his head. "Oh, no. You can have me. You can't have him."

"Norman. The bottom line is you didn't kill anyone, and you do have a wife and child. Things are tough, but they can get better. What you're doing now will ruin everything. We'll bust you, take your life apart, seize your assets, interrupt the cash flow to your son's treatment. You can prevent that. Give us the name of the man paying you off. That'll make you a witness for the prosecution, cut you some slack, buy your family time to heal, and take the son of a bitch who's exploited your tragedy off the street."

But he was stuck in his own reality. "That's just what you think you can do. The way I've set things up is the only hope we have."

I stood up, convinced of his determination. "You know we'll find him anyway. You're throwing away your only chance of salvation."

"You have to say that. You don't have a choice."

I sighed and looked out at the breathtaking view, pondering how such beauty could be host to such misery. "Okay, Norm, then I guess you better come with us."

CHAPTER TWENTY-ONE

LESTER SPINNEY FOUND ME IN THE BASEMENT OF THE MUnicipal Building, where I was putting the finishing touches on paperwork relegating Norman Toussaint to the police department's temporary holding tank.

"Conan Gorenstein just resigned as CFO of Tucker Peak, effective immediately. Linda Bettina thought you'd like to know."

I signed my name to the bottom of the form and leaned back in my chair. "Why?"

"Officially, because he got a better offer elsewhere."

"And unofficially?"

"Linda has no idea, but she smells a rat big time."

"I bet Win Johnston knows," I said. "Any news back from David Hawke on the vacuum bag?"

"Not yet. Should hear within a couple of hours, though. I called this morning and asked."

I gathered up the paperwork and rose to my feet, fighting what I knew was a juvenile impulse to forego Hawke's analysis and just move against Busco with what we already had. The contents of the bag were no longer as important as they'd once been, after all. Now they were merely Kathy's way of adding a pair of suspenders to the metaphorical belt of her legal case, and only that if Hawke found something incriminating among them. Still, I didn't want to piss off our own prosecutor, and a double sense of security was no bad thing. "I'm going to give Win a visit. Call me on the cell phone as soon as you hear, okay? I don't want the U.S. Marshals getting the jump on this. We have first dibs on Tony Bugs, regardless of what they think."

Win Johnston worked out of his home north of Brattleboro. His office was comfortable, roomy, well lit, and equipped with a pair of French doors leading out to a snow-covered deck overlooking a half-acre yard. It looked like the workplace of a semiretired CPA. In fact, Win ran an agency comprised of several investigators and a small secretarial staff, and owned a security service as well.

He greeted me with a cup of coffee and the offer of an easy chair. "What can I do for you, Joe?"

"Tell me about Conan Gorenstein."

He smiled thinly. "What about him?"

"He's the guy you've been investigating, he's been ripping off the resort by cooking the books on the condo rentals. Now he's out on the street purportedly because he got a better offer, which I doubt."

"And your question is?"

"Is your investigation completed and are those all your findings?"

He laughed. "You got me—that's not what I expected. I thought you were going to grill me for his identity."

A long pause stretched between us, during which my unanswered question hung in the air.

"Let me ask you something first," he countered. "If Gorenstein's now unemployed, what makes you think I haven't finished my job?"

"We caught the guy who rigged the ski lift and did some of the other sabotage. He also spilled the beans on what the TPL's been up to. If Gorenstein's only guilty of the condo shuffle, that leaves a big item unexplained. The man we have behind bars wasn't alone, he was being manipulated by someone else. I need to know if between you and us, we've done a clean sweep or not, or if a third party's still out there."

He pushed out his lower lip thoughtfully. "Huh. Good question."

"Was that all the dirt you could get on Gorenstein?"

He twisted in his seat and stared out the French doors for a moment. "Look," he finally said, turning back, "we both know how this works. You asked me that night in the parking lot to keep an eye open for anything that might help you out. I did that, and found nothing. Between you and me and nobody else, I was hired for the same reason I usually get hired by an outfit like that, and I found somebody's hand in the cookie jar. That was all they needed, and they acted on it. It's not like I have to build a legal case—in fact, that's exactly what everyone's trying to avoid."

"Did they tell you who to look at from the start?"

"Nope. They had no clue. It was just a feeling that they should've been grossing more than they were."

I frowned. "Hold it. How's that work? If they didn't know the condos were being rented out, how could they have been expecting extra revenue? From what I understand, Gorenstein was skimming off an operation he was running on the side, not dipping into general company income."

Win had been nodding in agreement throughout this question. "Right, right. That's only because a gut instinct isn't always based on the truth—sometimes it's just a flare for something that's vaguely out of whack. I studied the books, Joe—both sets of books, I should say. The condo scam was all I found, and it was netting him thousands of bucks a month. Not much if you're planning to rip off IBM, but handsome money for your average Vermonter. There was no indication he was involved in any sabotage."

"Who hired you?" I suddenly asked.

He paused again. "That's getting close to forbidden territory."

"Fine, play the stiff upper lip. I'll tell everyone what an uncooperative pain in the ass you are. So, who hired you?"

"Phil McNally."

That caught me off guard. "No kidding? When I mentioned you were prowling around, he pretended that was late-breaking news. He even suggested the Board might've hired you to check *him* out."

"You blame him? Actually, I was to report to the Board, not to him or Linda Bettina—so no one could say we were playing footsie."

"And he gave you a double-oh-seven license?"

"Free rein. McNally's a pretty straight-up guy. Plus, I think he arranged it like that so he couldn't be accused of stacking the deck. He hired Gorenstein, after all."

A small flurry of nagging questions kicked up in my head, none of which I wanted to share with Win right now. "You don't know where Gorenstein disappeared to, do you? I'm assuming he's not still clearing out his desk."

"No, he's gone, but he's probably just at home. As usual with these things, nobody's admitting anything—no fouls, no penalties. If he had the balls, he could probably ask for a reference, and they'd probably give it."

The phone in my pocket let out a muffled chirp, "Excuse me a sec," I said, and fished it out. "Gunther."

"It's me," Lester said at the other end. "We just got a fax from the crime lab on the vacuum bag. Looks like we've got all we need. Kathy Bartlett's on her way down here to tie the legal bow."

"Be right there."

I got to my feet and moved to the door, slipping the phone back into my pocket. "I gotta get going."

Win knew better than to ask why, but he did have one question. "How'd you figure out I was after Gorenstein and that he was scamming the rentals?"

"I met Mameve Knutsen. She told me how she reported the scheduling discrepancies between when people were supposed to be in the condos and when they were actually there. Said the man she talked to at the office was a newcomer with a habit of pulling at his earlobe when he talked. Got to watch those things, Win."

Johnston self-consciously touched his ear with a fingertip, as if to make sure it was still there. "Yeah. You have a good day, Joe."

I waved good-bye and pulled the door closed behind me. But outside in the hallway, instead of heading to my car, I paused to retrieve the cell phone and dialed Lester back.

"Do me a favor," I asked him when he answered. "It's a little off the topic, but send somebody over to Conan Gorenstein's house and have him brought down to the office. I want to have a talk with him. And see if you can find out who was supplying the equipment that was supposed to go into that cremated pumphouse. Also, locate the ski lift tower manufacturer and ask about the order they have with Tucker Peak."

I could tell from the background noises that Spinney was groping around his desk, presumably for a pen. "Right, ski lift towers. Got it. What the hell's going on?"

"Call it a follow-the-money hunch. I think we have more than Tony Bugs and Marty Gagnon in motion right now. And by the way, do not contact Phil McNally for any of these questions."

There was a slight pause. "How 'bout Bettina? It would speed things up if I worked through somebody over there. Being discreet'll take a lot more time."

I weighed that in my mind for a few seconds, and then went on pure instinct. "Fine, but same warning to her about keeping discreet. I want McNally left in the dark."

"Roger wilco."

"What've we got?" asked Kathy Bartlett as she dumped her briefcase on my desk and draped her coat across the back of a nearby chair.

I offered her the crime lab fax Lester Spinney had used to lure me back to the office and summarized the very advantages I'd been thinking of bypassing just hours earlier. "Traces of cocaine—lots of it. All vacuumed up by the cleaning lady into a factory-fresh bag, as attested to in her sworn affidavit. It's the third leg of the stool you were asking for to get us legally into Andy Goddard's—aka Tony Bugs's—condo. It should give us a rock-solid search warrant on its own merits, which in turn might give us something more than a fingerprint to connect him to Jorja Duval's murder."

She read both documents carefully, nodded once, and without having sat down, gathered up her things and headed back out the door. "I'll go round up a judge. What's your timing?"

"I don't want to rush things. I have to coordinate with Snuffy and the Marshals on how we pick Tony up." I checked my watch. "Is four hours from now okay?"

"I'll be here."

Spinney passed her on the threshold and nodded appreciatively after she'd left. "Very cool woman. Wouldn't like her as a mother, though."

I didn't ask him to expand on that. "Where've you been?"

He waved a computer printout at me. "Using the copier downstairs, wrapping up on your homework. Wild goose chase, as it turned out. I don't know what you were hoping to find, but both the pump and ski tower manufacturers came up empty."

"Meaning what?"

"Meaning they have contracts with Tucker Peak to work out general specs, all aboveboard. Plans are in place to move full steam ahead."

"General specs? The towers aren't in production right now?" I asked him. I began feeling the same satisfaction I got after locating a long-sought-after puzzle piece and fitting it into place. "I was told they'd be installed by helicopter this spring. They have survey crews out there now. And those pumps are supposed to have been finished and awaiting shipment, pending a new pump-house."

He looked at me blank-faced. I smiled in return, the conviction of what I was thinking spreading through my body like a warm glow.

"No," he said slowly. "They both told me they were just in the early stages."

"No money's changed hands?"

"Not beyond a down payment."

"That's what they think," I murmured, trying to counter my growing excitement. "Money's definitely changed hands, and I bet I know who's holding it. How was Bettina to work with on this?"

"Fine," he said. "She did ask me why she couldn't talk to McNally, but she didn't seem too surprised when I told her you'd fill her in later. What's going on?"

"I haven't figured out the details," I admitted, "and the evidence may prove me wrong, but I think we stumbled over an embezzlement scheme, with the CEO *and* CFO working as a team. Did you get someone to pick up Gorenstein?"

"Yeah. They should be here in an hour or so. I thought he'd just pocketed a few rentals on the sly. What're you talking about?"

"It looks clearer to me now than it did back then," I explained, "but the first time I thought something was wrong was when the sabotage at Tucker Peak went beyond the usual environmentalist high-profile pranks—maybe even before that . . . come to think of it, when I wondered why McNally didn't have Snuffy just throw the protesters off the property. That never made sense to me, even with McNally's good-guy reputation."

I rose from my desk and crossed over to where we hung our coats. "Want to take a field trip? I need to talk to Bettina face-to-face."

"Fine with me, but what about Gorenstein?" he asked, joining me.

"Leave a note downstairs to have him cool his heels till we get back. I don't mind him staring at a wall for a little while anyhow. If he gets antsy, tell whoever's holding him to invent a stall tactic—no car to take him back home or something. Meanwhile, you and I can coordinate with Snuffy and the Marshals via cell phone on busting Tony Bugs."

On our way through the reception area, we told Judy where we were headed and continued on down to my car, noticing that the second half of yesterday's snowstorm looked about ready to unload—at long last. Once on the road, I resumed my narrative. "Another thing was Win Johnston. He was hired by McNally—I think as a red herring—obvious enough that if Win hadn't approached me first, we would've heard about him somehow anyway. He was supposed to be a smoke screen, just like McNally's keeping the TPL around.

"Finally," I continued, "there was Norman Toussaint, twisting in his own guilt, eager to confess his sins even if he wouldn't snitch on his son's sugar daddy. He told us he'd done the chairlift and the water main and that TPL had dyed the storage pond, hung the banner, and the other benign stuff. But he had no explanation for the pumphouse burning and admitted someone else did in the generators."

"Couldn't that still have been the TPL people?" Spinney asked. "Betts doesn't seem to have a clue what they're up to, and he's one of the bosses."

I didn't argue the point. "That's possible, except for the kid's medical bills suddenly being paid and the overall timing. I thought it was an interesting coincidence that the pumphouse burned just before the pumps were supposed to go into it. In fact, McNally stood right in front of me and bitched that he'd have to pay storage fees on them until he could rebuild. That was after Bettina had told me her crew had finished building the shed two months ahead of schedule. Now you found out the pumps haven't even been fabricated—and certainly haven't been paid for."

"So, McNally was billing the resort while he was pocketing the money he claimed he was spending," Lester summarized. "But where's that put Gorenstein? If he controlled the books and was in cahoots with McNally, how come he only got caught for the condo rental deal?"

"Another smoke screen," I suggested, liking my hypothesis all the more, now that I was hearing it out loud. "Which is why I want to talk to Linda Bettina. My bet is that the consultants, engineers, feasibility studies, environmental impact statements, and everything else were mostly pure invention, the supposed costs of it all going instead into McNally's and Gorenstein's private account. What outsider can keep track of stuff like that? You can spend two hundred grand on a single research project and bury it in the back of a file cabinet. People do it legitimately all the time."

I held up my hand to stop him from repeating his question. "I know, I know—the condo shuffle. That's where I think they did their best work. Time was running out on their plan, see? Instead of milking this operation for the entire winter, like they'd hoped, the schedule had to be moved up because of the intensity of the TPL protests, and just maybe because we appeared out of the woodwork, looking to solve Snuffy's burglaries—plus, Bettina screwed them up by being too efficient, forcing them to burn the pumphouse. But the plan was still in place, and I think it called for Gorenstein to be fired for some minor infraction and allowed to vanish, explaining why Win was hired to find out about the condos. After that supposed 'embarrassment,' McNally was probably going to come up with his own excuse—maybe a better job offer or a bogus heart attack (meaning we better check the legitimacy of that heart condition)—and join his buddy in some banking haven where they've been sending the loot from the start."

"So, there're *three* sets of books," Spinney said, nodding at the logic of it. "One for public consumption, seemingly legit but hiding the condo deal; one fake backup set showing the condo rip-off, for Win Johnston to discover and get Gorenstein fired; and a third, truly accurate one that only McNally and Gorenstein knew about."

"Right," I agreed. "And which we'll probably never find."

The pager on my belt went off. I pulled it loose and looked at the number on the display. I was about to tell

Lester it was probably Judy telling us that Gorenstein had arrived under escort, when Spinney's pager ignited, also.

"Rains, it pours," he smiled, studying his in turn.

My cell phone started chirping, making us both laugh.

"Christ," I said. "No hands left to drive with."

I dropped the pager into my lap and answered the phone. "Gunther."

"Joe, it's Snuffy. Where in Christ's name are you?" His tone was close to panicky, unheard of in the man.

"Maybe fifteen minutes away from Tucker Peak."

"Step on it, then. All hell's broken loose. Some U.S. Marshal's been shot at one of the condos, and my people are going nuts. What have you been doing up there? And when did the Marshals get involved, or is that news to you, too?"

Didn't I wish. I leaned forward and hit the blue lights hidden in my car's front grille. "I was about to call you about that. Does the condo belong to a guy named Andy Goddard?"

"Yeah."

"Goddard's in the Witness Protection Program. We just found out about him. I was going to get with you and the Marshals to bust him later today."

"Thanks for keeping me in the loop," he commented sourly.

"The Marshals must've jumped the gun, Snuffy. I didn't know anything about it. When did this happen?"

"Right now. The Marshal was only wounded. He just called 911 a few minutes ago from Goddard's house."

Meaning there was still a chance. "Did you block the access road?"

"First thing, but my guys are feeling pretty lonely."

"Okay, spread the word. Tell the feds, the state police tactical team, see about rounding up as many snowmobiles as you can, and have somebody warn Linda Bettina about all this. Her crew could be at risk. That road's the only way out unless he goes cross-country some way." I paused and looked up at the dull gray sky. "It's about to start snowing here. Ask the National Guard if they can get a helicopter into this stuff—their infrared unit could give us a crucial set of eyes."

In response to all this, the phone simply went dead. Spinney looked at me questioningly.

"We're in deep shit now," I said in explanation. "Tony Bugs is on the run."

CHAPTER TWENTY-TWO

LINDA BETTINA MUSCLED HER WAY THROUGH THE SMALL cluster of cops standing around me in the parking lot in front of the lodge, which at this point consisted mostly of sheriff's deputies and a couple of state cops who'd responded to the general alert. Her eyes showed she was in high temper. "What the hell's going on? I heard somebody was shot, that the road's been cut off, and I just got a call from that fathead sheriff to take all my people off the mountain, but he wouldn't tell me why."

I tentatively laid a hand on her forearm, hoping she wouldn't feed it to me. "I'm sorry. That was my fault. One of the condo owners just shot a U.S. Marshal and disappeared. The road's blocked so he won't get away, but I was worried about employee safety. I know your folks are all over this mountain. I was afraid one of them might get hurt or killed for his snowmobile."

She shut her eyes briefly and shook her head. When she spoke again, she'd regained her usual composure. "Christ almighty. I thought I'd seen it all till now. I can't wait to get you bastards out of here. Look, you don't want my crew gone, you need them as extra eyes. The weather's about to turn shitty, and they know the terrain like the inside of the Butte's bathroom. My concern's more the guests. Who says your nutcase isn't going to use one of them as a hostage to get out of here?"

"That's what we were just discussing," I told her. "If he does, he'll have to announce himself, knowing full well we won't let him through. To be honest, right now, a hostage situation would be good news."

"And one I doubt he'll use," said a male voice behind us.

We both turned to see Al Freeman standing there, looking embarrassed.

I opened my mouth to voice my opinion about what had just happened, but he cut me off. "I know, I know. I'm sorry. It was a screwup, plain and simple. I didn't know Tony's case officer was in the area. We do that sometimes—run random checks on our clients. He had no idea of the situation, and we didn't know Tony had caught wind something was up. When Tony saw the officer at the door, he freaked. It was just Murphy's Law. We weren't trying to end-run you."

At this point, I didn't much care. I also knew that such things did happen, as unlikely as they might seem.

"How many guys can you call in to help?" I asked instead.

"I have eight coming from various corners—a couple of hours out at the most for some of them, and I can get more."

I turned to Linda as snowflakes began descending— fat, lazy, and very thick—guaranteeing we wouldn't be getting that helicopter. "You got a deal. We'll use your troops as eyes and ears, but I want them equipped with at least one cop each. They can come in to buddy up or we can send someone out to them on snowmobiles, but if you won't give me that, I am going to pull them all off the mountain. As for the guests, the best I can think of is to stop loading the lifts right now and hope that everyone who's up there skis off in the next forty-five minutes or so to give us a clear field."

She looked at me grimly. "Let's move to the dispatch room. We can reach everybody by radio or phone from there."

I motioned to Spinney. "We're going to Mountain Ops. Set up a command post right outside the garage and keep your radio handy."

He gave me a thumbs-up, and I followed Linda as she strode off toward her operational center. I was feeling the earlier adrenaline rush transform itself into an all-too-familiar, slightly slower-paced tactical tempo. The only thing I knew for sure about the near future was that this situation could last for days without allowing for much rest. As when I'd been in combat so long ago, it was time to think of conserving energy.

Less than half an hour had elapsed since Snuffy Dawson's phone call.

Twenty minutes later, Linda Bettina and I, now joined by Sammie Martens, Al Freeman, one of the state police troopers, and Snuffy's chief deputy were crowded into the resort's dispatch center—the true brains of Mountain Ops. It had radio, telephone, and computer links to all over Tucker Peak, as well as a bank of small television sets connected to a dozen or more surveillance cameras overseeing the area's primary gathering spots: parking lots, ski rack clusters, food service courts, and the lift buildings both near the lodge and at the top of the mountain. Before us, a huge whiteboard-mounted map of the resort covered the far wall and had already been sprinkled with cryptic notes in a variety of felt-tipped colors. Linda, a radio headset fitted over one ear, stood at the map, marking the locations of the teams we'd sent out. Over loudspeakers around the room, the air crackled with voices giving updates from the field, and on the TVs, the restaurants, bars, and lobby areas were filling with a growing crowd of confused guests. The whole setup looked like a scruffy movie version of a Pentagon war room.

Unfortunately, the exterior cameras only revealed a thick curtain of falling snow. Wherever Antony "Tony Bugs" Busco was right now, and whatever he was doing, it was going to be difficult getting a fix on him.

"What do you think?" Sammie asked me quietly. "He slip through already?"

"I don't see how," I told her doubtfully. "Linda says she's gotten no reports of a stolen snowmobile. We have watchers at the top of every lift and they haven't spotted him. I suppose he could either cross-country ski or snowshoe out, but that doesn't seem likely, not from what I've been told about his physical condition—he's no jock."

She seemed to absorb that for a moment, looking around the room, and then asked, "Where's McNally? You think he'd be here sweating bullets."

It occurred to me then that only Lester Spinney had heard my conspiracy theory in detail, although, having asked Linda about McNally's whereabouts myself a mere quarter hour ago, I was beginning to feel more confident of it. "He's apparently disappeared. Nobody knows where to."

Sammie studied my face, caught by something in my voice. "Except you, maybe?"

I shook my head sadly. "I wish I did. I think he's dirty, along with his CFO pal. I called Willy five minutes ago and told him to give Gorenstein the grilling of a lifetime to see if I'm right."

A deep furrow of confusion appeared between her brows.

"I had Gorenstein brought in," I explained. "I'm betting the condo rip-off was just the tip of the iceberg."

"You send somebody out to McNally's house?"

"I had Snuffy send somebody—Christ knows who. Right now, we're so stretched for personnel, McNally could probably hitchhike naked on the interstate and not get busted. He'll just have to wait his turn."

"Unless he's already out of the country," she muttered.

A clearly stunned and faltering voice over the radio loudspeaker suddenly brought all conversation in the room to a stop. "Base, this is Dick Russell. The deputy and me've been shot."

In the silence that followed, Linda calmly asked, "How bad, Dick? You okay?"

I left Sammie's side and crossed over to Linda, standing before the map. Soundlessly, she pointed at a red number marked high on the mountain's left flank, at the upper reaches of where the condos were located. Dick Russell was the same man who'd thrown me the crowbar during the ski lift rescue days before.

"I'm bleedin' pretty bad. I think the deputy's dead. The guy came out of nowhere with a gun. He got the sled."

Linda turned to me. "Cat's out of the bag. You nail this bastard or I'll make you sorry you didn't."

Feeling my face flush, I said, "Get me some outdoor gear." I motioned to Sammie to join us. "I'm catching a ride up there with the medical crew. Sam, you take over here and coordinate with Linda. Keep me informed on our own Tac frequency and have some kind of transportation hookup with me there. Got it?"

She knew better than to argue. "Right."

I began wrestling into the winter overalls and boots Linda handed me from a peg on the wall. "Get as many cops as you can to close in on that spot, and tell them to ditch their employee escorts. Even a snowmobile can't get everywhere on this mountain—shut down the major routes. And remember, he may be mounted now, but that also means he's making noise. Tell everybody to keep their ears open!" I paused and said to Linda, "We'll get Dick down in one piece."

She didn't answer, but her expression told me how much credibility I had left.

Outside the building, waiting with his engine idling, Bucky Arsenault sat at the controls of his Bombardier, one of several designated runners for an emergency such as this. On the back of the machine, with two state police officers carrying shotguns, the medical team was already piling their equipment.

I jumped into the cabin's passenger seat and told Arsenault, "Ready when you are."

He punched the accelerator almost immediately, sending the people on the slippery rear deck scrambling for secure handholds.

The trip up was far different from the last time we'd shared a ride. Bucky kept to his business, expertly cutting through the clotting veil of falling snow with an instinctive feel for the terrain beneath his caterpillar tracks. I paid attention to what was happening ahead of us, talking on the radio to Sammie and consulting the map I'd grabbed on the way out.

"Joe? Dick Russell just told us he saw the sled heading west when it left them, cutting across the face of the mountain."

"You got people there?"

"They're fanning out in a semicircle from peak to bowl."

"How 'bout above where Dick was?" I asked, staring at the map. "It looks like a straight shot up and over. Busco might've started west and then hung a left."

Linda Bettina's voice cut in. "He knows the territory better than you. There're rocks and ledges too steep to climb that way. He's got to go right or left before he can head for the summit."

Sammie's voice came back on. "Hang on, Joe. We're getting reports of a sled approaching one of our teams."

In the intervening silence, I saw Bucky staring straight ahead, having heard every word, his mouth clamped shut with anger under the flowing mustache.

"We near, yet?" I asked quietly.

The Bombardier took a hard lurch into a depression and ground up the far side. "Just a few hundred yards."

He reached for his own radio mike and asked, "Dick? This is Bucky. You hear us yet?"

"Gottcha, Bucky," came the weak reply. "Straight ahead."

"Sammie?" I asked. "You find anyone to pick me up here?"

"Yeah, a deputy named Doug Fleury. He'll be there in a few minutes. Wait . . . Hang on . . . listen to this." She must have held out her radio to the nearest speaker in the dispatch room, because I suddenly heard, "Base, this is Wilcox. The sled's coming right at us. I'm leaving the mike open."

Over my portable, Bucky and I heard the sound of an approaching engine, closing in like a furious insect, followed by a shouted challenge, several gunshots, and then a loud crash, abruptly cut off as by the snap of a switch— no doubt the open microphone being dislodged from where Wilcox had jammed it to transmit.

"Base, this is Wilcox." The voice was panting a moment later, almost breathless with excitement, and thankfully vibrantly alive. "We're out of it. He hit us broadside and broke my handlebar."

"Are you okay?"

"We're fine. He missed. We fired at him. May have hit him. Not sure."

"Which direction did he go?"

"He's angling up at a forty-five from us."

"You hear all that, Joe?" Sammie asked, her voice much clearer than what we'd been listening to.

The Bombardier came to a sudden stop, almost on top of a snow-covered couple of men, huddled together in a ball.

"Yes, I did," I answered, jumping out into the cold,

slowly fading gray light. The snow came up to my knees. "Where's my transportation?"

I staggered behind the red-clad rescue squad, which had vaulted off the back deck of the machine and was already surrounding Dick Russell and the inert deputy. I knelt beside them, watching them rapidly and expertly assess their patients.

"How's the cop?" I asked one of them.

"Still alive," was the terse reply, almost immediately overshadowed by the sound of a snowmobile drawing near.

A large, black Yamaha slid into view, bearing a helmeted police officer in a dark blue, padded jump suit labeled "Sheriff." "Which one's Gunther?"

I half ran, half fell over to him, clawing onto the rear of the machine. "I am."

"Doug Fleury. Hang on."

The difference between the Bombardier and the Yamaha was like comparing an aircraft carrier to a jet. Doug Fleury had obviously spent a lot of time riding snowmobiles, like thousands of other Vermonters, and handled it with the ease and self-confidence of a cowboy born to the saddle. We tore into the featureless white wash ahead of us, the snow whipping our faces and forcing me—without goggles—to bury my face into my driver's back for protection, racing at such speed that we sometimes left the ground, the engine howling with released energy.

"Sam?" I yelled into my radio, holding on to the strap at my groin for dear life with one hand. "I'm on the sled. What've you got?"

I had to hold the speaker flat against my ear to hear her say, "We're closing in on him. We got several hits on his engine noise. Looks like he's heading between the tops of lifts three and four."

Linda's voice came on. "That means you have him cornered. He's heading toward the windmill farm, and it's got a ten-foot chain-link fence around it, stretching across his path."

Sammie anticipated my next request. "I've got units closing in from both sides. You and two others are coming up the middle. Watch your butt."

I pocketed the radio and leaned forward to shout into Doug's ear. "We're coming up to the windmill farm's fence. That's where he's supposed to be."

Fleury quickly cut back on the throttle. "How're we going to know if he's to the right or the left of us?"

"We won't, but everybody's closing in. One of us'll find him."

We were both straining our eyes against the impenetrable gray curtain before us, looking for anything that would warn us against simply falling into the unknown.

Fleury saw it first and immediately killed the engine. "There it is," he said softly in the sudden silence. He pointed at the ghostly, intermittent watermark of a chain-link fence's crisscross pattern hanging before us in midair.

I could hear in the background the distant whining of more snowmobiles and groomers converging on the area, but more prevalent still was an otherworldly and rhythmic *whooshing* sound coming from someplace ahead of us. It was deep-throated, heavy and almost made the air vibrate, conjuring up images of a giant scythe swinging ever nearer.

"What the hell's that?" I asked.

Fleury swung one leg off his machine. "The windmills—give me the creeps."

He crouched by one side of the snowmobile and unlashed two pairs of snowshoes, handing me one. "How do you want to work this?"

"Nothing dramatic," I cautioned, attaching the snowshoes, "but being the ones in the middle, we should probably try to get a location on the guy. Don't engage him in any way, just look for his sled tracks so we can orient the others."

Fleury nodded once, tested his balance on the soft snow with a few hard stamps of his feet, and headed off toward the left, almost instantly becoming one with the falling snow.

I walked to the fence and cut right, my gun in one hand, the radio in the other, moving as silently as the gently floating elements all around me.

But not for long. I hadn't gotten ten yards before I heard a shout behind me and the sound of two gunshots. Turning clumsily, I started jogging in that direction, talking into the radio, "Shots fired midline along the fence. I'm going to investigate."

I almost fell over Tony Busco's stolen snowmobile, which was at a cockeyed angle. It was entangled halfway through the bottom of the wire fence, having smacked into it with enough strength to have punched a hole. Fleury's large footprints showed that he'd slipped through in pursuit, rather than waiting as I'd advised—

the cowboy image apparently not being restricted to his prowess on the back of a sled.

"Fleury, come in. It's Joe Gunther."

Nothing came back. I began squeezing through the ragged opening, noticing as I did a smear of blood across the machine's shattered plastic windshield.

"Fleury. Come in."

Still nothing.

"Gunther to all units. We may have an officer down inside the fence, about twenty yards to the left of our machine."

I continued walking, bent over double, studying the ground before me, breathing through my mouth as if that might make me quieter. With the specter of Tony Bugs in my head, looming up out of the murkiness, gun in hand, ready to take me out, I even turned the radio off so it couldn't give me away.

All the sound that remained was the ever louder, heavy, rhythmic chopping of gigantic blades slicing through the air, close enough now that I could no longer hear the whine of approaching reinforcements. To hell with Tony Bugs, I was thinking now, the image of Dick Russell and the wounded deputy fresh in my mind. I needed to find Doug Fleury and see if I could help save his life.

What I found first, however, stopped me dead in my tracks. Looming out of the cold, pale environment, revealed in a sudden gust of wind like a towering ghost rising from the ground at my feet, was a thin, white, tubular shaft impressive enough to make me think of alien visitors or a sign from God. Hanging a hundred and thirty feet over me, equipped with three huge, ponderous, black-painted, slicing blades, was one of the summit's distinctive windmills. Each blade, at least sixty feet long, came flying out of the sky, seemingly aimed at my head, only to reach the end of its arc with the sound of a diving aircraft. One by one, they thrummed by to vanish in the opposite direction, each one following on the heels of its mate, to begin the process anew—once every split second.

My instant and instinctive crouching down brought me almost eye-level to the ground—and to Doug Fleury lying half covered with snow a few feet ahead, one red stained glove clutching a wounded shoulder. Just beyond him, stepping out from behind the tower, a pistol aimed straight at me, was Antony "Tony Bugs" Busco, looking just like his mug shot.

"Drop the gun," he shouted over the steady beating overhead.

My own weapon was still in my hand, pointed halfway between the ground and him. I was struck by the sudden realization that because of both the protection program's harboring of this man and our own circumspection in drawing a net around him, this was the first time I'd actually seen him, even though I'd been pursuing his shadow from the very beginning.

"No," I said. "If you know what's good for you, you better drop yours. Cops are closing in on this spot from all directions. You can't get away."

"Maybe I don't give a shit," he said, but I had my doubts.

"Why not?" I asked him. "You protected yourself by entering the Marshals' program, by killing Jorja Duval to locate Gagnon and Lane—"

"Gagnon was blackmailing me," he cut in defensively. "That dumb hick. And she wouldn't tell me where he was—not at first, anyway. Greedy little bastards put *themselves* into that jam. Thanks for the assist with Lane, by the way," he suddenly added with a forced smile. "Didn't know cops could be so helpful."

Like an engine falling into gear, my brain latched onto his words and conjured up not only the ugly picture of Jorja Duval's cut throat, her usefulness over, but also the long-awaited realization, by implication, that Marty Gagnon was no longer unaccounted for. Perhaps Busco had run out of places to hide. Certainly his current protectors were going to throw him out. Still, I persisted. "It doesn't change that you're a survivor by instinct. Look at you now, still fighting to live. Put the gun down and make that happen."

"I killed four people, including two cops—three if that one dies."

"You *wounded* three cops. None of them're dead. It's not as bad as you think."

He tilted his head back and laughed, making me wonder if that might not be the instant to try to outshoot him. I was no longer under the illusion that my babbling would lead to his surrender.

But happenstance tilted the balance. With the sound of an enormous laundry bag sliding down a smooth chute, a huge wedge of rime ice suddenly released from one of the overhead blades and thudded into the snow just a few feet beside us. In the same instant that Tony Busco swung slightly to face this unknown threat, I leveled my gun and fired wildly, hitting him by pure luck in the leg and spinning him like a top, causing his own pistol to fly uselessly away.

Doug Fleury, the silent witness to all this, looked from Busco to me, and back again, before letting his head finally rest against the snow.

"Thank God," he muttered, and closed his eyes.

Amen to that, I thought, feeling suddenly very cold.

CHAPTER TWENTY-THREE

HE WALKED WITH A STUDIED INDIFFERENCE, FAKING A CA-
sual swing to his shoulders but revealing his tension with
the stiffness of his arms and neck.

And the look in his eyes. They moved back and forth
like a bodyguard's on alert, watching everyone's passing
face, sweeping the crowd for any signs of unusual movement.

Like my stepping out in front of him from behind a
kiosk of phone booths, located in the middle of the Man-
chester, New Hampshire, airport lobby. "Philip Mc-
Nally?"

His familiar smile was tight and artificial, and he
glanced nervously at Lester Spinney approaching from
another angle, and at a uniformed state cop closing
in from a third. "You know it is, Mr. Gunther. What's
up?"

As Lester stepped around behind him, took his bag and
began to frisk him, the New Hampshire trooper said,
"You're under arrest on a fugitive-from-justice warrant,"
after which he intoned the standard Miranda warning,

ending with, "Do you understand these rights as I have explained them?"

McNally's expression softened, much of the tension draining away, and he ducked his head slightly with a smile. "I guess I knew it wouldn't work. I don't know how you found me, though. Conan had no idea. I'm guessing you got him, too."

"Yup." I took his elbow and began steering him back through the security checkpoint. We'd already had his luggage removed from the plane.

"Actually," I admitted, "You told me yourself, when we first met. You said the hassles you were putting up with made Luxembourg look good, or words to that effect. That struck me as odd at the time—most people would've said Florida or the Bahamas or even Tahiti. I only realized it later, of course, after we thought you'd gotten away, but Luxembourg must've been on your mind for a specific reason. It didn't take long to find out that it had just the type of banking practices you needed, or to locate the travel agent you used to buy your ticket. You should know, by the way, that the U.S. and Luxembourg just signed a banking agreement allowing us access to your funds. Talk about bad timing."

We stepped out into the cold air of the airport's parking lot, where a couple of police cruisers were idling at the curb. Phil McNally stopped briefly and took in a deep breath of air, wistfully commenting at the end of it, "I came pretty close, though, didn't I?"

I put my hand on the rear-door latch. "You did better than that. You've probably destroyed an entire community—from the condo owners and Board members to the lowest lift ticket taker; you've ruined or damaged hundreds of lives. That's something the judge will appreciate, too."

I opened the door and shoved him inside.

Several hours later, I was back in Brattleboro, on the outskirts of town, in a long, low wooden building that had once been the nineteenth-century equivalent of a parking garage—a carriage house designed for up to twenty horses and their vehicles. It was a storage rental facility now, its erstwhile stable doors replaced with a row of heavy padlocked wooden ones, and it had been where first Ron Klesczewski and then a crime lab team had gone to paw through the ill-gotten gains of Marty Gagnon's career as a thief, early in the investigation.

We hadn't found much then. We had reason to think we'd find a bit more this time.

Snuffy Dawson stood next to me as we watched four officers in white Tyvek suits wrestling a heavy chest away from the far wall of an almost empty room, while a fifth stood by, taking photographs of each step of the process. Snuffy was now the happy recipient of much recent media attention, having held several press conferences in order to explain the Sheriff's Department's hat trick in solving a homicide and a major embezzlement case, and in busting up a local drug ring. I noted with satisfaction that he repaid our courtesy of keeping out of the limelight by mentioning our help. It was a political gesture on the part of an old pro, and I was hoping it would be useful in VBI's future interactions with other departments. That was probably wishful thinking, of course. Other cops would just think Snuffy had brought us in because he was losing his grip.

But it was another small step in our march toward legitimacy.

"Have you heard what they're going to do with Tucker Peak?" I asked him as we waited.

"Their board of directors hired a bankruptcy lawyer, if that tells you anything. There'll be the usual claims that the world is ending, and then they'll find a buyer at ten cents on the dollar and they'll start it all over again. The rich'll stay that way and the poor'll find other jobs."

"We found out McNally's heart condition was bogus, by the way," I said. "He printed the prescription label on his computer and filled the bottle with generic saccharin."

Snuffy snorted softly with disbelief. "Why did he add to the confusion? Burning the pumphouse, blowing the water main, sabotaging the generators? All it did was draw attention."

"But not to him. It just gave strength to the rumors about how messed up the mountain was—rumors they did everything they could to spread. Gorenstein's the better talker of the two. He said the plan was to degrade the resort's reputation, even push it into bankruptcy if possible. That way, the fake heart problem could believably flair up and let McNally leave gracefully, and the finances would be in such a mess that their little shoplifting might go unnoticed. That's the main reason McNally kept playing ball with the TPL. He needed them as cover. It was a long shot, but he and Gorenstein were hoping to get away with it free and clear—if they had, they could've stayed in the U.S., two mediocre businessmen who'd just been targeted by poor timing, bad luck, and in Gorenstein's case, a slightly soiled name. The burning of the pumphouse wasn't part of it, of course. McNally had to destroy it so no one would find out the pumps didn't exist. If Linda Bettina hadn't been so efficient McNally could've skipped adding arson to his list of offenses."

"What's Kathy Bartlett going to do with Norman Toussaint?" Snuffy asked after a moment's reflection.

"Nothing too awful, I don't guess," I told him. "There were mitigating circumstances. He'll probably be on probation forever, and owe a small fortune, but I doubt he'll do jail time. He finally rolled over on McNally, which helped. But the best news for him is that it may have all paid off—the treatments he was paying for seem to be working. I heard this morning that his kid's turned the corner and might be headed for a full recovery. To be honest, though, I don't think Toussaint'll be that lucky. He sold his soul in this deal, and that's going to haunt him the rest of his life. Too bad McNally doesn't have the same kind of conscience."

The chest now shoved aside, the team of four began tearing up heavy floorboards, all of which had already been sawed through to form a perfect four-foot-by-six-foot rectangle.

"Your two wounded deputies okay?" I asked.

"Yeah. Now they have bragging rights and their wives are ready to kill them both. Tough life. Lucky Tony Bugs was such a lousy shot. I bet he wishes you were a better one."

One of the men dropped into the hole with some rope and disappeared from view.

"I didn't shoot to wound," I admitted, although I was happy I had.

A few minutes later, the man in the hole reappeared

and handed several rope ends up to his colleagues. He re-joined them up top and they all four pulled as a unit, lift-ing a human-size, sausage-shaped bundle wrapped in multiple layers of tarp and plastic, much like a poor man's mummy.

"Well, there you have it," Snuffy said quietly, "as ad-vertised. At least Tony Bugs gave us that much."

I looked at the packaged remains of Marty Gagnon, the small-time hood who'd thought himself capable of mov-ing up from simple burglary to blackmailing a mobster whose identity he'd discovered by pure fluke.

"God," I sighed. "What a species we are."

Snuffy Dawson smiled. "You gotta love it."

ARCHER MAYOR lives in a Vermont village, where he is town constable. He writes full-time and volunteers as a firefighter/EMT. Before reaching this happy state, Mayor lived all over the U.S. and Europe, variously employed as a scholarly editor, a researcher for Time-Life Books, a political advance man, a theater photographer, a newspaper writer/editor, and a medical illustrator. He is the author of eleven earlier, critically acclaimed Joe Gunther novels and two books of American history.

More
Archer Mayor!

Please turn this page
for an excerpt
from

The Sniper's Wife

available
wherever books are sold.

Nathan Lee swung out the door and stepped lightly down the stairs of the apartment building fronting Amsterdam Avenue, a wad of cash tight in his back pocket. He'd known a man who needed a job done, and knew another man who could do it. That was largely the nature of Nate's existence nowadays, hovering in the middle of as much action as possible, like a party balloon being swatted from one table to another—he made it his business to pass between disparate people, and made sure that with each swat, he got a small percentage.

He looked up and down the sidewalk with a smile. It was long after midnight, which for him was mid-workday, and he was in the mood to see if he couldn't hit two scores in one night.

He turned south toward 155th Street and headed for his office, an all-night, pocket-sized general store selling everything from cigarettes to playing cards to soda and candy bars, and whose owner, Riley Cox, he'd known since Riley was a kid.

Nate had been a street hustler even back then. Part of his success now, in fact, lay in how old he was. White-haired, bandy-legged, and skinny as a pole, he was the epitome of the elderly black caricature, watching life passing by on the stoop of a brownstone. Except that he had too much energy for that. The combination of his appearance and his natural enthusiasm made him hard to resist, and more importantly, harder to target as a fall guy when things went awry. The tough people he often dealt with either protected him or dismissed him, but they rarely held him to blame. It was a blessing he nurtured and never took for granted.

He entered 155th and walked west, his feet moving to a tune that kept echoing in his head, something he'd heard on the radio last week. He saw Riley's sign in the distance, a yellow beacon offering friendship, comfort, and maybe a hot lead.

Now snapping his fingers to the tune, he rounded the newspaper rack outside and pulled open the glass door into a wall of warm, aromatic air, as embracing to him as a home kitchen on a winter day, even though the odors were of dust, cigarette smoke, and stale humanity.

Nate caught Riley's eye as he stepped inside and felt his opening one-liner die on his lips. There was nothing amiss about the tiny store. It was as busy as always, and even Riley looked almost normal. But you didn't know someone for decades without sensing that single element's being out of place. Nate stopped in his tracks, the door still open in his hand, and readied himself for a fast retreat.

"Hey, Riley. How's it keepin'?"

In response, Riley shifted his gaze to the nearest of the two aisles inside the store, the one that was just out of Nate's line of sight. Nate silently leaned to his left in order to get a better view, his hand still on the doorknob. Slowly, the aisle came into view, revealing a thin, hatchet-faced man with intense dark eyes and a shriveled left arm.

Nate, whose business was faces, didn't hesitate, even after all the years. He broke into a wide smile and released the door. Riley visibly relaxed. "Why, if it ain't Officer Kunkle."

"Long time, Nate," Willy answered.

Nate approached him with an appraising eye. "Not to be rude, but you're lookin' a little rough, if that's all right to say."

Willy let out a small snort. "Can't argue with the truth."

"What happened to you?"

"Took a ride along the bottom a few years back."

Nate stuck out his hand, and Willy shook it, enjoying the warm, smooth feel of it.

"And the arm?"

"Bullet wound," Willy answered shortly.

Nate nodded sympathetically. "Oh, my Lord. So, you're not with the police anymore."

Willy smiled thinly and gave an indirect answer. "You don't get that lucky. They can't fire you if you can still do the job."

Nate tried to hide his skepticism. "Hell, given some of your brothers, they're not even that picky. Why're you back, after all this time?"

They were looking at one another straight in the eyes, as if reading the real dialogue between them.

"Favor for a favor?" Willy suggested.

Nate chuckled. "I didn't forget. That's why I'm still here to talk to you. What're you after?"

Someone squeezed by them to pay at Riley's counter.

"You up for a walk around the block?" Willy asked.

Nate glanced over his shoulder at Riley and raised his eyebrows.

"It'll keep," Riley answered enigmatically.

That put Nate back in his good mood. He was intrigued by Kunkle's reappearance, but he doubted it would fatten his wallet. Riley's comment, however, implied the night might still be young, as he'd been hoping.

Nate patted Willy's right elbow. "Follow me. I got just the place."

He led the way down the block and up a side street. Before a dilapidated brownstone with the front door attached to the sidewalk by a set of broad steps, Nate ducked to the right and climbed down a narrow metal staircase to what had once been the service entrance. It was so dark at the bottom of this trench that Willy could barely see the back of the man before him.

Nate gave the door a coded knock and waited. A small, weak light went on overhead for no more than two seconds before the door swung back just wide enough to let them both into a small, quiet antechamber that reminded Willy of an airlock. A huge, barrel-chested man with no hair and a goatee gave Nate a broad smile and a pat on the shoulder. "How're tricks, Nate? Keepin' busy?"

"You know it, Jesse. How's your sister?"

"Much better. I'll tell her you asked."

The man's voice was friendly and relaxed, but his eyes hadn't left Willy's face since the moment he'd come into view.

Nate laid a protective hand on Willy's shoulder. "This is Willy, Jesse. An old friend who did me a big favor a long time back."

"And the man," Jesse said simply, his smile only half in place.

"That's true," Nate agreed. "You got the eye. But he's still okay."

Jesse weighed that in his mind for a moment, then gave a single nod with his large head. "Well, then I guess he's okay with me, too."

He took one step toward the rear of the small room and pushed a button Willy didn't see. A back door opened with a click, and they were instantly met with the sounds of laughter and music and of ice chinking against glass. Nate had taken them to an after-hours bar, the new century's equivalent of a Flapper-era speakeasy, and as big a business during the predawn hours now as any of its predecessors had been all through the 1920s. New York prided itself on being a twenty-four-hour town, and it wasn't going to let any arbitrary bar curfew stand in its way.

Nate exchanged greetings with half a dozen people as he led the way around a pool table and down a row of booths to a bar at the far end of the room.

There the bartender asked them, "Place your orders, gentlemen," as if they'd just arrived at the Ritz. The place wasn't that fancy, but it wasn't a dive. Dimly lit and simply but tastefully decorated, it could have held its own against any of its legitimate brethren. There was also a decent CD player leaking out good jazz, and since almost everyone present was over fifty, there was the mellow feeling of an old-fashioned men's club.

Nate ordered a rum, Willy merely bought an overpriced tonic water and was handed a warm bottle without a glass.

"Over here," Nate said, indicating a tiny table wedged against the far wall near a back door labeled, OUTHOUSE.

They settled down, comfortably far from the music, and sat almost knee to knee.

Nate had the contented look of a man watching an old home movie. He shook his head, took a sip of his drink, sighed with a contented smile, and said, "Officer Kunkle. Man, oh, man. I wasn't sure I'd ever see you again. I thought maybe you were like the nomad in the desert or somethin'—the righteous man who delivers the word of truth and then vanishes forever." He pointed at the arm, and added, "And I guess if you'd been standing a few inches in the wrong direction, that'd be the fact of it, too. You ever get my letter?"

"I got it." Willy didn't detail its effect on him.

"Well, I meant every word in it, and I still do. That was an act of grace in an ungenerous world. You did yourself proud that night."

"That's just because it was your bacon I spared. You would've called me a patsy if I'd cut someone else the same slack."

Nate laughed and took another drink. "I am disappointed at the depth of your cynicism, but I can't deny your point. In any case, you did me the big favor, and I will always be grateful."

Willy removed the evidence photo he'd stolen from Ogden and laid it on the table before Nathan Lee. "You know where this stuff comes from? It's called Diablo."

Nate looked at the picture without touching it, his face suddenly grim. Narcotics were what got him in touch with Kunkle the first time, and he'd never dabbled in them again. The fact that the same man was back and wanted to discuss the same topic didn't bode well.

"I know what it's called," he said shortly.

"Comes from around here, right?"

"Why you want to know?"

Willy hesitated. A cop's first impulse in a conversation is never to volunteer anything. Every word you say is to get the other guy talking. And you sure as hell never reveal anything personal.

But Willy was the one asking favors here, and, training and paranoia aside, there wasn't much to be lost sharing a little with Nate.

"My ex-wife was found dead with that shit in her arm."

Useful or not, the effect of this admission was telling. Nate's eyes opened wide, and he stared at Kunkle in amazement. "No wonder you're lookin' a little ragged. She live around here?"

"Lower East Side."

That surprised the older man. "Huh. It happens, but usually a home brew like that doesn't travel far from home. The local appetite's enough to keep the dealer happy."

"So, it is made nearby?"

Nate ignored the question, trying to step back a bit first. "Officer Kunkle, I know I owe you, so don't get me wrong, but is this something you want to do?" As Willy's face darkened, he quickly added, "Now, hold on, don't get me wrong. I'll help you out. I will. But see it from my side, too. That's all I'm askin'."

Willy's expression didn't soften, but he didn't say the harsh words that first came to mind. Instead, he asked, "What do you want?"

Nate waved both his hands at him. "Nope. That ain't it, either. I don't want a thing. But you come back after all this time, and you got one arm messed up and you say you're still a cop and then you show me the picture and say that dope killed your ex-wife. If you were me, you gotta ask yourself: What's goin' on here? You see what I'm saying?"

Once more, Willy fought the urge to react impulsively and tell him to mind his own business, but struggled instead to address Nate's concerns.

He took a swallow from his warm tonic water and then explained, hoping for the best, "I am a cop, but not from here anymore. I work in Vermont."

Nate's eyebrows shot up. "Vermont?"

Willy cut him off. "Yes, Vermont. I'm kind of a state cop up there, like a statewide detective. It doesn't matter, for Christ sake. The point is, I got a phone call that my wife had died, and I had to come down. They're writing it off as an accidental overdose— locked doors, needle in the arm, history of drug abuse. They just want to clear their books."

"They wrong?"

"I don't know for sure. I think they might be." Willy knew Nate would've liked more, but he was disinclined to hand it over. He also wasn't sure he actually wanted to air his misgivings, for fear they might lose credibility even to him.

Fortunately, Nate seemed comfortable working with that little. "I do know somethin' about this Diablo. That's why I was surprised you found it downtown. It don't really go there. She have a reason to come up here to get it?"

Willy thought of his brother, but he couldn't see how that fit. "Not that I know of. We've been apart a long time."

Nate stared at the tabletop thoughtfully. "Sounds kind of funny," he finally admitted, looking up. "Especially if it wasn't an accident. I don't know how much I can do, though. It's not like these people keep records, you dig?"

Willy opened his mouth to say something when they both heard a loud crash at the bar's entrance. The large bouncer was being propelled backward into the room by a flying wedge of men in uniform.

Willy responded first. "Shit. Cops."

Nate recognized them more specifically. "Vice," he said and grabbed Willy's good arm as patrons and cops began falling over each other near the front. "Head out to the bathrooms and take the second door on the right."

Willy left his seat like a sprinter out of the blocks. "You coming?" he asked over his shoulder.

Nate merely flashed a smile and said, "Too old. Good luck."

Willy slammed through the OUTHOUSE door and found himself in a short, dark corridor. With the noise escalating behind him, he pulled open the second door on his right and plunged through without hesitation, stumbling over a couple of steps and sprawling into the middle of a dimly lit landing with a staircase leading upward.

Scrambling back to his feet, he took the stairs two at a time, and had climbed two floors before he heard the door he'd used crash open and the sound of voices shouting.

"Upstairs, upstairs. I hear one of 'em headin' up."

Using his right hand on the banister to help propel himself, Willy increased his speed, peering into the gloom for some alternate way to what was looking like a straight shot to the roof. But every door he saw appeared shut tight, and he didn't have time to do more than look. He was pulling ahead of his slower, more heavily laden pursuers, however, so if the door to the roof was open, there might still be some way to escape.

He wasn't optimistic, though. New York was nothing if not a haven for the security prone. Home of the fox lock, the Lojack, pepper spray, and more miles of razor wire than it took to tame the West, this city wasn't known for having rooftop doors left open.

Except when they'd been propped that way by a

strategically placed brick. As soon as Willy made this discovery, now six floors above the speakeasy, he remembered from the old days how some drug runners would leave themselves a way out, just in case they needed an emergency back door.

Silently, he thanked this particular guardian angel's prescience, stepped through the door onto the gravel-covered roof, and shut the door behind him, hearing with satisfaction the spring-loaded lock snap to.

The roof was flat, bordered by a three-foot-high wall, and pinned in place by an enormous, ancient, otherworldly water tank that stood in the center on lacy legs of steel and loomed overhead like a captured blimp. It was as symbolic of New York as that odd sound manhole covers seem to make only when taxi cabs hit them at high speed, and was duplicated a thousandfold all across the five boroughs.

The light was better up here—the city's perpetual ocher glow a veritable sunshine compared to the darkness of the stairwell, and Willy took advantage of it to jog to the edge of the roof, step over it onto the neighboring building, and continue trying to distance himself from his starting point.

Just as he was beginning to think he might have pulled it off, however, he saw his luck begin to sour. Simultaneous to hearing a heavy ram repeatedly smashing into the door he'd locked behind him, Willy saw the beam of a flashlight clear the top of the distant fire escape he'd been aiming for, followed by the silhouette of a cop carrying a shotgun and rolling commando-style over the top of the low wall to vanish from view against the darkness of the roof's surface.

Willy began looking around for another way out, already knowing in his gut that he'd run out of options. He hadn't made five steps in a new direction before the door flew open and a voice from the fire escape yelled, "*Police. Don't move.* Get face down on the ground with your hands above your head. *Do it. Now.*"

Willy instead ducked briefly into the shadows cast by one of the water tower's legs, quickly removed his wallet, his shield, and his weapon, and slid them all under a flap of tar paper he found extending from the footing of the tower leg.

"Get out into the light, you son of a bitch, or I'll blow you away where you are."

Willy stepped out where they could see him, his right hand up. "Okay, okay. You got me. My left arm is paralyzed. I can't move it."

One of the cops, winded, adrenalized, and angry at having given chase in what should have been a routine bar sweep, came up behind him, threw him to the ground, wrenched his left hand free of where he parked it in his pocket, and kicked him in the ribs for good measure, frisking him roughly for weapons and contraband. Grunting with the pain, Willy also had to admit he would have done the same thing had the roles been reversed.

The cop finished his search by handcuffing Willy's wrists behind his back and rolling him over to shine a light in his face.

"What the hell did you think you were doing, asshole? You think we haven't done this before?"

He didn't wait for an answer. Instead, he looked up at someone Willy couldn't see and yelled, "We got him, Sarge. Any others up here?"

"Negative," came the distant reply. "Nuthin' with two legs, anyway. You got anything on that guy?"

The answer, Willy thought, was telling: "Nah, just looks like a cripple rummy. No ID, no nuthin'. Better search the area to make sure, though."

He was yanked to his feet and escorted back down the stairs, less troubled by the jam he was in than frustrated by the fact that his investigation would be put on hold.